Praise for

THEY ALL FALL
DOWN

"Part high school drama, part mystery, this fast-paced novel will appeal to a broad range of readers who will have a difficult time putting it down." —*SLJ*

"St. Claire keeps the tension high as she slowly uncovers the mystery and builds to a thriller-level climax."
—*Kirkus Reviews*

"St. Claire ropes in readers from the opening pages, creating a taut thriller that keeps the audience turning pages and guessing until the end." —*VOYA*

"A suspenseful mash-up of Indiana Jones and *Pretty Little Liars*." —*The Bulletin*

"Bestselling author St. Claire makes her YA debut with a thriller in the tradition of Lois Duncan and R. L. Stine."
—*Booklist*

"The combination of a determined, guilt-ridden heroine with esoteric knowledge and an evil conspiracy with ancient roots should appeal to fans of Ally Carter's Gallagher Girls series." —*Publishers Weekly*

ALSO BY
ROXANNE ST. CLAIRE

Don't You Wish

ROXANNE ST. CLAIRE

THEY
ALL
FALL
DOWN

YA

EMBER

Text copyright © 2014 by Roxanne St. Claire
Cover photograph copyright © 2014 by Timothy Devine/Gallery Stock

randomhouseteens.com

Educators and librarians, for a variety of teaching tools,
visit us at RHTeachersLibrarians.com

The Library of Congress has cataloged the hardcover edition of this work as follows:
St. Claire, Roxanne.
They all fall down / Roxanne St. Claire. — First edition.
pages cm
Summary: Kenzie's life is transformed when she is voted one of the prettiest girls in
school, but when the girls on the list start to die, Kenzie is determined to uncover the
deadly secrets of the list before her number is up.
ISBN 978-0-385-74271-9 (hc : alk. paper) — ISBN 978-0-307-97700-7 (ebook)
[1. Popularity—Fiction. 2. Beauty, Personal—Fiction. 3. Murder—Fiction. 4. High
schools—Fiction. 5. Schools—Fiction.] I. Title.
PZ7.S774315Th 2014
[Fic]—dc23
2013038933

ISBN 978-0-385-74272-6 (trade paperback)

Printed in the United States of America

10 9 8 7 6 5 4 3 2 1

First Ember Edition 2016

For Mia, my daughter,
my inspiration,
my best friend:
Sine te nihil sum.

PART I

Bene qui latuit bene vixit.

He who has lived in obscurity has lived well.

CHAPTER I

I run away from home in a downpour.

Guilt wends its way through my belly, knotting things up before catapulting into my throat, making it impossible to swallow or breathe. But I have to breathe. I have to exhale the taste of those words my mother and I just slung at each other.

You can't go, Kenzie. It's dangerous! You could die.

It's a freaking bus to Philadelphia, Mom, not a rocket to the moon!

Buses crash! There are no seat belts! What if the driver is drinking?

You're suffocating me! I hate you! Hate!

My parting word had cracked like a gunshot, punctuated by the slam of the front door behind me. But she'd followed, calling my name in breathless desperation—*Mackenzie Grace Summerall! Don't you dare drive in this weather!*

I ignored the order, the rain drowning out her last whimper

as I vaulted into the front seat. Even then, I refused to turn to get a glimpse of her.

I don't really hate my mother. But I loathe that haunted, sad, scared, pained look that turns Libby Summerall's gray eyes into two burned-out pieces of charcoal. What I hate is her fear. I don't want to fear life—I want to live it.

The echoes of the fight fill the car and I don't try to erase them with music, letting the pounding rain on the roof do the job. I never yell back at her—tonight was an exception. Usually I just simmer under the pressure of her protection, understanding it enough to accept the weight of it, only throwing off the heavy blanket whenever I have to escape.

I squeeze the steering wheel and work my way through the darkened streets of my western Pennsylvania neighborhood until I can turn onto Route 1, grateful for the lights of a strip mall and a few traffic signals to guide me through the blinding rain. Not many cars, though. Not on a night like this.

I press the accelerator and barrel into the left lane, that lane of peril my mother wouldn't let me venture into for the year I had my learner's permit. But I have a license and freedom now, and a car I bought with tutoring money and some help from Dad. Now I pretty much live in the left lane.

I pick up a little speed despite the rain, the tires sloshing through puddles and potholes, the eleven-year-old Accord feeling all of her 140,000 miles. The light ahead is green, so I give it some gas, hydroplaning for a split second, enough to send a flash of panic through me.

That's not calming me down. I need happy, soothing thoughts. I need something I understand, something absolute to relax me.

Between the swipes of my windshield wipers, I go to that more comfortable side of my brain, away from guilt and worry and arguments I can't win. I decline the Latin word for "strong."

Fortis, fortis, forti, fortem, forte . . .

The language grounds me, almost instantly. The rules might be complex, but they make sense. I love things that make sense, that are exactly as they should be time after time. No surprises, no random twists, no pieces that don't fit. Latin makes sense in a way that my world rarely does; it rolls off my tongue so smoothly I sometimes wonder if I didn't live in ancient Rome in a previous life.

Which is why, if only I could get a damn bus to Philadelphia for the Latin competition, I could be number one in grammar in the entire state. But no . . . that would make too much *sense.*

The reminder of what started our fight makes me mad at Mom all over again. She wouldn't even *read* the parental release, let alone sign it and have it notarized. So I'll miss state competitions.

Because my leaving home has become Mom's worst nightmare. Well, one of them. There's also driving alone, taking a shower in a storm, crossing the street, using a knife, going on a date, or . . . living. Basically, my mother is terrified of life because . . . *accidentia eveniunt.*

In other words, shit happens, and that could be my mother's motto. Except she is bound and determined to stop any accidents from happening. *Ever again.*

A wisp of a memory curls through my chest, a frustrating and elusive clip of Conner's voice. I can still remember a lot of things about him, but I can't quite capture his voice. I try for anything—the sound of his laughter, the way he said goodbye when we parted at school.

Go get 'em, Mack.

As if I could get *anything* the way he could—with ease. He'd been so accomplished. So big in life. And still big in . . .

Mors, mortis, morti, mortem, morte . . .

Declining "death" didn't help me, either. I blink into the darkness, barely able to make out the next light about a half mile away. It's green, I think, but it might be yellow by the time I get there. I hate making that decision, never sure if I'll make it through the intersection in one piece.

Listen to you! You sound just like her.

Lights flash behind me, the high, bright halogens of an expensive SUV. Cursing softly, I swerve into the right lane to let it by, the wipers clearing the glass just long enough for me to catch a glimpse of one of those stupid stick-family decals on the back of the SUV. Why do people insist on advertising how perfect their little family is? Mom, Dad, soccer boy, and ballerina girl. All perfect. All . . . alive.

On the next pass of the blades, I reach the crest of a slight hill and see a pickup truck approaching from the side, probably going to hit the intersection the same time I do. I may have only had my license for a month, but I know the universal rule of trucks: they *will* cut you off at any opportunity. So I stay in the chickenshit lane and tap the brakes—

And hydroplane wildly. With a gasp, I shimmy the steering wheel to correct myself, splashing rooster tails of rain under my tires and shots of adrenaline in my stomach. In the next puddle, I'm tempted to smash the brake pedal, but

I clearly remember the page in the driver's ed handbook on maneuvering in the rain. *On a wet surface, tap brakes repeatedly to avoid . . .* something. Flooding? I don't know which car part could flood, but I'd rather not risk it. So I touch the pedal again, applying light pressure, once, twice. But nothing happens. In fact, the car is picking up speed on the downhill slope.

"Crap." The wipers fly by and I see the truck, the traffic light, but rain blurs my view again. "Come on!" I scream, willing the windshield wipers to move faster and clear the glass. They do, and I touch the brakes again.

Nothing.

With a soft inhale of surprise, I fight a wave of panic and press the brakes a little harder.

Nothing. This car isn't slowing.

And neither is the black truck. The light turns yellow and I slam my foot on the brake so hard the pedal collapses onto the floor. I brace for my back end to fishtail, fighting the urge to squeeze my eyes shut, accepting the unacceptable: *I have no brakes.*

My Accord is flying now, spraying water like wings on either side of the car, barreling toward the yellow light with scant seconds before it turns red. The truck is twenty feet from the intersection and so am I.

"Stop!" I scream at him and my stupid car and everything in the world. But nothing stops. The wipers smack at the rain as the car soars forward and the damn truck isn't slowing down. I stab at the console for the emergency brake, but there's no time and I can't get my shaking fingers around the grip.

Five feet from the corner, the light turns red and I stomp

the useless brake pedal over and over and over again. A scream wells up inside me as I steal a glance to my right, blinded by the beams of the truck hauling ass right at me.

"Stop!" I cry again, finally yanking the emergency brake handle with every ounce of strength I have, looking left and right for an escape as I careen right into the intersection.

I can't hear my own scream, but I feel everything. My muscles tense like steel in anticipation of the crash. Ice-cold terror washes over my body. The car's moving like a roller coaster down a ramp and all I can hear is the piercing and relentless shriek of a pissed-off truck driver's high-pitched horn.

Everything whips to the left, then the right, and I close my eyes as the world spins and twists and my chest is squeezed by the seat belt that keeps me squashed to the seat.

My only thought is . . . *Conner.* Is this how my brother felt when the conveyor belt yanked him down? When his neck snapped? When his world went black and cold and—

A thud stops everything. The car, the spinning, the dark thoughts. There's just a steady pounding of rain, a mechanical clicking, and a low hum with a soft ding that resonates through the silence.

It takes a full five seconds for me to turn to the side, peer through the rain to see the bright yellow arches, and realize that the McDonald's sign is right side up. Then I must be, too. And best of all . . . I'm alive.

But I don't move, doing a silent, swift inventory of my body, waiting for the howl of pain . . . somewhere. But nothing hurts, and the only sound is a repeating hum on the seat next to me.

My phone, my addled brain realizes. A text.

Mom! Joy and horror collide in my chest as the what-ifs

play out like a movie. Mom . . . hanging on by a thread as a police officer knocks on our door with the worst news . . .

It would kill her to lose another child. But we averted tragedy this time. Somehow. The only bad news is my car definitely has no brakes and probably will never see a hundred and fifty thousand miles, but who cares? I'm alive. And, oh, God, I'm sorry for saying that I hate my mom.

Desperate to talk to her, I flatten my hand on the passenger seat, rooting around until I find my phone. My hands are trembling so badly I can barely slide the screen lock. I manage to get to the texts, looking for Mom's picture at the top of the message list, but it's a phone number I don't recognize.

I shake my head, not caring about anything but calling my mother, apologizing, getting home, and figuring out a way to downplay this near miss so she doesn't freak out completely. Like that's even possible.

The phone dings and vibrates in my hand, another number I don't recognize, and I see the message attached to it.

Caveat viator, Quinte.

I'm a little off my translation game, but I squint at the screen as my brain registers the Latin words. *Let the traveler beware, Fifth.*

What the hell? I look up and try to see through the rainwashed windows. Did someone see me? Is that a warning? A fifth warning? A joke from someone in my Latin class? Someone who just saw . . .

Very slowly, lights come into focus, moving up the opposite side of Route 1. High, bright beams on a . . . big black pickup truck.

I don't know why, but instinct makes me duck. No, not instinct. Common sense. That jerk tried to mow me down.

I lie on the console, my heart hammering into the emergency brake handle that just saved my life, when my phone vibrates and dings again. I refuse to look at the text, squeezing my eyes closed and praying for someone to help me. Someone . . . not in that truck.

My phone vibrates again and I let out a soft whimper. Another text. And another. And another. What is going on?

Finally, I have the courage to look at the texts, letting out a soft cry of relief when I read *Molly Russell* at the top. My best friend would come to my aid. Then I scan the rest of the texts. More from Molly. But there are at least twenty new texts from kids in school, names I recognize, some I barely know, and a couple of unknown numbers.

Why was I text-bombed? I thumb Molly's text first.

OMG, Kenzie! Answer me! Did you see?
You're FIFTH on the list!

The list. The list? Not the . . . No, that wasn't possible. I could never make *that* list. I touch more texts, barely processing a single message, because all I can do is stare at one word that pops up over and over and over.

Fifth.

CHAPTER II

*T*his morning, the aftermath of my accident has almost died down, but Mom is still wrung out from the long night. After I called her from the car, she got Dad to pick me up and file the accident report. In spite of their separation, which has had him living in a town house a few miles away for the past year, he performed his dad duty and took care of everything, including the tow to a garage.

As always, he was the calm during our family storm, exactly what my mother needed to get through the ordeal. And as always, I had to wonder why those two can't rise above the statistics that say parents who've lost a child inevitably divorce. They're on their way to the inevitable, it seems, but haven't yet signed the papers. So I remain hopeful, although my car accident last night did nothing but rip scabs off barely healed wounds.

I leave Mom to nurse those wounds and wait outside for

Molly to pick me up for school. She arrives at eight in her VW Bug, and I jump in to escape the late-October chill.

"You don't look any different," she says when I slam the door shut.

"I didn't get hurt," I reply. "I told you last night, it was just a spinout."

"I mean, you know, the list."

Oh, God, the freaking Hottie List. "There was so much going on, I forgot about it."

"You forgot?" Molly flips a honey-blond strand, making me notice that she's not wearing her usual ponytail today, and . . .

"Do you have makeup on?" I ask her, unable to keep the disbelief out of my voice.

She shrugs. "I figure we'll get a lot more attention today than usual."

I almost snort over that. "Because of that list?"

"Kenzie, don't you get it? That list makes royalty out of ten junior girls every year and you are *on* it." She can't keep the awe out of her voice and I can't say I blame her, but not because I am suddenly "royalty." I'd known the list was coming out this week—every kid in Vienna High knew that. But I never, ever dreamed I'd be on it.

With dark-brown hair that always has an annoying wave despite the flatiron, blue eyes that rarely get much cosmetic attention, and unremarkable features, I'm not a girl who stops traffic. I can't imagine how I ever landed on a list of the most attractive girls voted on by the entire male population of Vienna High.

"Oh, please. Royalty?" I scoff. "First of all, that list is obsolete, meaningless, and unbelievably immature, starting with

12

the cringeworthy name of Hottie List. I mean, who even says that anymore?"

"They said it in the eighties when they started voting on the list."

"Started, I'd bet my life, for no other purpose than sexualizing and stereotyping girls, not to mention getting them to do God knows what for votes."

"I heard Chloe Batista gave blow jobs to the entire lacrosse team."

I roll my eyes. "My point exactly."

"And she only got second."

"Must have given second-rate blow jobs," I mutter, tucking my bag under the dash.

"Well, Olivia Thayne was kind of a shoo-in for first place, wouldn't you say? I mean, she's gorgeous."

I try not to look south on Route 1 when we turn, relieved we're going the other way and I won't have to pass the scene of last night's accident. "Whatever, Molly. It's not like being on that list is something I can put on my college app."

"No, but that list is still a ticket to a better life."

I shoot her a look. "A better *life*, Moll?"

"Better than what we have now. You're going to get to go to *list* parties, Kenzie. I've heard they're so much fun and every cute guy from miles around goes to them. Don't you want a boyfriend?"

"Not as much as I want to get into Columbia."

"Still Columbia, Kenz?" She can't hide her disappointment. Since middle school, we've talked about being roommates at Pitt, but that was before I was old enough to realize that the town of Vienna, where we live, is really a bedroom community of Pittsburgh. The university is less than forty-five minutes away—too close to Mom for me to breathe.

"Oh, I won't get into Columbia." I try for casual, but my voice cracks. Because I *might* get in. "Anyway, we have a year to worry about it." I don't want to hurt Molly by admitting just how badly I want to get as far, far away as possible from everything in Vienna. The only way I can justify that is if I get into an Ivy League—no ordinary college would be enough for Mom to let me move away—and live with relatives. My aunt Tina has already offered to let me live in New York with her, so Columbia is my ticket to freedom. Of course, there's a fifty-thousand-dollar-a-year price tag on that ticket. "Don't forget, I need a scholarship."

"You could get one."

I might be smart, but an academic ride to Columbia is next to impossible unless you're National Merit, and I'm not. I don't play sports, either. "I'd have a shot if I won the state and national Latin competitions. Then I might be able to get a classics scholarship, but you-know-who won't even sign the form to let me go to State in Philadelphia this winter."

"Might snow on the roads?" Molly adds a smile to her joke, but that does little to ease the sting of the truth.

"Yeah, and she pulled out the drunken-bus-driver line."

"Always." Molly nods with pity, long aware of my mother's obsessive nature and the reason behind it. She was next to me on those dark days after Conner's accident, and she knows I live with the specter of a lost sibling. Of course, she doesn't know . . . everything. No one knows exactly why Conner went down to that storeroom. No one except the person who asked him to go . . . *me*.

14

"It's still a big deal," she says.

I pull myself back to the conversation, stuffing guilt and grief into their proper boxes. "To get a scholarship to Columbia? No kid—"

"To make the list!" She sighs, exasperated with me. "Kenz, enjoy the moment, will you? You're a year from even applying to college, and that is going to be the very year you reign on the list."

"Reign?" I snort out a laugh. "It doesn't make me some kind of princess, Moll."

"And fifth! Not tenth, Kenzie." She's totally not listening to me. "You are hotter than five other really hot girls. Big names, too."

"Oh, yeah, Chloe Batista and Olivia Thayne are virtual celebrities. Watch out for all the paparazzi in the junior parking lot."

She ignores my sarcasm. "You got more votes than Shannon Dill."

"Dumb as a rock, that one."

"And Bree Walker! They're superpopular, pretty girls. And we're . . ." She trails off and I have to laugh.

"We're not," I finish for her, stating the obvious.

"Well." She manages a laugh. "We're nerds."

"Speak for yourself. I'm not in the band."

"You're the president of the Latin club, take four AP classes, and tutor calculus. Card-carrying nerd."

So I'm a little geeky. "I don't see how a stupid list changes that."

"You're fifth!" she exclaims again, like she just can't say that number enough. "I mean, you are right after Kylie Leff and

15

Amanda Wilson, captain and cocaptain of the varsity cheer-leading squad, and homecoming princesses three years running." She recites their positions like she's reading their resumes.

"Together on the list as they are in life. Don't those two ever separate?"

"Don't change the subject. You know our lives are about to change." She throws me a grin. "Yeah, I said 'our lives.' I hope you don't mind me riding your coattails to popularity, 'cause I'm totally on that train."

"By all means, climb on the train of mixed metaphors."

She shrugs. "Joke all you want. This is big."

"I guess you're right," I concede. "Otherwise I wouldn't have been text-bombed last night."

"Really?" She repositions herself in the driver's seat like a bolt of excitement has just shot through her. "Anybody good? Read me some."

"Some . . . interesting."

"Like?"

"Just, you know, kids." I'm not sure I want to read that weird Latin one to her. But last night, before I went to sleep, I read every single message, and that one was still the most bizarre.

Caveat viator, Quinte.

Sent from a number that didn't show up on Google, anywhere. An area code I couldn't even find in the United States. It had to be some bonehead in my Latin class. But why was "the traveler" warned right after I had an accident?

Ignoring the full-body creeps that shudder through me, I reach into my backpack on the floor to get my phone.

"Let's see," I say, scrolling through the list. "I got texts from, oh, mostly the lunch crew and Latin club members. Drew Hickers said, 'Grats, girl.'"

"Grats?" She gave a good guffaw. "Who *says* that?"

"Icky Hicky," I reply, calling up our seventh-grade name for the first boy I ever kissed. "It's mostly everyone trying to hide their utter amazement and not insult me with a 'how did this happen' even though we all know someone probably miscounted the votes and I got three. Counting Hick-man."

"I don't know. I heard the vote tallying is closely watched. But who knows? That list is shrouded in secrecy."

"'Shrouded in secrecy'?" I choke out a soft laugh. "Who says *that*?"

"Well, it is. Do you know who counts the votes?"

I don't answer her because I'm still scrolling. I've been through the whole list and can't find the Latin text. I start from the top again.

"I heard that the guys really get pressured to vote," Molly says. "Like there's hazing or something if they don't cast a ballot."

It's gone. The text I read first after the accident is gone.

"And someone once tried to start a movement to get the list name changed to the Hot List, but . . ."

I barely hear her. How can that be? Texts can't disappear, and I certainly didn't delete it. Did I?

"They were killed."

"What?" My head shoots up in shock.

"I think that's just band-room folklore," she says with a sheepish grin, her dark eyes sparking with humor. "C'mon, we're almost there. Read me the messages. Did anybody really popular write to you?"

"Molly!" I know she's always been a little more obsessed with popularity than I have, but this seems over the top. "Why is it so important?"

"Because for the first time, some doors are open that have always been shut and locked," she admits quietly, pulling into the junior lot behind the gym. "So sue me if I'm a little excited to elevate my social standing. Hey, you gotta have a list party! At least I know I'll be invited to that one."

"As if my mother would let fifty beer-drinking lunatics into our basement for a list party."

"Then you better take me to the ones you go to."

"I will," I promise, knowing my mother won't let me go to parties anyway. I return to the phone, determined to find that text.

"Swear it," she demands. "You will not get popular without bringing me along."

"I swear it." Could I have imagined the text after the accident? I was pretty dazed. But, no, I read it again before I went to—

A loud thwack on the trunk makes me jump, and Molly lets out a shriek.

"Oh my God, Kenzie," she whispers, looking into the rearview mirror and grabbing my arm. "Look who it is. No, don't look. Yes, look. But be cool."

Without moving my head, I slide my gaze to the side-view mirror, blinking into the morning sun to see a tall silhouette. Very tall, broad, and sporting a Wildcats varsity jacket. I know that silhouette; I've watched it from every imaginable angle.

"Well, what do you know, Miss I Don't Care About That

List," Molly says, turning to me with an awfully smug expression on her pixie-like features. "It's Josh Collier, man of your dreams."

"He's not—"

She points a finger in my face. "Don't even try to lie to me. You've crushed on him since eighth grade"

"Seventh," I correct her, fighting a smile.

"Grats, Kenz!" Josh pounds the roof this time and lopes around to my side.

Molly and I just stare at each other. "Who *says* that?" we whisper in perfect best-friend unison.

"Kenzie?" He taps on the window and I turn, blasted by his slightly crooked, seriously cute half grin as he grabs the handle and yanks the door open with an air of possessiveness.

"Hi," I say. Beside me, I hear Molly let out a soft *ugh* of disappointment. What did she expect, witty banter?

"Damn, girl," he says, bending down to sear my face with eyes the color of a summer sky. "You made the list."

I give him an unsure look. "That's what I've heard."

"You know what that means?"

Molly's grinning as she gets her bag from the back. "She's starting to find out," she says with a bit of an "I told you so" singsong.

"It's a big deal," he says, his attention all on me. "Nice placement, too. Fifth." He winks, sending a weight sliding right down my stomach and spine.

"Thanks." I reach for my backpack on the floor, aware that Molly is taking her sweet time getting out, no doubt to eavesdrop. "But really, it's no big deal."

"I voted for you," he says softly, a tremor of disappointment

19

in his voice, as though I haven't taken the honor seriously enough.

"That's . . ." Kind of unbelievable. "Nice."

"You almost came in fourth."

My eyes widen. "I thought the vote count was some big secret."

"It is, but I'm *connected*, babe."

Babe? Did Josh Collier just call me *babe*?

He straightens as I get out of the car and then angles his head toward the school, those incredible silver-blue eyes still locked on me. "Can I walk over with you?"

I turn to look at Molly. "Go ahead," she says, giving us a finger wave.

"No, come with us, Moll." After all, she wants to ride the Popularity Train, and you don't get much more popular than Josh Collier.

"Well, I kind of have to go into the band room. . . ."

He ignores her and steps close to me. "Bet you were stoked to see the list," he says.

Molly backs away and catches my eye. "You go on, Kenz. I'll see you at lunch."

After an awkward beat, she takes off, leaving me alone and inches away from the guy I used to pillow-kiss when I first knew there was such a thing as kissing and that pillows were for practicing said art.

"Weren't you psyched?" he presses.

"I guess, yeah." I sling my backpack over my shoulder, painfully aware that the cool girls carry tiny purses and far fewer books . . . but they aren't trying to get a classics scholarship to Columbia. I push aside a lock of my hair with my free hand, a little resentful that my breath is tight and my palms are damp and I didn't have the foresight to put on some makeup, like Molly.

"You don't seem very happy," he says, his casual hand on my shoulder burning through my jean jacket.

"Well, I . . ." I dig for something other than *You leave me speechless*. "I kind of wrecked my car last night."

"Seriously? That blows."

"No kidding."

"Congrats, Kenzie!" A girl whose name I don't know holds up her hand for a high five as she passes.

"Thanks," I say, brushing her hand. Is this what today is going to be like? Is this the power of the list?

"You going to the game tonight?" Josh asks as we approach a set of wide, trapezoid-shaped steps. Right now, my legs are so wobbly I'm not sure I can navigate what we call the crooked steps.

"The football game?"

He laughs softly. "No," he says, layering on the sarcasm. "Girls' volleyball."

"No, I . . ." I shake my head. I don't want to insult him because I know he's on varsity, but I haven't been to a high school football game . . . since Conner played and I was still in middle school. "Maybe," I say, hedging bets left and right.

"Kylie and Amanda are throwing a list party afterward. You want to go with me?"

Holy, holy—

"Hey, Collier!" Another kid in a football jersey jogs over to us, giving me a tipped chin in greeting. "'Sup, Kenzie."

Tyler Griffith wouldn't have acknowledged me yesterday, let alone said my name.

21

"Dude, you're killin' my game here," Josh jokes, with a pointed look at me.

"I'm saving you from being benched is what I'm doing," Tyler says. "Coach wants us in the weight room for first period."

Josh mumbles a soft curse, then puts a hand back on my shoulder, turning me away from his friend. "So, see you tonight?"

The list might be incredibly tacky and dumb, but a date with Josh Collier is . . . rare. Hell, a date is rare.

"Maybe, if I can."

"I'll text you." He leans closer and puts his mouth near my ear. "Fifth."

CHAPTER III

I don't get it. Indefinite integrals and Riemann sums make zero sense no matter how furiously I take notes in Calculus. Actually, not that furiously because I'm still getting texts—did my phone number get published on someone's Facebook page? Every message that's from an unrecognized phone number gives me a little flutter, but each text is more congratulatory and friendly than the last.

Molly's right about the royalty factor. It's crazy and weird and, okay, not completely horrible.

Under my desk, I skim through a few more texts.

Three people text to tell me the girls who got ninth and tenth were calling the voting fixed. And apparently Austin Freeholder is so pissed off his twin sister, Alexia, isn't on the list that he's demanding a recount.

"Is it, Kenzie?"

I look up at the sound of my name, a quick squeeze of dread

when I see Mr. Zeller lift his reading glasses to get a better look at me. Is what . . . *what?*

He angles his head at my blank expression. "Is it a horizontal asymptote in that case?"

I close my eyes and shake my head. "Can I get a hall pass, Mr. Zeller?"

He lets out a typical Zeller sigh of disgust, but he likes me and isn't going to be a jerk about letting me off the hook.

"Hurry up so you don't miss the homework assignment." He tears a yellow slip from the pad and I take it, mumbling thanks as I rush into the silent hall dying for a gulp of solitude.

I'm suddenly hit hard with a memory of what it was like to be on the radar. After my brother died, almost two years ago, people stared at me. Not with envy, but with pity. And, of course, sadness, because I reminded them that one of Vienna High's brightest lights had been snuffed out in a freak accident. But I'd been a freshman, swamped by grief and overwhelmed by high school. I actually don't remember much of my freshman year. By the time I became a sophomore, no one noticed me anymore.

Until today. And now the looks aren't pitiful or sad. All morning, I noticed kids checking me out. During class changes, I could just imagine their thoughts. *That one made the list? The skinny one with brown hair? I guess from a distance she's got nice eyes and a decent smile, but . . . is she listworthy?*

Some of the looks, though, were from boys, eyeing me like a new target has been added to their game. I'm not sure how I feel about that, even from Josh Collier. After all, I'm the same girl I was yesterday, minus the list placement.

There's a bathroom not too far away, but I'd rather take a longer walk, so I slip into the stairwell, going down to the first floor toward my locker bay.

In my pocket, my phone vibrates again, but I ignore it. I consider texting Molly to meet me to take a walk across the quad for air, but she's in History and I know Moriarty won't let her leave.

Rounding the corner, I'm relieved to see an empty hall, and as I pass each classroom, the sounds of teaching and laughter and even the quietness of test taking somehow soothe me. This part of school makes sense: the learning, the classrooms, the teachers, the homework.

Unlike my brother, who personified the "big man on campus" cliché, I've never been very adept at navigating the social stuff. Conner never met a stranger, but I've battled shyness my whole life, and it only got worse after he died.

So maybe this list isn't a bad thing. Maybe this *will* change life for Molly and me. Holding tight to that thought, I wander past the biology lab, the faint scents of formaldehyde mixing with the lingering smell of freshman boys doused in Axe. My feet follow the blue-and-white-patterned linoleum floor, circa 1940.

Before I reach the new wing of the school, I turn into the last locker bay, nothing more than a dead-end hall with about forty lockers and two bathrooms. Molly and I celebrated at registration last summer when we got this choice location, usually reserved for seniors. The lockers are as ancient as this original part of the building, with a row of glass blocks along the top of the wall that lets in natural light on sunny days. No one cares that the lockers are rusty; these alcoves are old-school (literally) and they are off the beaten path. And right now, I couldn't love that more.

Facing the lockers, I put my hand on the cool cobalt metal and take a deep breath. What is going on with me today?

Is it just the list business that has me feeling so weird? The accident last night? The fight with my mom that preceded it? The fact that Josh Collier asked me out and kids who never acknowledged my existence are now fist-bumping me when I walk by?

So much has changed in the last twelve hours, and I'm reeling a little. A *lot*. I didn't ask for this sudden notoriety, and while a part of me wants to bask in the glow of something I've never known before, the other part of me wants to run far and fast.

I lean my head forward, letting it touch the locker as I sigh.

"You okay, Mack?"

I spin at the sound of a boy's voice so close the hairs on the back of my head flutter. The sunlight through the glass block hits his face, highlighting long lashes around shockingly dark eyes and forming shadows on his hollowed cheeks. I don't know how he sneaked up on me or why he'd call me by a name no one uses—well, not anymore, not since Conner died—but I know exactly who he is.

Levi Sterling.

"I'm . . ." I don't think I've ever been this close to him. If I had been, I wouldn't forget it any more than I'd forget a personal brush with the devil. "Fine."

"You don't look fine."

"Just . . . you know." No, how would he know? We've never talked. We've never exchanged a look. Levi Sterling is bad news, and the fact that he's still enrolled in school at all is kind of remarkable.

He's been in fights, he's been in handcuffs, and he's been in juvie. And right now, he's zeroing in on me in a way that actually steals my breath.

"I know." He takes a step closer, making me want to back into my locker. He's not super tall, like, say, Josh Collier, but he's strong. He's . . . a force. "You made the list."

I lift one shoulder, trying really hard just to look into his eyes and not linger over every feature, from the dark brows to the cleft chin, or study every lock of thick black hair that looks like it air-dried on his motorcycle, falling into silky strands that brush his shoulders. *What is wrong with me?*

"It's no big deal," I say, possibly for the twentieth time today. I want to turn back to my locker and let him do whatever he came into this bay to do—which I'm certain *wasn't* to corner me and make me go all gooey inside—but I don't. His eyes essentially pin me against the wall, and all I'm capable of doing is staring back like a helpless baby deer in the face of a forest fire.

"So how's it feel to make school history?"

I can't think of anything clever, so I go for honest. "Lame."

He gives me a slow smile, revealing perfect white teeth and, holy cow, a dimple on one side. Really, God, was that necessary? "It is lame."

Finally, one person in the whole school with common sense. With a record, too, but still. "It's all anyone's talking about," I say.

"Because they're not on the list," he says. "Making them losers."

"Pathetic losers," I agree.

That makes him laugh, a short, low rumble in his chest. "You gotta be the only girl in school who doesn't think the Hottie List is a big-ass accomplishment."

"It's not. Although I'm sure you voted like everyone else."

"I'm alive, aren't I? I voted."

But probably, I muse, not for me. Still, he's the first boy who's talked openly about the voting, and curiosity gets me. "So is there a ballot with names on it or are they all write-in?"

He tips his head, the softest moan of disappointment in his throat. "You *do* care."

I actually feel like I've let him down, which is crazy. "Not in the least," I say too fast. "I'm just curious because I don't belong on that list."

"I'd argue with that."

The compliment surprises and warms me as an awkward beat passes. He doesn't move, so basically we're a foot apart staring at each other.

"Anyway . . ." I move my eyes left and right to indicate our surroundings. "What are you doing here?" His locker's not near this bay, I'm certain. Levi Sterling doesn't fly under anyone's radar. If his locker were around here, I'd know it. Then again, a kid like him probably doesn't need a locker because he doesn't bother with books. Rumors have always swirled about him. I once heard a girl in his old school cut his name into her thigh with a razor blade.

"I'm skipping class."

I nod, like skipping class is something I understand and have done.

"You?"

"I just escaped AP Calc."

A glimmer of amusement dances in his eyes at what could be the nerdiest admission *ever*.

"AP Calc?" He raises his eyebrows. "And I'm failing Advanced Topics."

Math for Morons. I'm grateful that the school name for his pathetic class doesn't pop right out of my mouth. "Math can kill you," I say, managing not to cringe at how stupid that comment is.

He inches a little closer, rubbing his chin as he studies my face. "You know what's killing me?"

You. You are killing me. I shrug. "Not a clue."

He's so close now I can barely think. "The word problems," he whispers.

The word . . . does he mean in math? I let out a hollow laugh because hating the word problems is so cliché and because he's so . . . close.

"Yeah, they're pretty tough."

"I bet you breezed through that shit."

My eyes shift to the floor. "Word problems aren't that hard."

"So you're pretty *and* smart," he says.

I look up at him, not quite sure what's going on here. "Both are subjective."

"And I heard you're an expert in dead languages."

I blink for a minute before it processes. "Latin? I don't know about expert."

His gaze moves over my face from top to bottom, lingering on my mouth. "Are you . . . *flirting* with me?" I ask with a nervous laugh.

"Trying."

And honestly? Succeeding. A slow heat creeps up my chest,

a mix of trepidation and excitement fluttering through me, along with— No, it can't be.

But it is. Attraction.

To him? I should run for dear life, not flirt with him. I sure as heck should be in my math class. "I don't flirt," I say, feeling as awkward as that sounded.

"You're doing okay."

For the first time in my life, I understand the meaning of the word *swoon*. And I don't like it. Swooning is dangerous, helpless, and it doesn't feel so great. For all I know, this kid's rap sheet could include rape and murder.

I finally turn to my locker, expecting him to walk away when I start opening the lock. But he just leans on Molly's locker, to the right of mine, totally undeterred by my clumsy brush-off.

I feel his gaze on my hands. No doubt he's memorizing the combination . . . and noticing my hands are trembling.

"What are you scared of, Mack?"

You. "No one calls me that," I say, finishing the combination. Only my brother did, and since I can't even remember the sound of his voice, I don't want to hear his nickname for me. I yank the lock and grunt softly when the damn thing stays firmly closed.

"Here." He nudges me aside with his shoulder, an assault of male and muscle and something that definitely isn't Axe. With confident fingers he spins the lock, stopping at fourteen, passing it to twenty-one, and twirling right to five.

Click.

"How'd you do that?"

"My hands aren't shaking."

30

Dang it. "But how'd you get my combination?"

"Photographic memory." He grins at me. "And practice breaking and entering."

I don't know if he's kidding, so I put my hand on the side of my locker, steadying everything in me that isn't steady. "Guess I better change that lock," I say.

He slips the lock out and dangles it over one finger, very slowly lifting the latch and opening the door. "Not necessary." He gives me a slight nudge with his shoulder. "I'm a lot of things, but not a thief."

"Maybe not," I concede. "But you are a flirt."

He leans on the open locker door and crosses his arms, facing me. "I could teach you."

"How to flirt?"

"It's a skill that could come in handy with your newfound status."

I can't really disagree with that, so I just stare into my locker trying to think of what I could get out. I didn't even need to come here.

"And in exchange," he says, dipping just close enough that I can feel his breath near my ear, "you can tutor me."

"In math?"

He lifts his eyebrows, leaving the question unanswered.

"Why don't you just cheat?" I ask.

The quickest flash of hurt darkens his eyes. "That's not how you flirt, Mack. You don't insult your target."

A new kind of heat curls through me. Shame. How does he do that, this bad boy with the record and the reputation? How does he make *me* feel ashamed? "Sorry," I mumble, and I mean it.

"If you were sorry, you'd tutor me."

I freeze in the act of reaching for a notebook I don't need. Tutor him? Now, there's a bad idea. Bad on so many levels.

"My tutoring hours are pretty . . . full."

He nestles a little closer, so we're both practically in the locker. "Don't tell me I wasted my time following you here so I could get this favor from you."

He followed me here? A chill sweeps up my back, tingling the nape of my neck. I let go of the notebook, pressing my fingers against the frame of the locker as I dare to turn and look right into his eyes.

"No," I say simply. If I have to tell him the truth, I will: he scares the crap out of me.

This boy is menacing and intimidating and way too good at flirting. My mother would probably faint at the sight of him.

Josh Collier? Yeah, he's just a guy who's popular and jocky and harmlessly attractive. Levi Sterling? He's a threat to the heart, the mind, the sanity, and quite possibly the virginity.

"List go to your head already, Mack?"

The comment makes me inch back and grip the frame of the door a little tighter, my fingers slipping right above the hinge. "Nothing's gone to my head." *Other than whatever soap you use and those sinfully long eyelashes.*

He narrows his eyes, so close I can feel his breath and count the stubbly hairs on his chin. *That's hot, too*, my traitorous brain thinks.

"Then tutor me." He presses closer, his whole body against the inside of the locker door.

"I don't— *Ow!*" White-hot pain fires to my brain like an

electrical shock, making me yank my hand from the hinge that just crushed my middle finger. "Oh my God!"

He jerks away instantly, realizing his weight has made the door pinch me, and I turn in a full circle, clasping my right hand, biting my lip, and holding back a wail of agony.

"Shit, I'm sorry, I'm sorry." He tries to reach for my hand, but I snatch it away, embarrassment and anger as sharp as the pain.

"Just . . . leave it." I shake my hand and look at it, cringing.

"Oh, God, look at that," he says, grabbing my hand. The skin is sliced, and the whole nail is bright, screaming red. "Damn it, you gotta see the nurse."

"I'm fine."

"Mack." He steps forward.

I shake my head. "Stop calling me that!" I yell. Irrational, I know, but the pain is insane and I can't think beyond fighting the tears that are threatening. "Just leave me alone."

"I feel like shit. I'm sorry." He closes the locker door. "Let me look at it."

"No." I just want to get away from him. I don't belong around a kid like this. He makes me nervous and . . . A new thought settles. Did he do that on purpose? Because I wouldn't tutor him?

"I'm fine," I say again.

He replaces the lock with a firm click that reverberates through the empty alcove. "I'll take you to the clinic."

"No thanks." Squeezing my wounded hand, I take off, heading into the hall just as the bell rings and the classrooms empty, swallowing me up in the crowd and separating me from a boy who admitted he followed me.

33

Why? Because I'm fifth on a list he just told me he doesn't care about? Because he was looking for a tutor? Because he thinks I'm attractive? So he could break my finger if my heart didn't happen to be available? None of those options seems plausible, but I can't help wondering.

CHAPTER IV

The parent volunteer in the nurse's office has put me in a holding room that smells like bleach. Was the last person in here so sick they had to disinfect? The thought makes me a little queasy—but maybe that's just the throbbing, bleeding, purple middle finger on my right hand.

Not that it really hurts so much. The cut isn't that deep, and the really nasty bit under my nail is almost numb. Even though I wrapped it in some paper towels I got from the bathroom, I know it looks wretched. It's bad enough that I didn't bother to hunt down Molly for a second opinion—or third, if you count Levi Sterling, perpetrator—before I headed straight to the office for some antiseptic and a Band-Aid.

I perch on the edge of a vinyl cot and close my eyes, reliving my conversation with Levi, feeling stupid for being so caught up in his eyes and his game and his suggestion I tutor him that I didn't realize I'd stuck my finger in the locker door. So I can't really blame him for hurting me.

Although . . . he's been known to hurt people. At least, that's the rumor. Put a guy in the hospital, they say. Disappeared to a truant school for a while. Oh, hell, I've heard he's robbed banks and stolen cars and, basically, if it's a crime in Vienna, he's the cops' go-to guy.

Why would he even talk to me? He admitted he wasn't all about some idiotic Hottie List. Or was that a line?

A tap on the door interrupts my thoughts. "Kenzie Summerall?" a woman calls as the door inches open.

"You can come in."

The school nurse enters and gives me a quick smile, brushing back a strand of frosted blond hair that has slipped from her clip. "What's the problem?" she asks cheerily. "You hurt your finger?"

I hold up the whole hand because just showing her the one finger could get me a detention.

She reacts with raised eyebrows. "Bleeding?"

"A little."

She comes closer, searching my face. "You're very pale."

I touch my cheek, which is cool. "I just need to clean this out and get a Band-Aid."

"Let's take a look." She sits across from me, her considerable size making the chair squeak as she reaches for some latex gloves from a box.

"Am I going to lose that nail?" I ask when she takes hold of my hand, dreading the answer, because right now, that's my biggest fear.

She shakes her head, plucking at the slice in the skin. "How'd it happen?"

Flirting accident. "Locker injury."

She looks up, a gleam of humor in her pretty blue eyes. "We don't have a lot of those."

"I was . . . distracted." No way I'd admit the truth to her.

"All the attention around the list, I assume."

I jerk my hand a little, stunned. "The faculty knows about that?"

She sets my hand back down on my lap before getting up to go to a cabinet, opening it to block her profile from me. "Some do. Of course, I'm in the *in* crowd." She leans away from the open cabinet so I can see her tilt her head in a movie-star pose that's a bit weird, but kind of cute, too. "Number nine, 1988." She winks. "And that makes me forty-two if you can do math."

"You were on the list?" I instantly regret the shock in my voice, knowing exactly how that sounded—and really knowing how it must feel.

"I know, tough to believe. But I was a rockin' hundred and ten pounds back then, and the baby-oil-and-iodine-laden summer afternoons hadn't taken their wrath out on my skin yet." She brushes her face wistfully. "And sometimes the most surprising people get on that list."

Like me. "Was it a big deal back then?"

"Oh, yes." She places bandages and a bottle on a sterile tray, then settles back down in front of me. "Everyone looks at you differently."

"Tell me about it," I agree. "But I'm no different."

She takes my hand and lets out a sigh. "You're in a very special club."

I hiss in a breath when the disinfectant stings. "No offense, Nurse Fedder, but I really wasn't that interested in getting into this particular club. I'm more concerned about getting into college."

"No offense taken." She dabs lightly. "I was no great beauty, trust me, so getting voted onto the Hottie List was kind of a stunner."

"That's how I feel."

She scrutinizes my face again, this time with a less clinical eye. "You're pretty."

The way she says it makes me laugh. "Pretty average."

"No, pretty." She adds a slow, sad smile. "You look like your brother, and I mean that as a great compliment."

I keep myself from reacting with anything but a simple nod, mostly out of habit. I've heard it a hundred times. A thousand. We shared coloring and face shape, but Conner was somehow beautiful and bright, on the inside, too.

"He was a very nice boy."

"Yeah, thanks."

"Loved to talk."

I can't help but smile. "There was never a quiet moment in our house." But now it's stone silent most of the time.

"It's been about two years now, hasn't it?"

I try to swallow. "Just about."

"I'm sorry." She pats the hand she holds. "I just want you to know I thought he was a really outstanding young man."

No surprise there. Everyone loved Conner. *Everyone*. "He was," I agree, my voice gruff.

"Such a shame and shock, that accident."

Please, no. Don't go there. Don't take me there. I know she feels my hand stiffen in hers because she adds a quick, tight smile. "And no," she assures me. "You will not lose this nail." She unwinds a long strip of gauze. "But now you can really give someone that finger if they say you don't belong on the Hottie List."

"I don't"—I wince when she starts to wrap—"care about it," I finish.

"Oh, you will," she says confidently.

"Really, it's not that important to me." Maybe it was the highlight of her life. Maybe she peaked in high school. But that wasn't going to be me.

"It's not being on the list that's important," she says as she finishes the wrap. "It's the friends you make for life."

I sincerely doubt I'll be friends with the likes of Olivia Thayne and Chloe Batista.

"I'll tell the others I met you," she adds.

For a second, I'm not sure I heard her right. "What others?"

"The other hotties." She lets out a soft laugh. "I know it sounds crazy to call ourselves that when some are in their forties, but once a hottie always a hottie, we say."

"There's a club?" Which would be, *whoa*, another thing I don't want to be in.

She just smiles. "Celebrating the thirtieth year, too. We have an email loop, meet when we can, even attend weddings and . . ." She shakes her head. "A few heartbreaking funerals."

"Do I have to be in this club?"

"You *are* in this club." She puts the final piece of tape on the big white lump of gauze that used to be my middle finger. Without looking at me, she stands and begins to put her supplies away. "Like it or not." I hear her sigh deeply.

"Not," I say quickly.

"When you're ready, you can contact me." This time her look is quite serious, all humor absent from her eyes and replaced by something that looks a little . . . sad. "I won't be able to answer everything, of course, but over the years, we've learned a few things."

Like how to be weird. I stand and nod my thanks, so ready to get out of there. "Am I done? Do I have to see a doctor or get a note or something?"

"Keep that covered for a day or two and treat it gently, and the nail will heal. Get a pass for whatever class you're missing at the front desk."

"Okay, thanks." As I reach for the doorknob, her hand lands on my back, and I jump.

"And, Kenzie?"

I don't move, bracing myself for a parting shot about my wonderful, unforgettable, dead brother. "Yes?"

"Don't be afraid. . . ."

I turn to meet her eyes as she passes me in the doorway. "Of what?"

"Most of us have been lucky. But . . ." She lifts a shoulder. "Beware."

Did she say "beware" or "be aware"? The text message dances in my brain.

Caveat viator, Quinte.

Traveler beware. I try to act as casual as possible. "What are you talking about?"

Her smile is tight. "Just call me if you need . . ."

"What?"

She keeps her mouth sealed and that fake smile in place, her lips pressed so tight it looks like she's fighting to keep from saying anything else. Before I can ask again, she continues into the hall, disappearing around the corner.

I stand for a moment, trying to replay and understand the conversation. Why would I call her? What would I need? Something about Conner . . . or the list? Or this injury? Unable to decipher what she meant, I go back to the main office and head out.

"Excuse me! Kenzie!"

I turn, ready to face Nurse Fedder again, but it's the lady at the front desk, waving a pass I need to take to my physics teacher.

"Thanks," I say, taking the slip of paper.

"And he's here for you."

I glance in the waiting area, sucking in a breath at the sight of Levi Sterling on the couch, legs propped on a coffee table, my books and handbag next to him.

"I stopped into Zeller's room and got your stuff," he says, like it's the most normal thing in the world for him to have done. "And, no, I didn't go through your wallet." He's trying for a joke, but the humor isn't there. Can't be easy knowing everyone assumes the worst of you.

"Thanks," I say.

He stands, looking at my hand. "Nice."

Of course, I give him the finger. "This one's for you."

"I'm sorry," he says softly, and damn it, I believe him.

"'Sokay." I reach for my books and bag. The move is awkward with my newly bandaged finger, so he scoops up the textbooks for me. "Thanks," I say again, willing myself not to blush when his hand brushes mine.

Good God, Kenzie. Not only is he out of your league and dangerous—he just smashed your hand in your locker.

Beware.

41

I shake the nurse's weird warning out of my head. "I'm late for class, so I better go."

"I'll see you Sunday night, then."

I feel a frown form. "Sunday night?" Was there something going on that I didn't remember?

"For tutoring."

"At night?"

He laughs at my incredulous tone. "Yeah, at night." As I start to shake my head, he holds out his hand to stop my argument. "I talked to Mr. Zeller, and he thinks it's a great idea and the only way I'm going to pass the test next Monday."

I forgot Zeller also teaches Math for Morons. "I can't, sor—"

"He said he'd give you extra credit."

"I don't need it."

He leans his shoulder into mine. "Liar."

"I'm not lying. I have a—"

"You have an eighty-nine. I saw his grade book."

I blow out a breath. "I have a ninety-eight, so maybe your issue with word problems is the reading, not the math." I smile, a little smug with my clever banter.

But the smile fades as I read the expression in his eyes. "Yeah," he says softly, looking away. "Maybe."

He gives me a nod and takes a step in the other direction, leaving me with a sensation of . . . Crap. Why did I say that to him? Maybe he really does need help to pass and I'm the one who'll keep him from robbing a bank or being a garbage man. He's two steps away from me now, and my face grows warm as I try to remember all the reasons to say no. Juvie, motorcycle, trouble, bedroom eyes . . . nothing is actually making enough sense to use as an actual excuse.

"Saturday afternoon would be better," I say quickly, bringing him to a stop. At least I won't have to see him at night.

"I can't, I have someone—something else."

Someone else. We both know he was right the first time.

"Meet at Starbucks across from the Giant Eagle?" he suggests. "Sunday at eight."

That's close enough to my house that I can walk. "For an hour," I say.

"That'd be good, Mack. Thanks." He gives me the faintest hint of a wink, or maybe I imagined that. Either way, I don't know what I just got myself into, but I'm not as scared of him as I should be.

CHAPTER V

When Molly drops me off at home after school, the driveway is empty and so is the garage. I feel guilty for having a silent minicelebration, but my alone time is rare, even though it's just Mom and me in the house. She works as a legal assistant right in Vienna, and her boss is usually pretty cool about letting her leave around four, so I don't often get to enjoy being a latchkey kid.

Before Dad moved out last year, she'd sometimes coerce him into coming home from work early if she had to work late. The thought of their separation weighs on me as I yank open the mailbox at the end of the driveway. Dad still spends an awful lot of time here, fixing things and even sleeping on the couch if it gets too late. They don't really want to be apart, but any love they had somehow got swallowed up in grief after Conner died. Dad wants to leave this house and the memories—he has to, I think. But Mom feels that's being disloyal to the son she raised here.

I just want to be a family again.

Of course, that can never happen. Our family will always have a hole in it. If only Conner hadn't died. If only he hadn't gone into that Pharm-Aid basement storeroom. If only he hadn't reached into that crevice for my necklace. If only I hadn't dropped it. If only he hadn't been such a damn good brother who cared because I was crying. If only. If only. *If freaking only!*

My throat closes as I yank the bills and brochures from the box, barely looking at what I'm holding. I hate when I fall into the "if only" spiral. Pulling myself out, I round the house to unlock the side door.

I toss the mail onto the kitchen table and dip down so my overloaded backpack thumps on the top of it all, practically knocking the spice rack over in the process. Of course, I'm carrying a library's worth of textbooks. Bet none of the other list girls lugged home Calc, Latin, and AP US History books.

Before I take another step, I turn around and lock the door so as not to experience the wrath of Mom when she comes home. An unlocked door is somewhere between undercooked burgers and a slippery bathtub on the "tempting fate" scale that directs my mother's every move and thought.

I snag a can of Pringles from the pantry and a Coke from the fridge and head up the narrow stairs to my room, already considering how I can convince Mom to let me go to the football game. I'm pretty sure "the cutest guy in school asked me" isn't going to fly. In a few minutes, I've got Pandora playing some Mumford tunes and I log on to Facebook.

Holy cow. One hundred and four new friend requests.

I zip through the list of people who couldn't have cared less about following my woefully infrequent posts yesterday.

I accept them all. Just like I replied to the texts from people I didn't ever consider friends but who now want to hang out sometime. Why not? They'll forget about me when this list business dies down.

I also check Instagram, where I see hashtags like #hottielist and #topten and, oh my *God*, #kenziesummerallfifth have been created and used by many of the Vienna High students who thought it was perfectly okay to take random pictures of ten girls at school today.

I blink at the shot of me talking to Josh Collier in the parking lot. Someone took my picture? I don't have any recollection of that, no awareness at all that my picture was being taken. If I had, maybe I would have at least tried to wipe the wondrous look of teenage rapture off my face as I stare up at him like he's Zeus dropped down to Vienna High to break some hearts.

Which he kind of is. And he's never so much as thrown me a wayward smile, yet today I got sidelined in the parking lot, touched on the shoulder, and asked on a date.

That right there is the power of the list. It just gets attention, and some of it I don't want.

Like Levi Sterling. I can't help but compare Josh to the other boy who stole a lot of my thoughts today. Could they be any more different? At least on the surface, Josh seems so bright and harmless and golden. And Levi is dark and scary and sexy. All I know about either one of these guys comes from rumors and distant observation, so of course I turn to a reliable source of teen information: Facebook.

Since they're both in the group of 104 new friends, I go creeping. I'm pretty good at this, I have to say. I know how to sift through friends and family and find pictures and tags that tell me all about a person. And I'm not limited to the Vienna High crowd, either. I've learned how to stalk people who study classics at Columbia, even the professors who should be more private but aren't. I'm always picking up little tips I think will help me on my application.

Stalking Levi and Josh should be more fun than that, especially because we're Facebook friends now, so I can really dig beyond friend lists and pictures and see their posts. Except Levi rarely posts. His pictures are a couple of years old, and not very plentiful. Not a single picture of his family or his house. No activities, party pictures, or goofy shots. Guess he wasn't allowed to post while *he was in juvie.*

Josh, on the other hand, posts kind of stupid sayings almost daily, like "Guns don't kill people, people kill people"—does he think he made that up?—and tons of pictures of him in football, basketball, and lacrosse uniforms and, of course, having fun with his legions of friends.

So, suddenly this popular boy is interested in an unremarkable Latin club geek like me? I know why, of course, but I'm not sure if I like it. Why wasn't I good enough to talk to before this list came out? Did he need the approval of "votes," or is he just simply seeing me for the first time? Should I give him the benefit of the doubt? Why not? What's the harm in it?

Still curious, I find an album called "Christmas" on Josh's page and dive in, ready to see his family. No siblings, it seems, and no pictures of his parents. Just more friends and an older man named Rex Collier, who I assume is his grandfather, with all that white hair.

I click through a few more photos, hearing the kitchen door

open just as Pandora jumps to a commercial. I know I should call out to Mom, but I don't want my solitude to end yet. And I really don't want to deal with the discussion we're going to have when I ask if I can go to the game.

Forget the fact that most kids my age wouldn't even ask— they'd just go. But most kids didn't bury their brother, so I'm different that way.

I spend more time clicking through Josh's pictures, looking at one of him standing next to the brand-new sixty-thousand-dollar Audi he got for his sixteenth birthday. *Someone* has money in that family.

That reminds me of my old Accord, and I get off Facebook with a hard keystroke. I should call Dad and find out what the damage is going to be, but I don't really want to know. Shutting off the music, I hear Mom in the kitchen and wait for her to call me. I know she won't come up here; she never does.

I glance at my hand, which doesn't really hurt anymore, but the injury will probably send her into a tizzy. *How did it happen? Who did this to you? Why weren't you more careful? Was the door rusty? Do you need a tetanus shot?*

My throat closes and the weight presses down on my chest, familiar and unwelcome. The suffocation of Kenzie Summerall is about to begin, and it's already making me freakishly tired.

It's quiet downstairs, so I close my eyes, wondering why Mom hasn't hollered up here yet. Bad day at the law firm? Sometimes the legal secretaries in the office make her nuts with all their gossiping, and I get the brunt of it in the form of a lousy mood. More often than not, though, she's just anxious to hear about my day and make sure I survived it. Literally.

48

I'd already decided not to tell her about the Hottie List. My parents didn't grow up in Vienna and don't know anything about this particular high school tradition, and frankly, there's no reason to tell. She'd just find something to worry about. *Oh, Kenzie, what if all that publicity brings some pedophile after you?*

I fall back onto my bed and feel my body drifting into the softness of an afternoon nap, but in the distance, I think I hear the door again. Did she go out? Leave something in the car? I wait for what feels like an eternity, but the exhaustion of the day seems to be pressing down on me.

Images of Levi Sterling and Josh Collier collide in my head, all dark and light like the embodiments of evil and good. My brain's playing tricks on me, giving them animal faces.

Hac urget lupus, hac canis.

The Latin words float through my head and I have to dig a little harder than usual for the literal translation. But it comes to me: *On this side a wolf presses, on that a dog.* I know that means trouble on either side, but isn't a dog a bit safer than a wolf? Levi is definitely the wolf. But he's also the one that makes me a little . . . a lot weak inside.

I let out a yawn so giant it cracks my jaw and makes my whole body shudder, slipping me even deeper into nothingness. I'm so unbelievably tired. I have to sleep. I have to . . .

Next to me, my phone rings, close enough to my ear to jar me awake. Wow, this being-popular business is exhausting. I turn my head, which feels like the most I can possibly do, and read the screen.

Mom.

Mom is calling. Wait? What? How can that be? She probably locked herself out while taking out the trash or something.

That's so like her, the overlocker. I reach for the phone, vaguely aware that my afternoon nap left me with a headache and . . . the scent of rotten eggs. Gross. What is that smell?

I grab the phone. "Hi."

"Honey, I'm so sorry to be this late."

I blink myself awake, which is no mean feat. "What do you mean?"

"Mr. Hoyt had a deposition and made me stay until the client left. I know you've been home alone for, what, an hour? Everything okay?"

"Didn't I just . . ." My voice trails off as every hair on my arms and neck rises slowly. "You're not . . . home yet?"

"Where are you, Kenzie?" she asks sharply.

"In my room." I roll over on the bed, aware that my heart is jackhammering my ribs. "I fell asleep."

After I heard you come home.

"Are you sick? Do you have a fever?"

I never, *never* cop to anything that makes her worry, but . . . didn't I hear someone downstairs?

I know I locked the door. I remember putting my bag down, turning the latch, dropping the mail . . . or did I? My brain is like a blanket of sleepy fog.

"Kenzie? Are you all right?" Her voice rises in a familiar note of grade one panic. Not anywhere near her potential of DEFCON 5 (saved for left turns, no matter how far away the oncoming car is), but she is now alarmed.

Of course, that just means she is now breathing.

"I'm fine, Mom, just sleepy." But I'm staring at my open door, half expecting an ax murderer to jump into the room. I know I heard something.

50

I squeeze my eyes shut, as adept at stopping my own fears as I am at sidestepping hers. I must have totally imagined that noise.

"Did you sleep last night? You didn't tell me you had a bad night. Anything going on at school?"

Oh, here we go. "It's a nap, Mom, not a coma."

I hear her sigh at my sarcasm. "I'll be home in less than half an hour."

"'Kay." Then I remember the football game. "Oh, Mom, did you have any plans for tonight?"

"Just burgers and fries, honey. I thought we could watch a movie."

My eyes shutter heavily. She's lonely, I know, and when Dad doesn't come over, I'm all she's got. Whose fault is that? Mine. "Oh, okay."

"Why?"

"I just thought . . ." That smell dances up my nose again, putrid and stronger. "I was thinking about going to the football game at school."

"Oh, Kenzie." I hear her already digging for reasons why no safe or sane person should go to a high school football game. "Do you think that's a good idea?"

"Yes, Mom." I try to dial back the bitchy, but it gets so hard sometimes. What I want to say is, *I think going to a football game on a nice autumn night when you're sixteen years old and the hottest guy on the team asks you is a grand idea.* It's not respect that stops me; I just don't have the energy for a fight right now.

"We'll talk when I get home, Kenzie. Be careful."

I don't respond because I feel like crap and my head hurts even worse now. Anyway, "be careful" is just her everyday sign-off. I learned long ago that it was her substitute for "I love you" and stopped waiting to hear the real thing.

I hang up, still staring into the hall. The other door is visible, but closed, of course. Conner's room remains exactly as it was the day he went to work after school and let me tag along because I didn't want to be home alone.

I stay still and listen, but a bone-deep exhaustion still presses, despite the adrenaline rush. I know that if I don't move, I'll be asleep again in a minute. Fighting the same physical pain that I feel when my alarm goes off at 6:30, I slowly roll off the bed.

I have to go downstairs and make sure I locked the door.

Shaking my head clear, I walk across the room, drawing back with a face when I get another whiff of that rancid smell. What the heck?

My pulse is loud enough in my head that I don't hear my own footsteps, let alone any downstairs. I hold the handrail and peer down.

"Anyone there?" I say, feeling incredibly stupid. And just a little . . . sick.

A wave of nausea swells in my stomach and I grip tighter, taking each steep step slowly.

The house is dead silent, but the smell is stronger. I hesitate on the last step, continuing to steady myself with the handrail. This is crazy. I've spooked myself for no reason.

I leap around the stairway wall, landing in the empty, quiet dining room.

Now I really feel stupid. And, whoa, dizzy. I walk to the kitchen because I was absolutely sure I'd heard Mom in there. But the room's as quiet and still and empty as when I came in. I go straight to the door and check the latch, which is firmly horizontal and locked.

Okay, totally an overactive imagination. But what is that smell? Good God, did someone blow one in here?

I turn in a circle, my gaze stopping on the lock, my book bag, the mail, the partially opened pantry door. Did I leave it like that?

Another set of chills rises over my arms because I swear, I did not leave that door open. I take a step closer and then I hear something.

A low, soft, slow . . . *hiss*.

What the hell is that noise?

I look at the stove to see that the back burner knob is twisted to the right—*on*—but there are no flames. What does that mean?

It means that poisonous gas has been seeping through the whole house, and if I hadn't just noticed, I'd have been dead in about ten minutes.

CHAPTER VI

Throwing myself at the stove, I flip the knob so hard it pops off in my hand. With a small shriek, I lean closer, listening for the sound of escaping gas.

Everything's off. But how—

No. Not yet. If I think, I'll freak. I have to move. Or worse—I'll faint.

If Mom hadn't called I would have died in my sleep!

I lunge toward the stove-top exhaust fan, turning it on max, then bolt to the kitchen door, unlocking it with trembling fingers to throw it open. I don't care who's out there, or who was in here. . . .

Yes I do.

I fill my lungs with air, gulping and gasping like a person who's been held underwater. Instantly feeling clearer, I look side to side, not even sure what or who I'm looking for, a million thoughts at war in my head.

Did someone break in? Did Mom leave the stove on all day? Was Dad here? Or was it someone else? Did I bump the knob by accident? Did I really lock the door? What did I hear when I thought it was Mom?

But the questions are all just background noise to the words my brain is screaming.

I almost died. I almost died. *I almost freaking died . . . for the second time in less than twenty-four hours.*

The side yard is empty except for the trash cans, neatly closed and lined up the way Mom likes them. The way Mom likes everything—orderly. She's obsessive about neatness. And safety. And timeliness. And she checks the stove about ten times a day, including before bed and before leaving the house, even if nobody has cooked on it.

It's her thing.

So who messed with the stove? The whole place could have exploded with one stray spark!

I'm thinking more clearly now, breathing steadier with a heart rate approaching . . . No, not normal yet. But I venture back inside and stand very still to try to re-create what on earth happened in here.

I can't. There is absolutely no answer. No one was in here.

But I *heard* footsteps. Didn't I? I was so sleepy. . . . Of course I was! I was inhaling poison and knocking on death's front door.

With a whimper of fear, I open the cabinet under the cook-top, not even sure what I'm looking for, but immediately I see an electrical cord hanging there, pulled from its plug in the wall. I vaguely recall Dad talking about that when he installed the new gas cooktop for Mom. Something about an igniter? Something that makes sure there's a flame and we don't breathe gas.

How did that get unplugged? And how did the burner knob get turned on?

After fixing the plug, I drop into the chair. The exhaust fan is loud enough to drown out that thought, and I'm certain the smell of gas is dissipating. But I have to clear out this house and I have to . . .

Tell Mom.

In the distance, I hear the soft ding of my phone, still upstairs, alerting me to a text. Mom in high worry mode, no doubt. And with good reason. I jog back upstairs to assure her I'm still alive—and for once, I'm not kidding. The phone's on my bed next to my laptop. I unlock the screen to see an unknown number.

Another new friend? Another invitation to hang out with someone I barely know? I tap the message and read.

Lares et penates, Quinte? Aut viam inveniam aut faciam.

What? The last phrase clicks into place instantly—*I will either find a way or make a way.* Every Latin student learns that in the first semester of phrases.

But what does this mean? Who sent it? And *lares et penates*? I got nothing there. Still shaking, I seize my Latin textbook and manage to get to the glossary in the back, praying the translation is there. I might know this, but I can't think. I can't . . .

The *lares* and *penates* are the Roman gods of the household. My eyes sting as I read the short paragraph. "Gods who looked after the safety and well-being of the home." Slowly, I lower the textbook because I just can't stand what this is telling me. Whoever texted knew what just happened.

Then my eyes fall on the last sentence: "The *penates* are the gods of the storeroom with the duty of keeping the house free of danger."

I grab the phone and back away, blindly smashing the button that turns the device off completely, if only to prevent the horror of another text. I turn to the door, certain I'm going to meet the eyes of a killer. No one's there . . . just the closed door to my brother's room. *My brother who died in a storeroom.*

A bolt of horror jerks me and I run out of the room and down the stairs, my whole body vibrating. The place still smells and Mom will be home soon. And she will freak with a capital *F*.

What's worse? This . . . stalker, or Mom discovering I almost died? Knowing the answer, I open the kitchen windows, still seeing the words on my text. He called me *Quinte*.

Fifth.

The house phone rings, making me jump a foot and yelp like a frightened cat. Instantly, the fear rolls over me again. No one calls our house phone, ever. We use cell phones for everything; the only reason we have a landline is in case cell service is down and we need to call 911 to tell them where we are.

The shrill ringing doesn't stop. What if it's another Latin message? What if whoever was in the house is now calling to tell me . . . *caveat.*

Beware.

I grab the receiver with one thought: we can trace a landline call.

Bracing myself for the absolute worst mouth-breathing and hair-raising warning, I pick up the phone. "Hello?"

"Kenzie, there you are." I almost faint at the sound of my father's voice.

Maybe I should tell Dad. Dad could help, right? Dad would take this seriously but not freak out.

"Yeah, I'm right here," I say, my head whirring.

"I called your cell phone about four times." He sounds more weary than angry.

"I left it upstairs." I close my eyes and try to come up with the words to tell him what's happened. I fail.

"I wanted to talk to you about your car. I got the estimate."

I can tell from his voice it's bad news. But worse than *I almost died at the hands of a crazed Latin-speaking killer*? "Is it bad?" I ask weakly.

"Very. But, Kenzie, I'm more concerned about the situation with your brakes. Don't you read your dashboard?"

"Of course I do."

"Then why didn't you see the warning light that said you were out of brake fluid?"

I close my eyes, picturing the dash. "There was no light."

"There had to be," he insists.

"Dad." I know my own dashboard. "I never saw a warning light. What happened?"

"Can't tell now. The accident screwed up the car enough that we can't see how your brake line cracked or ruptured, but you leaked enough fluid to have a failure."

I blow out a breath. "I didn't see a warning light, Dad. How did it happen? How does that line crack?"

"You hit something, usually, or natural wear. That car has a hundred and forty-some thousand miles on it."

"I know that." I press my hand to my temple, a completely

different kind of headache throbbing now that the gas is clear. Something is buzzing in there, nagging at me. I have to know. "Could it have happened any other way, Dad?"

He snorts. "Short of someone cutting the fluid line? No."

Oh, God. I grab a kitchen chair for support.

"You need to get those brakes checked regularly, young lady."

"Okay."

"You do not want another accident."

But I almost just had one.

"Is your mother there?"

"Not yet. She had to stay late."

"Yeah, Mr. Hoyt had a deposition today." It doesn't really surprise me that he's up on Mom's schedule. "Listen to me," he says gruffly. "Under no circumstances do you share this with your mother about the brake line."

"I know she'd go ballistic, Dad, but—"

"No, Kenzie. Don't do that to her. She'll just worry herself sick."

He really cares about her. This is not news, but it never fails to twist my heart and give me an extrabrutal kick of guilt and sadness. If it weren't for Conner's death, they'd still be together.

"She can't handle that this week," he adds.

"What's this week?"

He sighs. "Just don't tell her. And I'll cover the cost of the bodywork on the car. We'll work it out later."

Without another word, he hangs up. I realize that I'm still holding my cell phone, so I push the top button to bring it back to life, instantly getting a vibration of a new text. No, not again.

But this one's from Olivia Thayne, hottie number one.

Party at Keystone Quarry tonight. You in?

I tap back to the text list to brave another read of the Latin message, but . . . Damn it. There is no such message. Did I imagine that? A result of partial gas poisoning or something?

My gaze falls to the date in the corner of the phone, giving me a start. How could I have forgotten what was coming up and why Dad would be worried about Mom? The two-year anniversary of Conner's accident is next week.

The accident that happened because he was doing me a favor.

The sound of Mom's car door pulls me back to the moment, and I know exactly what I'm going to do tonight. Not the football game. Not the quarry party. Nope, it's burgers, fries, a movie, and companionable silence with my mom. I owe her at least that.

CHAPTER VII

Mom's already asked me to spend Saturday with her, which will mean a trip to Sam's Club, also known as my personal hell in a big-box superstore. I don't want to fight with her, especially since we made it through the night without an argument. Yes, she did a low-level flip-out over my bandaged hand. *You could get MRSA! How qualified is that nurse?*

But after she undid the bandage and examined the bruise, she came down from the crazy ledge and managed to relax a little. We both did, thankfully. Of course, I didn't tell her about the gas incident. Or the car.

By the time I went to bed, I'd convinced myself of the obvious—someone accidentally knocked out the igniter plug when putting a frying pan away and I had bumped the stove dial with my backpack when I took it off. The noise I heard? The old house settling. The text? Obviously, the gas leak had played with my head, because when I looked at my phone, the text was gone. Texts don't delete themselves.

But I can't take a day of shopping with Mom. Molly comes to the rescue with an invitation to spend the day and night at her house. Which Mom won't like, but I'm ready with all the reasons why I should. I eat Cheerios and wait for her to come in.

She does, moving slowly, looking far, far older than forty-four years, making little effort to fight her graying hair and softening jowls. That just makes me feel guilty again. Two years ago, when our house was vibrant and our family whole and Conner Summerall reigned as the golden boy in our home and outside of it, Mom reflected his light as a happy, pretty, healthy woman. That woman died the day she buried her sixteen-year-old son.

"Sam's today?" she asks, an attempt at brightness that I always think is faked for my benefit.

"I'm going over to Molly's."

She starts to frown.

"And tonight," I add, just so we get that out there first and fast, "I'm sleeping over."

She draws back, ready to put a stop to that. "Can't she stay here?"

That was always her solution. I could have sleepovers, if she was there to monitor the potential hazards. God, I want to be normal. I want to go to parties and football games and on dates. And for the first time—thanks to the list—some of that actually awaits in my future. I have to shake her fears.

"She can't," I say. "I have to go over there."

She goes through the motions of making a cup of coffee, something about her expression indicating she's actually thinking about saying yes. I hold on to that hope.

"You'll miss Dad. He's coming over for dinner."

Hey, that's almost a yes. "Well, okay. That way you won't be alone." Because deep down in my gut, I don't want her to be alone in the house. And I know Dad will of course sleep on the sofa in the family room, because he'll have a drink and Mom won't let him drive. In fact, if I'm not here, maybe he'll sleep where he belongs . . . in his room with Mom.

"What time would you be going?" she asks.

"A little bit later. You don't have to wait for me. Molly can pick me up or I'll ride my bike."

She gives me a quick look. "Wear your helmet."

Yes! But I keep my cool and smile with a thumbs-up, so glad I stayed home with her last night.

Sumo vestri proeliis. Choose your battles, baby. And I won this one.

An hour later, I'm on my bike riding to Molly's house, wind in my hair (totally ignoring the helmet command—such a rebel), my backpack holding only clothes for the night and not a single book. This is huge for a dweeb who studies all weekend, and I can barely wipe the smile off my face.

Because, hey, dweebie life changed yesterday. Guys hit on me, the entire school knows me, my social networks are overflowing with new friends, and even Mom seems to have gotten the memo that Kenzie Summerall has moved up the popularity ladder. And I'm taking Molly with me.

Jazzed by that, I pedal harder, dying to share everything with her.

The last shreds of a decent autumn have washed the world in amber tones under a rare blue sky. I wind around the curves and over the hills, humming a tune in my head.

I'm not looking at the brick houses or almost-bare trees,

though, and there isn't enough traffic on these streets for me to worry about cars. Instead, my mind drifts to Levi Sterling and pretty much stays there as I bike past Cedar Hills Middle School, my alma mater and the halfway point between my house and Molly's.

I cut through the teachers' lot and past an outdoor basketball court, where a bunch of younger boys are shooting hoops. On the other side of the gym, I pull out to cross Baldrick Road, bracing my foot to hit the crosswalk button at the light even though there are no cars on this quiet Saturday morning in the rolling neighborhood of Cedar Hills.

This light takes forever because it's in front of a school, I know that. So, what am I waiting for?

I look left and right—not a car in either direction. So I force my foot down on the pedal and pull off the curb, my eyes on that still-red Don't Walk sign I'm disobeying. I hear an engine, glance left, and catch the front end of a dark vehicle coming out of the school lot.

Praying the vehicle doesn't turn right, I press harder, the pedal suddenly so hard to push it feels like I'm riding through mud, but I reach the middle of the southbound lane. I can't get back to the curb now. There are three lanes left to cross and that engine revs louder, making me look over my shoulder just as a truck pulls onto the road, heading directly for me.

I freeze for a second, whirring through my options. I can't back up; if I go forward he could hit me, so please . . . *stop*.

But the pickup keeps coming, and my bike wavers in the middle of the intersection as I make the instant decision to try to beat him to the other side of the street. Heart pumping in my ears, I pound the pedals around, sliding into the northbound lane just as the truck zooms by behind me.

Was that necessary, asshole? Yes, I was in the wrong by crossing on a red, but really? I whip around to glare at windows tinted so dark it's impossible to see a face. Still, I stare with righteous indignation, losing my balance and wobbling to one side.

I manage to get my foot on the ground before I fall, looking again as the truck gets farther away. Just before he turns at the next intersection, the driver's window rolls down and a hand reaches out to wave at me. He *waved*?

What a *jerk*!

Shaking, I slip off the bike and walk it onto the sidewalk, still staring down the road, but the truck disappears. Did he just wave at me like this was his idea of a joke?

I frown, the image of his hand spread out wide still burning in my mind. No, that wasn't a *wave*. That was . . . the number five.

Delivered by the driver of a dark pickup truck very much like the one that nearly killed me the other night.

I grip the handlebars to stay steady and catch my breath. I have to stop. My imagination, always a tad hyperactive and now fueled by my wack mom, is in overdrive. I have to stop this.

There are a thousand dark pickup trucks in Vienna, and all that guy meant was he was sorry. Right? He was probably on the phone or texting and didn't see me until he passed.

Let's not forget I was in the middle of the intersection when I should have been waiting for the light to change.

No one just tried to kill me, damn it. I just tried to kill myself.

If there's any hope for me in this life at all, I have to stop letting every normal day loom like an accident waiting to kill me. And I sure can't let those old worries get tied to the meaningless Hottie List just because he held out five fingers.

Molly will help me, I tell myself. She'll play up the positives of the list, too. New friends, new popularity, a possible new boyfriend!

I bike hard and fast up the hill to Molly's house, so angry at myself I barely notice how steep it is. With each strained pedal pump, I intensify the lecture in my head.

So I had a car accident the other night. So I got a couple of weird texts and accidentally deleted them. And I had a little brush with a gas leak yesterday. And I made a stupid mistake on my bike.

I will not turn into my mother.

I've got my eye on Molly's redbrick split-level house at the top of the hill, making it my goal, when I see her running into the driveway, waving frantically at me.

"Hey!" I call, breathless and laughing at how much effort it takes to make that last hundred feet.

"Kenzie, hurry!" she yells back. A frightened note in her voice makes my heart catch. Something's wrong.

She runs toward me, meeting me before I even reach her yard. Her hands are over her mouth and her eyes are wide with shock and fear. Something is most definitely wrong.

I slip off the bike seat. "What's the—"

"Did you hear about Olivia Thayne?"

I can only stare at her, my throat closed so tight no words can come out. I shake my head.

"She hit her head diving into Keystone Quarry at a party last night." Molly reaches out to me. "She's dead, Kenzie."

66

CHAPTER VIII

"Everyone is going to school," Molly says an hour later while we're still combing social media and reading texts, trying like crazy to make sense of the shock. "Look."

She turns her phone to me so I can see the latest post on the #rememberolivia hashtag that's been flying through the Twitter stream for the last twenty minutes.

"Why?" I ask.

"To talk about it, I guess." She rolls off the bed and starts digging around her clothes for a jacket, but I don't move.

"I don't want to go to school today, Moll." I want to digest this some more. And, God, I want to tell her all the weird things that have been happening, so she can totally make me see how dumb it is to even try to connect the accident, the gas leak, or that car that buzzed me on Baldrick. And now Olivia's death. But for some reason, putting that into words is so incredibly lame I can't mention it. Why would I even go there?

"Not *in* the school," she says. "Everyone's in the junior lot. We need to be there. We're her classmates, Kenzie." She sighs. "Well, we were."

But I was never close to Olivia Thayne, unless I count the fact that she invited me to the party at Keystone Quarry. Where she died.

Molly pops out of a pullover hoodie and fluffs her hair in the mirror. "Would it be wrong to wear makeup?"

"Wrong? It would be out of character and . . . Why?"

She pivots, narrowing her brown eyes. "Because that's what cool girls do." She lets her voice rise on the last word, almost a question, as if she's not sure at all what cool girls do.

"I wouldn't know," I say dryly.

"Well, you better find out since you're one of them now. And if you are, I am, right?"

"Right."

"And by the way . . ." She returns to the mirror, picking up a brush and running it through her shoulder-length hair. "Josh is there."

I wait for my heart to skip or soar or at least do a little tap dance at the thought of seeing Josh. Nothing. "Really?"

She smiles, catching my eyes in the mirror. "Want to go now?"

Do I? "Kind of sick to use the tragic death of a classmate to see a guy."

"So that's a yes?"

"I don't know. We wouldn't have gone two days ago, would we?"

She frowns, not following.

"The list," I say. "You think we belong where all the kids are gathering like I have some kind of entrance pass because of the list. We're still the same band/Latin club/uncool kids we were on Thursday."

"I am, you aren't." She kneels on the bed and looks hard at me. "Anyway, Olivia was like a, you know, sorority sister to you."

I give a dismissive wave, thinking of Nurse Fedder's comment. *Most of us have been lucky. Beware.* The warning echoes, but I don't share it. There is some weird tug at my heart, though. As if I should go to school in a show of solidarity for my dead listmate.

"Well, think about it, Kenz," Molly says. "There are, what, four hundred and forty kids in the junior class? The list is less than . . ." She screws up her face. "A small percent."

"Two point three," I supply.

"Smartass."

"I am. I'm smart and I'm quiet and I'm boring and I'm not hot, so I don't belong on that freaking list!" My voice gets a little too loud, and she draws back at my outburst.

"How can you say that? You're pretty." She pulls me off her bed and turns me to the mirror. "You have beautiful blue eyes."

I squint, not seeing anything beautiful.

She takes two handfuls of my hair and lifts it like angels' wings. "You have gorgeous mahogany hair."

"Mahogany?" I laugh. "Who *says* that?"

"Me. And look at that face." She takes my chin, angling my head. "Not a zit in sight."

"That doesn't make me pretty."

"Kenzie! What is wrong with you? You got voted onto the list, why don't you just embrace it? The world—and the boys

69

in it—sees you differently than you see yourself. It's time to break out of that bad habit, and I know just the trick."

"What?"

"A boyfriend. Josh Collier."

I can't help but snort. "He's just being nice to me, Molly. I'm not girlfriend material. Not for a guy like him."

"Then who?"

I have to get Molly's opinion, so I risk it. "How about Levi Sterling?"

She chokes softly. "I assume you're kidding."

Am I? "You know how I told you what happened at my locker? Well, right before I got hurt, he asked me to, um . . ." I make a show of using her brush and fixing my hair, just to avoid looking at her. ". . . tutor him."

Her jaw slackens, her eyes turning into slits. "You wouldn't do that, would you?"

"He needs help in math."

"You can't help a kid who's going to fail anyway. He's a serial class-cutter."

Was he? "Well, he asked me, and—"

"Kenzie, that kid is a zero." Now she raises her voice. "He's trouble. Nothing but a truant on his way to jail. Where he's already got a cell with his name on it, I hear."

"You *hear*," I say. "But do we *know*? We have no idea what happened in his old school."

"Other than that some chick cut his name into her boobs with a razor blade."

"Thigh," I correct her. "And oh my God, does that ever smell of urban folklore."

"All those stories can't be folklore," she fires back. "He

70

steals, he does drugs, he deals drugs, he rides a motorcycle. I heard he put a kid in the hospital in a fight."

I'd heard that, too. "You know, when I hurt my hand, he seemed really concerned."

Instantly, Molly is in my face. "He's the one who leaned on the locker and gave you the injury," she says, eyes wide. "He's nasty, that boy. He's trouble."

"He's hot."

Her jaw falls so hard I'm surprised I don't hear it hit the floor. "Yes, if you're into the ex-con type."

"Molly."

"Kenzie! You can have your pick of Vienna High boys now that you're on that list. You can do a heck of a lot better than a thug like that."

A thug who wants tutoring? "He might be misunderstood."

She grunts with disgust. "You'll get over this madness the minute you see Josh. C'mon." She scoops up my jacket. "Let's get to school and join the vigil."

I can't get my head around her twisted logic. "No, I don't want to go hang out in the parking lot and grieve over a girl who never said boo to me until last night."

"What did she say last night?"

"She texted me and invited me to the party at Keystone Quarry."

Molly gasps, grabbing my phone from where I left it. "I can't believe you didn't tell me that! Let me see. That could have been the last text she ever sent!"

I take the phone and unlock the screen for her, shaking my head. "I doubt that." I scroll through, looking for Olivia's text.

"People will want to read that," Molly says.

71

"What people?" I look up. "Like the cops?"

"No, like her friends. Her last text could be, you know, important."

"Oh." I read the phone again, flipping through my text list, my heart falling as my head gets a little light. Not again. "I can't find the text," I say softly. "I've been losing a lot of messages lately."

"Never mind." She tugs the phone from my hands and urges me up. "Let's go. I want to go."

"Why is it so important, Molly?"

She sighs and bends down to meet my gaze. "Kenzie, I'm just this side of a social outcast. I have never run with the in crowd and I—*we*—have a chance. They're expecting you at this thing. Let's go and, what do you Latin kids say? *Carpe diem*?"

I just smile. "Yeah, that." Maybe I should seize the day— and find out exactly what happened to this girl and make sure it was merely a freak accident. "C'mon, Molly, you're right. Let's go."

The junior lot at Vienna High is a special place on a normal day. The area isn't designated only for eleventh graders who drive to school: it sits on a slight hill looking down over the buildings, with shady trees and wide spots perfect for those of us who haven't mastered tight parking slots yet. The seniors have their own lot, closer to school, but the junior lot includes a few picnic tables where kids hang out in the morning or have lunch. The crooked steps that connect the lot to the school are now peppered with cellophane-wrapped bouquets, stuffed animals, and homemade signs, many of which include pictures of Olivia and one that says #1 IN OUR HEARTS.

Molly gestures to it as we leave her car to start mingling. "You think that's a reference to the list?"

"I'd like to forget about the list," I say. "Let's just find out what happened to her."

A group of girls are standing arm in arm in a huge circle, rocking back and forth and singing some sappy song. One of them catches my eye and gives a halfhearted wave. I think she's about to call us over, when her gaze shifts to Molly and her hand drops.

I feel Molly stiffen next to me and I know she saw it, too. "I don't want to talk to them," I say quickly, even though I suspect she does. No, I *know* she does.

"You should," she says. "They're all on the list."

She's right. Amanda Wilson and Kylie Leff are anchoring the sides of the group like the cocaptain cheerleaders they are. Between them, I spy Dena Herbert and, next to her, Chloe Batista. Do I belong in that group?

Someone thought so. I'm surprised at how torn I feel about going over there.

Chloe trains her gorgeous blue eyes on me and adds a slow nod of permission.

Molly nudges me. "You've been tapped by the queen bee. Better step into the honeycomb."

"Or the hive," I mumble. "I'm not going over there without you, Moll."

But she hesitates, holding back. "Why don't you go make nice with your listmates, and you can slowly get them used to

73

the idea that you're a living, breathing BOGO. Buy Kenzie, get Molly for free."

I shoot her a smile, feeling a rush of affection for her. "I'll do that," I promise. We separate and she goes off to talk to some of the band kids while I make my way to the circle.

"Kenzie!" Dena Herbert, one of the most visible girls in class, who's a popular jock but also parties hard, gestures to the spot next to her. "Come on."

"Hey, Kenzie," Amanda calls over to me. "Glad you're here."

She is? I refuse to give in to the small thrill that simple acceptance sends through me. We're here because a teenager is dead, and no one knows as well as I do how horrible that really is. But I can't help it. Being part of a group, a clique, a circle of friends who are considered popular is . . . fun. Just plain fun.

"If I die young?" Kylie, Amanda's best friend, calls out, making me swing around in shock. What did that mean?

"Perfect choice," chimes in Candace Yardley, a gorgeous Asian girl with waist-length hair.

"Oh my God," Shannon Dill squeals. "I love Taylor Swift!"

Amanda gives her a cutting look. "Actually, it's the Band Perry. Sing, everyone."

Shannon rolls her eyes at the correction, but in another few seconds, someone is singing the first line to the sweet pop ballad "If I Die Young." The choice is inspired, I have to admit, and almost immediately, I find myself swaying with them, singing off key about being buried in satin on a bed of roses.

The words, most of which I don't know, sucker-punch my heart anyway, squeezing tears from my eyes and planting a far-too-familiar ache deep in my belly. I look around at the faces—strangers, essentially—and feel the weirdest sense of belonging, a comforting warmth that I let wash over me for the duration of the song. When we're finished, I impulsively hug Dena, and when I look over her shoulder I see Molly sitting on top of a picnic table with some other kids, watching us.

I don't want to belong to any group at the expense of my best friend. Pulling away, I give Dena a quick smile. These aren't exactly optimum circumstances for expanding my social circle, anyway. After all, there were ten girls on that list and only nine of us are alive.

The thought kind of buckles my legs, but Dena grabs me and offers support. "I know, man. This sucks."

I look at her. "She was number one."

Dena pales a little. "Let's hope the bad luck stops there."

Next to her, Chloe leans in. "Don't scare her, Dena."

My heart rolls around, caught in a very tight band around my chest. "What do you mean?"

Chloe just lifts her eyebrows mysteriously. "We'll talk," she says to both of us. "But not here."

The group starts to disperse and I use the opportunity to go back to Molly.

Over the next half hour, we hear ten different versions of the story. The best I can tell, the kids who were at Keystone Quarry weren't from Vienna High, making me wonder why I got an invitation from Olivia and no one else did. They were partying and someone suggested jumping off the cliff, about twenty-five feet above the water.

Olivia jumped and never came out.

And that's where it gets murky. Rumors and speculation beat anything like the truth, and stories were flying like bullets across the parking lot.

She was totally shit-faced and fell.

She jumped on a dare.

A few of the boys jumped in to find her and her leg was trapped between two boulders.

The only thing that sounds real is that the paramedics and rescue team brought her body out after someone called about the accident. Whatever happened, it's awful.

Molly and I end up with the kids we eat lunch with and a few stragglers I don't really know. Sophie Hanlon, a supershy but very sweet girl who is Molly's close friend from elementary school, is there, along with Kara Worthy and Michael Kaminsky, who are both in Latin club with me.

Across the lot, I see a group of guys and instantly spot Josh Collier, who stands nearly a head above the rest.

Molly catches me looking and elbows me. "Told you he'd be here."

"Yeah, yeah." I look away, chewing my lip. "What do you think really happened, Moll?" I ask.

"She got drunk and fell."

"I hope so."

Molly's eyes widen. "What the heck does that mean?"

"What if someone pushed her?"

"This is Vienna, Pennsylvania, Kenzie. Crime is low."

"I hope so," I say again. "Because what if . . ." Oh, man. I'm really about to sound like my mother, looking for trouble where there is nothing but an imagination on steroids.

"What if what?"

I lean a little closer. "What if she was killed 'cause she was on the list?"

I get the exact look I expected. Incredulity mixed with a smile. "Hey, I'm the one who thinks it's a big deal, and even I don't think any of the two hundred–some girls who didn't get on the list would kill over it," she says. "Anyway, it's not like that leaves an opening or something."

"I don't know," I say softly. "It's just scary."

"Death is scary," she agrees, looking over my shoulder. "You know what else is scary?"

"What?"

"Levi Sterling."

I snap around without thinking, meeting his smoldering gaze, locked on me. Inside, everything sort of shifts . . . my heart, my stomach, my center of gravity. I'm vaguely aware that seeing Josh had no such effect on me.

He barely notches his chin at me, very cool, very subtle, *very* sexy.

"Talk about killers," Molly mutters. "If anyone could have given poor Olivia a push, it's him."

I feel the strange desire to defend him. And . . . kiss him. I force myself to look away and my gaze lands on Josh. He's cute, too, and slightly above me on the food chain in the sea of high school, but Levi Sterling? He's a great white, and right now, he's looking at me like I'm a guppy.

Levi stops directly in front of me, ignoring all the others sitting on the table. I instinctively cross my arms like a protective shield and stare right back at him.

"Mack." He speaks one word—one I don't particularly like—and I'm warm despite the October chill in the air. I feel the eyes of my friends moving between Levi and me, as if they can't believe we're talking.

I just look up at him, not moving, my seat on the top of the picnic table still not high enough to put us eye to eye.

"Come with me," he says. And I fight the urge to push myself off the table and go anywhere he wants. I don't answer, not because I think I'm being cool. I really don't trust my voice not to come out in a croak.

He puts his hand on my knee, giving it a slight squeeze. "You're not still mad at me, are you?"

I can practically hear Molly's jaw unhinge.

"I wasn't mad at you."

Lifting my hand, he takes a good look at the Band-Aid I used to replace the gauze my mother had unraveled. "How is it?"

"Hurts." Kind of like it does to look into his eyes. But I do anyway.

He brings my hand close to his mouth and it takes me a second to realize he's going to kiss my fingertip. I can't draw back in time and his lips touch the Band-Aid.

Still holding my hand, he tugs. "Please. It's important."

I don't bother to argue, and I don't look at Molly. I slip off the top of the table, my sneakers landing on the asphalt next to his black boots. "I'll be right back," I say to Molly, still not daring eye contact.

I walk next to Levi along the perimeter of the lot. He doesn't say anything for a few minutes, making me feel super awkward, so I fuss with a hair that's fallen out of my ponytail and then wonder if that makes me look like an airhead hair-twirler, so I let my hands fall to my sides.

"Don't be nervous," he says softly, as if he can smell my discomfort the way I can smell leather and soap and rain on autumn leaves all over him.

"I'm not," I lie, finally tucking my hands into my jacket pockets and looking around like walking with Levi Sterling is the most normal thing in the world. I glance to my right and instantly lock eyes with Josh Collier.

There's nothing casual about the way he's looking back. Despite the fairly standard "what's up" nod from him, I can see everything in his expression change, even from twenty-some feet away. Disgust, distrust, disapproval.

Of course guys like Josh Collier don't like guys like Levi Sterling. Actually, no one likes Levi Sterling: I don't think he has a single friend at this school. But he only came in the spring of last year.

"Over here," Levi says, either oblivious to or completely unconcerned about Josh. He leads me down a row of parked cars to the very edge of the lot, far away from any of the kids. We stand for a second and I rub my jacket sleeves, aware that I'm hugging myself.

"So what's up?" I ask.

Standing in front of me, he blocks my view of the rest of the parking lot. No, what he does is command all my attention so that the lot and the kids and the cars and the noise all fade away and one hundred percent of my focus is on Levi Sterling.

He doesn't speak for a minute but searches my face carefully. "You're upset," he finally says.

"A girl died," I reply, hoping he doesn't think that being alone with him has a deep impact on me. "What's up?" I ask again.

I see him suck in a slow breath, then let it out with a long, soft exhale, looking over my shoulder into the distance, a struggle drawing thick brows and tensing his jaw. God, his jaw is beautiful.

"I need a favor."

The request pulls me out of my reverie about his bone structure. "More tutoring?"

For a second, he doesn't say anything, but somehow manages to get closer. "Where were you last night?" he finally asks.

My whole stomach twists and tumbles. Why does he want to know? The question, the tone, the proximity actually make me a little dizzy.

"I was home," I tell him, leaving out the part about a movie with my mom.

He eyes me, almost as if he doesn't believe me. "Then why did you text me?"

"What?" I choke the reply. "I don't even know your number."

His dark eyes narrow in confusion. "I got a text from you."

"You're mistaken."

He reaches into his pocket, pulling out a phone. "Look." He taps the screen and starts searching, squinting as he thumbs through. "What the hell . . ."

"Maybe you were loaded and imagined it."

He gives me a sharp glare. "I don't get loaded," he corrects. "And I didn't imagine that you told me to meet you at the Keystone Quarry."

I hiss in a breath. "What?"

"It's gone, damn it. I didn't delete that text."

A dark tendril of concern slips through me. "That's happened to me recently."

He lets out a frustrated sigh. "Well, if you didn't send it, then I guess you can't help me."

I'm still curious and tamping down a little rise of concern. Who texted him and pretended to be me? "Help you with what?"

Giving up on the phone, he sticks it into his back pocket and pins me with a smoky look. "Explain what I was doing there if anyone asks."

"So you were there at the quarry when she died?"

"I left before . . ." He scuffs his boot on the ground and looks around, his eyes distant. "She was alive when I left."

"Oh," I say, not really sure of the right response.

"But who's going to believe that?"

"Why wouldn't they?" I ask.

He snorts softly, as if the question is rhetorical. "Would you say that you asked me to meet you there?"

A soft gasp escapes me. "You need an *alibi*, Levi?"

Something like amusement, then disappointment, flickers in his eyes. *"Et tu, Brute?"*

Did Levi Sterling just speak clichéd Shakespearean Latin to me? "Me too, what?"

"You're thinking the worst of me."

I don't want to think the worst of him, but I kind of do. "How do you know what I'm thinking?"

He gives a dry laugh. "By the fact that your face is as transparent as it is pretty. I've seen that look before."

I almost touch my face, wondering just what in my expression is giving away my thoughts. "So why do you need someone to lie about where you were?"

"I didn't ask you to do that," he says. "I asked you to explain

81

to someone why I was there in the first place. Because you texted me."

Except I hadn't. "Someone like who? Your parents?"

"Hardly."

"Then who?" He doesn't answer, so I push it. "If not your parents, then who? The cops? Or . . . what?"

"What," he answers softly, the little break in his voice so surprisingly vulnerable it catches me off guard.

But what—who—does he mean? "Does not compute."

He shakes his head again, finally taking a step backward. "Never mind, Mack. Forget I asked."

Like that was going to happen.

He stuffs his hands in his pockets, sighing and eyeing the parking lot, probably looking for the next female victim he can coerce to lie for him. I follow his gaze, watching the ever-widening circle of crying, singing girls.

"It's sad, isn't it?" I finally say.

He nods. "She was a nice girl," he says.

"Did you know her . . . well?"

"Pretty well, yeah." He almost smiles and I get the distinct feeling "pretty well" could loosely be translated into "intimately." Which is strange, because I would never have put those two together. I can't even imagine them talking, let alone . . .

"We went out last spring when I first got to Vienna."

Dating.

"Hey, Kenzie." At the sound of a guy's voice, I turn and spot Josh shouldering his way through the cars, heading toward us.

"I better go," Levi says, surprising me by touching my chin ever so softly to keep me from looking at anything but him. "See you tomorrow."

82

"Tomorrow?" He still wants me to tutor him?

"Yeah, nothing's changed. Please be there."

I don't answer, but I can't look away.

"I want to see you again," he whispers. "I need to."

"Kenzie!" There's more urgency in Josh's call this time.

Before I can answer, Levi slips behind me and takes off without even acknowledging Josh.

CHAPTER IX

Josh looks like he might have been crying, and that trips my heart a little. Levi certainly wasn't grieving Olivia's death . . . just shopping for alibis with fake texts that were never sent.

And still the spot on my chin kind of burns from where he touched it.

"What are you talking to that kid for?" Josh asks as he approaches, his open varsity jacket making his shoulders look even broader. He's so tall I have to look up to meet his gaze, and I suddenly feel very small.

I open my mouth to tell him everything, then stop myself. Some innate sense that I don't understand tells me to stay quiet about the Levi situation right now. I don't know why, but no one feels trustworthy at the moment.

"I was talking to him about . . ." I give him a simple smile. "How sad this is."

He chokes softly, as if he doesn't believe Levi could understand sadness. "Kid's a problem, you know?"

"How's that?" I ask, hoping to hear something concrete and not just another piece of Levi Sterling folklore because so far, he wasn't exactly living up to his bad-boy rep.

"Well, look at him."

That's pretty much all I've done for the last ten minutes. "What about him?"

"He's a fu—freak, Kenzie. He'll be lucky if he graduates and doesn't end up in prison."

"Why is everyone so certain Levi Sterling is going to jail?" I demand.

His blue eyes spark. "You like him?"

"I don't even know him."

"Well, you shouldn't. He's bad news and I don't want him . . ." His voice trails off and his cheeks flush.

"You don't want him what?" I really, really want to know.

"I don't want him near you," he finishes.

I feel my jaw loosen, a hundred different emotions going to war inside me. Resentment, excitement, shock, and maybe just a little anger. "You don't *want* him near me?" I repeat, changing the emphasis entirely.

"I don't . . ." He shakes his head and tries to shrug off the topic. "Never mind."

"So, were you friends with Olivia?" I ask, just as happy to have the subject of Levi closed for the moment.

"I knew her, sure. We had Spanish together for two years and her father's company has done some construction work on my house." He looks off into the distance, his eyes moist. "She was a really cool girl."

I nod sympathetically, supposing that's a legit enough connection for a guy like Josh to shed a few tears. Levi didn't seem to be in mourning, and he dated the girl.

"How about you?" he says. "Good friends?"

Was he kidding? Girls like Olivia and the rest of them on that list didn't hang out with nerds like me. But guys don't always know that. "Just well enough to say hi," I tell him. "We nodded to each other yesterday, after . . ."

"The list came out," he supplies when I falter.

"Yeah." 'Cause now we're in some kind of club.

"Yeah," he agrees, the moment suddenly awkward because he's looking at me too intently for a boy who's never said more than a few words to me before yesterday. I muster up the courage to ask him about that. *Why now? Why me?* I open my mouth, but am silenced by his arm around my shoulder, a strong hand pulling me into him.

"I missed you last night," he says right into my ear, with a secret, sexy voice that should have every cell in my body jumping up and down. "Where were you?"

"I had . . ." Movie night with Mom. "Something else to do."

A flicker of distaste crosses his expression as he considers what could possibly have been more important than his game, and his gaze shifts in the direction where Levi had been. "Out with your parolee?"

"I was not with him."

"Good thing, 'cause they're saying he was there and was having a deep and heated conversation with Olivia before she died."

Really? "Who said that?"

He eyes me. "Ready to defend him?"

"Just trying to find out what happened last night."

He relaxes his hand on my back, sliding it down, the touch too familiar and unsettling. "Good thing you weren't with him."

I look up at him, my throat dry. "Why is that good?"

"I can take my shot with you," he says with a wink.

I don't answer, not sure what to say.

"And I never miss a shot," he adds. "Listen, I know it's not going to be really fun under the circumstances and all, but a bunch of kids are getting together at my house tonight. Will you come?"

The invitation throws me for so many reasons. My first instinct is to say no, of course. My mom and parties? Not happening. But then I remember that I'm staying at Molly's and her mom is . . . normal.

"I'm hanging out with my friend Molly tonight," I say. And boy, would she love an invitation.

I know he's flipping through whatever he knows about Molly and deciding if she merits an invite. Whatever he says, it's going to make it or break it with this guy. I don't care how cute he is, how popular, how crushworthy. If he says—

"Bring her along." He underscores the perfect answer with the perfect smile. "I want to be sure you show up this time."

"Okay."

He leans forward and surprises me with a soft kiss on the forehead. "See you tonight, Fifth."

God, I hate that nickname even more than I hate *Mack*. Can't these guys call me by my name? But I see Molly watching impatiently and I'm eager to deliver the news that we've been invited to a party at Josh's house, so I just nod and smile. "See you tonight."

It's hard to imagine Molly's room any messier, but getting ready for a party where we want to fit in and yet look like we really don't care takes a lot of work. We've got her music playing loudly, and she's kicking discarded tops around the floor to make space as she models wedges and skinny jeans.

"Yes?" she asks.

"Maybe a little too dressy." I glance down at my own jeans—well, a pair I've borrowed from her—and a simple navy T-shirt, also borrowed.

"Only 'cause you're in sneakers and you don't want me to dress up."

"Only 'cause I can't fit in your tiny shoes. I'm fine in these." I lean back on her desk chair and wiggle my worn Nikes.

"We could swing by your house and—"

"No!" There's no way in heaven or hell I'm going home to get clothes or shoes. "And alert the worry police? Once she's done fainting and listing all the things that can and will go wrong at a house party, she'll follow us there."

Molly giggles as if I'm actually kidding. "You must get so sick of that, Kenz."

"You have no idea."

The door pops open with a loud noise. "Are you guys deaf?" Molly's twelve-year-old brother screams at us. "We're eating!"

"Get out of here, Hunter!" Molly lunges at him. "We're changing clothes, you freakazoid!" She slams the door in his face. "Oh my God, I hate him."

But I know better. There's no hate in the Russell family. There's noise and laughter and friendly teasing and a lot of love.

A few minutes later, I can practically taste all that stuff as I sit in the chair usually reserved for Blake, Molly's eighteen-year-old brother, who left for Ohio State this fall. Of course, he was friends with Conner, so I'm always relieved when he's not here. I don't like to imagine what Conner would be like now, in his first year of college.

Around the table, I'm joined by Hunter and nine-year-old Kayla and Molly's amazing parents, who never pass each other without a quick touch or even a kiss.

Not going to lie: Molly's family makes my shattered home look even worse than it is.

After we pray and the rush to scoop up lasagna and salad begins, Mr. Russell turns his attention to Molly. "A party, you say?"

I feel myself tighten; is he going to talk us out of going? That's what would happen at my house. But this is the Russell home and the rules—and conversations—are different here.

"At Josh Collier's house," Molly says, a bit of pride in her voice, as if she's longed to go to a party like that since we got to high school.

"Oooh," Molly's mom coos. "I'm jealous. That is a gorgeous house."

"Is his dad loaded or something?" Hunter asks as he serves himself enough lasagna to feed a small country. "'Cause you should marry him, Molly, and have him buy me a Corvette."

"Aww." Molly angles her head and gives him a pitying look. "Did your anti-idiot pill prescription run out?"

"Molly," Mr. Russell says softly.

"It's his grandfather who's loaded," Mrs. Russell informs us. "His parents passed away many years ago."

I look up from my plate. "Really?"

"Oh, yes, tragic accident."

My first bite of lasagna threatens to lodge in my throat, so I grab a sip of milk.

"What happened?" Molly asks for me.

"Terrible boating accident while they were on vacation somewhere off the coast of Virginia. I don't remember where, but it made the news because the whole family was on a yacht that sank."

"Oh, wow," I manage.

"Sad," Molly says.

"Cool, a yacht," Hunter adds, getting a vile look from Molly.

"Josh was a baby and his grandfather rescued him from drowning, as I recall. But both parents were killed. They never found the bodies, either. So awful."

"I've heard Josh is really close to his grandfather," Molly says.

"The better to get in the will," Hunter jokes.

"You're a jerk."

"Molly . . ."

The teasing and chiding continue, but I just stare at my plate. *Accidentia eveniunt.*

"What did you say?" Hunter asks me.

I look up, not aware I'd spoken out loud.

"Kenzie talks to herself in Latin," Molly explains.

As Hunter hoots, impressed, I smile. "I said 'accidents happen.'"

Mrs. Russell sighs. "You know, I tried so hard to get the job to decorate that house a few years ago, but lost out to some big New York design firm. There aren't many houses like that in Vienna."

"Want me to take secret pictures so you can see what the other designer did?" Molly asks.

"Yeah," Hunter says. "You could steal ideas for Mom."

He earns a dark frown from his mother. "I don't have to steal ideas, young man. But . . ." She turns to Molly. "Yes. Take a ton. I never got into the house but I've heard it's amazing, with an indoor swimming pool and a ten-car garage, adjacent to some of the prettiest parts of Nacht Woods."

"So what banks did this guy rob?" Molly's dad asks.

Mrs. Russell nods, clearly knowing her Collier family info. "The grandfather, who's retired, of course, made a killing on Wall Street, as I understand it. Really hit it huge in the go-go eighties."

"Where'd they go-go?" Kayla asks, making everyone laugh.

I eat quietly, listening to the banter, trying not to let it hollow me out because there isn't anything like this at my dinner table, even on the nights Dad comes over.

"I still think it's odd to have a party when a girl's dead," Mr. Russell says.

"Oh, Tim, they're kids." Mrs. Russell holds out the lasagna dish to me with a smile. "More, honey? And it's probably very healthy for all of them to get together and remember this girl." She shakes her head. "I can't imagine what her mother is feeling tonight."

Her mother! I suddenly remember mine. I haven't checked my phone in hours, but since she hasn't tracked me down here, I'm going to guess that my mother hasn't heard the news yet. How will she act when she learns that a classmate of mine died in an accident?

Of course, I can assure her I'm not going to get drunk and jump off cliffs, but still, this will tilt Mom sideways.

"Has there been anything else about Olivia on the news?" I ask.

"They're saying it was a freak accident and they'll be

91

reinforcing the fencing around the quarry so kids can't go there to party," Mr. Russell says. "The No Trespassing signs apparently aren't enough."

"What about . . ." I push some salad around, looking down, thinking of Levi. "The kids who were there? Do they know who they were yet?"

"I don't know," Mr. Russell says. "They haven't released any names. Those kids could get in trouble for trespassing."

Was that all they could be in trouble for? "So they're sure it was an accident?"

"So far," Mr. Russell says. "I guess they're still investigating."

Mrs. Russell shakes her head, sending a warning look to Molly. "Those kids were drinking and smoking pot."

"Duh," Molly says with a sarcastic choke.

But her father is eyeing her just as hard. "Will there be drinking at this party tonight?"

"I don't know, Dad," she says. "But Kenzie and I don't party. No worries."

"It's not you I worry about," he says. "It's the idiots who can't handle the peer pressure. But, okay, you girls use common sense."

"And call if you need anything," Mrs. Russell adds. "Even a ride."

The conversation is so foreign to me, I'm in stunned silence. My mother would have gone ballistic over the whole topic. This is so much better, so much easier and nicer and more normal. God, I want that. I know our family's broken and we can never fill the void of Conner's death, but couldn't we at least try?

"We're good, Mom," Molly assures her, pushing away from the table. "Let's get going, Kenz."

I get up with her. For the moment, anyway, I'm at the Russell house and I'm going to a party and I just want to revel in the fun and normalcy of that.

"Hey." Hunter grabs his sister's arm. "Saturday is your cleanup day."

Her face falls and she looks at her mom. "Can't we switch for tomorrow?"

Mrs. Russell nods and shoos us away. "Come and say goodbye before you leave."

Hunter starts to balk, but Kayla jumps up to offer to do Molly's cleanup. A little chaos ensues while we slip out of the kitchen and I'm surprised at how much I'd love to just sit around that table for hours with a family that is so whole and happy.

But I have only myself to blame for that.

CHAPTER X

*H*oly crap, the Colliers are rich. Molly parks her car at the end of what feels like a half-mile-long driveway, lit up by fake gas lamps. At least fifty cars are in the drive and along the street. Some I recognize from the lot at school, some I don't. This "little gathering" has to have a hundred kids already, and we're early.

"Hey, Kenzie!"

I turn at the sound of a girl's voice and see one of them emerging from a group of kids, coming toward me. In the dim light, I can't quite make out who it is.

"It's Chloe Batista," Molly supplies under her breath.

She's wearing superskinny jeans and boots, her cropped top riding high on her bare midriff. She's cute—and has to be freezing—but, really, nothing extraordinary to look at. "How did she ever get number two?" I whisper.

"Are you forgetting the blow jobs?"

Oh, yeah. "Hi, Chloe," I call back to her.

"Hey, you," she says, super friendly, as she threads long blond hair highlighted with pink tips through her fingers. When she reaches me, I can see a tiny nose stud and false eyelashes that she didn't have on at the school today. Guess a lot of us tried a little harder for the party tonight.

"Hey, do you know Molly Russell?" I ask Chloe.

Forced to acknowledge my friend, Chloe barely nods. "Hey." Then she takes me by the elbow and guides me a few feet away. "Can I talk to you, like, privately?" she asks.

I turn to Molly, ready to say *No, she's my friend and stays with me*, but Molly nods. "I'll see you in there, Kenzie."

"No, Molly, come on," I insist.

Chloe squeezes my arm and gives me a purposeful look. "We can't, Kenzie. List rules."

I open my mouth to say *Screw the list*, but Molly holds up both hands to stop me. "Seriously, Kenz, I'm fine. Come and get me when you're done." She gives a quick smile to Chloe, not quite hiding the disappointment in her eyes.

Before I can stop her, Molly takes off and Chloe slips her arm through mine, a whiff of lemon body spray emanating from her. "We're going into the woods."

"Why?" I ask, walking with her because curiosity has gotten the better of me and I'm still hoping for answers about what happened to Olivia.

"Because it's where we meet." She tightens her squeeze a little and checks out my confused face. "We, the sisters, hon. Except, of course, we're missing one." She snorts softly, as if she's amused by the irony. "Number one."

The complete lack of sadness in those words—so different

from the tears in the junior lot today—creeps me out and slows my step.

"Let's go. I've been waiting for you," she says, tugging my arm.

So I follow her across the vast lawn toward a dense forested area that's more or less the everyday scenery in this part of Vienna. Nacht Woods is made up of miles of pine-filled paths, creeks, and cliffs. The woods are a haven for hikers and even hunters, as beautiful as any state park, but not a place I'd venture into at night.

Yet I'm venturing right along with my new friend, Chloe. Leaves crunch under my sneakers and the light grows dimmer as we get farther away from the Colliers' house.

"You party, right?"

I just look at her, clueless at how to answer because the truth will be . . . uncool. I've never had a drink in my life.

"I mean you drink, right?"

No way I'm copping to my total geekiness, not at my first party with this crowd. "Once in a while," I reply with a shrug.

"Well, this is once in a while, Kenzie." She still has me by the arm and gives me another squeeze, pulling me along.

After an awkward silence, I say, "It's so sad about Olivia."

"Yeah, jeez. What an idiot."

I hesitate again, and not only because we've reached the tree line and I don't see anyone nearby. How far are we going into these woods? "Why would you say that?" I ask. "You were just singing her funeral dirge this afternoon."

"And I meant it, I'm sad. But come on. Who does that? Drunk boys from West Virginia jump off cliffs, not normal girls like Olivia Thayne. But I guess I'm like the leader since now I'm at the, well, top." Her voice trails off as we round a thick group of evergreens, the needles scraping my jacket as she guides me in. "We're at Meesha Mound." She leans closer and lowers her voice. "Indian burial ground, you know. Cool, huh?"

"Very."

She misses my sarcasm and takes me down a dark path. Almost instantly, I see the lights of a few cell phones and make out a small circle of girls sitting in a clearing at the foot of a hill.

"Guys, I got her," Chloe says. "Number five."

It's weird to be introduced that way, but I fold down in the place Chloe indicates, right between Amanda and Dena, who are numbers four and six.

"Welcome, Five," Dena says with a soft giggle, the smell of beer oozing off her breath.

"All right, we're all here," Chloe says, sitting down across from me. "The Sisters of the List."

I can't help snorting a laugh, figuring this *has* to be a joke.

But eight pairs of pretty damn serious eyes look back at me.

"Is that the name we picked?" Amanda asks.

"We picked a name?" I blurt out.

Chloe sighs as if she has to explain something to a child. "Every year, the list girls give themselves their own name. You know, like our secret club."

"Okay," I say slowly. How does she know that happens every year?

"I like Sisters of the List," Kylie Leff says, leaning into Amanda. "We've been blood sisters since kindergarten." She holds up a single knuckle and Amanda meets it with one of her own in the most feminine and lackluster knuckle tap in history. "So it's perfect."

"Should we vote on the name?" Shannon Dill, number seven, asks.

"We don't need to vote," Chloe says. "I decided."

Dena sputters. "Who died and left you in charge?"

Two girls gasp at the question; the rest of us stare slack-jawed at Dena. She throws both hands over her mouth and lets out a little cry. "Oh my God, I didn't mean that."

After a beat, someone laughs nervously. "It's okay, Dena. We know you didn't."

Chloe produces a frosted bottle from a handbag behind her and holds it high. "We don't need to vote," she says again, ignoring Dena's faux pas. "Tradition says you drink on it. And our tradition is now"—she turns to read the bottle—"Three Olives grape-flavored vodka, thanks to my sister's boyfriend." She unscrews the top and sniffs. "Thank God I'm allergic to peanuts and not grapes. Girls, you're gonna like this tradition."

"Tradition?" I say, unable to keep the derision out of my voice. "Why would there be a tradition?"

"I'm second generation," Chloe says proudly, like that explains anything at all.

"You mean your mother was on the list?" Bree asks.

Chloe gives one confident nod. "She was number four in 1990. They called themselves the Babes of the New Decade."

I laugh again, and Dena does the same, only her reaction is a loud guffaw.

"You think this is funny?" Chloe snaps.

All the others are looking at me, and I glance at Dena, who has somehow become my partner in this, courtesy of one hug this afternoon and a shared laugh tonight.

98

"Well," Dena says, dragging the word out. "I think it's a little silly."

"Thank you," I whisper under my breath.

"Did you think it was *silly* when Olivia drowned after falling off that cliff?"

My head jerks around to see who posed the question. It's Candace Yardley, number ten, who up to this point has been virtually silent. Once again, I take a second to admire her dark good looks; she is runway perfect. How I ever beat her on a list of hot girls is a question for the ages.

"Of course I don't think Olivia's . . ." Dena shakes her head, clearly unable or unwilling to say *death*. "I don't think it's funny. But that didn't have anything to do with this list or some secret club."

One of Candace's perfectly waxed brows rises. And something in my chest slips.

"You think it does?" I ask quietly.

And no one says a word, the silence just long and heavy enough for me to feel the individual bumps rise on my skin. The weird, anonymous texts dance before my eyes. The feeling of the brakes giving way. The shock of smelling the gas leak. The truck that almost ran me down on the way to Molly's house.

All after the list came out.

"You guys," I whisper. "Are you saying that . . ."

"We're not saying anything," Chloe says sharply as she sticks the bottle in the middle of the circle. "We're drinking vodka in the name of the Sisters of the List. If you don't join, then . . ."

I wait, aware I'm holding my breath.

"Then what?" Dena asks, her voice rich with sarcasm. "We're going off the cliff like Olivia?"

"I hope not." Chloe closes her eyes, lifts the vodka, and takes a healthy sip. Then she hands the bottle to Kylie. "Three?"

Kylie does the same, wincing, her drink a little longer. She smiles at her best friend. "Four?"

Amanda drinks and hands the bottle to me. "Five?"

Part of me wants to run, part of me wants to giggle nervously—my first drink!—and part of me wants to tell them about the weird things that have been happening. But some other part of me decides to stay quiet. I take the bottle and let a few drops touch my lips, the flavor like bitter grape cough medicine.

I hand the bottle to Dena and hold her gaze. "Six?"

"You bitches *cray*." She sings the last word on a laugh. "But I need to get fried." She takes a long, deep drink, finishing off with a satisfied sigh before turning to Shannon Dill. "Seven?"

Shannon drinks, then gives the bottle to Bree Walker, who passes it to Ashleigh Cummings, who finally hands it to Candace. She flips some of that long black hair over her shoulder and raises the vodka like she's going to make a toast.

"Here's to you, Olivia. I hope to hell that really was an accident."

CHAPTER XI

I don't drink any more, and in a few minutes, the group disperses and heads toward the party. Dena sidles right next to me as we walk to the house.

"So, sis," she says, a little giggle in her voice. "What do you think about all this?"

I just roll my eyes.

"You think the list is stupid?"

"It's not anything I ever wanted or thought I could be on."

"I'll admit, you were a dark horse for me."

I shoot her a look. "Did you really, like, sit around and wonder who'd be voted in this year?"

"Of course. Didn't you and your friends?"

I shake my head and squint toward the house. "Speaking of friends, I kind of ditched mine and I have to find her."

Dena grabs my arm, stumbling on the grass. I catch her and look into her eyes. "Are you okay?"

"Tipsy," she admits, laughing. "But I'll be fine."

"You sure?"

Her amusement disappears. "I don't know. Didn't that conversation kind of freak you out? About Olivia's accident?"

Should I trust her? Should I tell her about the texts and the weird things that have been happening to me? "Yeah, it kind of did. Makes you wonder, huh?"

"Like, did she get punished for being on the list or something?"

I consider that, and shake my head. "It just makes you realize how fragile life is," I say. "Could be taken away any second."

"No shit. Yesterday my hair dryer shorted out and I damn near burned down the whole house."

"Seriously? What happened?"

"Hell if I know. My dad said our electrician effed something up in the outlet."

"And weren't you . . ." *Scared to death?* "Concerned?"

She shrugs and gives me a grin. "YOLO, baby girl. Which translates into 'have some fun.'" She shoulders me into the house. "Like, now."

Inside, the house is such a showplace it's overwhelming and difficult to take in. Plus it's packed with kids. So much for the somber little get-together of grieving teenagers.

I can smell beer, and the sound of rap is barely drowned out by loud boys and girls laughing. Really? On the night after the girl they all planned to vote for class president next year has died? They either don't care or . . . they don't understand death.

That's how they can be so cavalier. They don't know how permanent death is. But I do.

Shaking that thought, I peer past the bodies, trying to find Molly, when a hand snakes around my waist and pulls me into a big, strong, masculine chest.

"Hey, Fifth." I can feel his mouth close to my ear. "Thought you'd never get here."

Dena, next to me, observes the whole thing and gives me an amused look. "Like I said . . . YOLO." She winks at me. "I'll find your friend. I know who she is. You relax and have fun."

She's gone, and for a second I stand really still, my stomach tightening under Josh's arm.

"That's good advice, you know." He slowly turns me around. "Relax and have fun."

Holy cow, he looks good. His dark-golden hair is mussed and his eyes look smoky blue in this light, even more attractive now that they're zeroed in on me with interest.

"Hey, Josh," I say.

He gives me a slow smile. "Seventh grade, huh?"

I frown, trying really hard not to let my eyes drop to the way his plain white T-shirt fits his shoulders and hugs his biceps. "What about seventh grade?"

"The crush you've had on me since then."

Oh, Molly. You traitor. I consider a fast and furious denial, but I can see the laughter in his eyes. And something else. Satisfaction.

"Shocking, isn't it?" I try for a flirtatious tease.

"You know what I remember about you in middle school?"

My braces? My breastlessness? My inability to get a boy to notice me? The list is long. I shake my head, not sure I want to hear this but oddly excited by the conversation.

"You were hydrogen in our Dress Like an Element Day in science."

Oh, God, I went to school dressed like a giant raindrop. "Probably not my finest middle school moment."

"I thought you were cute."

I look up at him, letting the compliment wash over me. "Then we're even," I say quietly, giving myself an inner high five for a banter win.

"Want a drink?" he asks, inching me away from the entry-way toward a lavish-looking living room.

"I thought this was supposed to be some kind of gathering to mourn Olivia."

"She'd want us to be happy," he replies. "Come and meet the king."

"Who's that?"

"My grandfather."

"The king?" I laugh. "That's what you call your grand-father? What happened to Poppa and Gramps?"

He rolls his eyes. "So not my grandfather. Anyway, his name is Rex. You're the Latin expert. Come on, he lives to meet pretty girls."

The way he says it makes me feel like I really am one of those pretty girls. As we walk through the house, I spy Molly in a game room with a bunch of kids surrounding a pool table. She's laughing a little too loudly, her eyes bright with excitement, a red Solo cup inches from her mouth.

"Wait—I want to kill her, er, say hi."

He laughs. "Don't be mad at her. I made her tell me. And she's deep into a beer pong match, so don't bother her. Come this way."

Taking my hand, he leads me to another part of the house, a two-story great room connected to a massive kitchen, also peppered with groups of kids, and I don't think I know a single one.

"Isn't this a Vienna High party?" I ask.

Josh nods a "'Sup?" to a few guys and stays ahead of me, our fingers locked as he tugs me along. "I know kids from everywhere because of sports. I play on two travel teams—hey, Ryan—and lots of these kids are from all over this side of the state."

At my surprised look, he adds, "They all crash here tonight. We've got plenty of room, and tomorrow we'll probably play touch football all day long." He adds a slow smile and pulls me a little closer. "You should be here so I can tackle you."

"I thought it was touch."

Laughing, he closes the space between us. "It can get pretty dirty."

I don't have to answer because we stop and talk to a few kids I don't know who are from a town on the other side of Pittsburgh. And I thought Molly had a fun house. This is a whole different world—weekend parties, kids from all over the place, and a grandfather who apparently doesn't care if they play beer pong on his pool table.

"And who do we have here, Josh?"

I turn at the sound of a man's voice, meeting eyes the same gorgeous blue as Josh's, only icier and feathered with crow's-feet.

"This is Kenzie Summerall." The way he says it, I know they've already talked about me.

"Kenzie." The older man nods in approval. "Of course."

Flashing an easy, wide smile, he looks down—way down—at me. Instantly, I can see where Josh gets his gifts—his height, the build, the sort of raw masculinity mixed with charm that rolls off him. That's hereditary, I suppose.

The older man puts a familiar hand on my shoulder, and I'm immediately at ease. Another gift. "Rex Collier," he says, studying me like nothing could make him take his eyes off my face. It's disconcerting, and flattering. "You were absolutely correct, Josh. She is a refreshing change."

Josh just shakes his head, laughing. "And you thought you wanted to kill Molly?" he asks me. "How do you think I feel right now?"

Rex shoos his grandson's comment. "Nothing wrong with honesty, young man. Haven't I taught you anything?"

"You've taught me everything," Josh says, a respectful note in his voice. "Including how to pick quality girls."

"Indeed." The older man gives me one more thorough inspection. "Quality, and an improvement."

I feel my eyes widen. "Over what?"

That makes Rex laugh, wrinkling his face but not making him any less imposing or regal. "Over the ones that have their bosoms spilling out and wear makeup like Cleopatra." He lifts a glass. No Solo cup for the king; he's got a crystal water glass filled with something amber over ice. "I'm guessing you don't drink beer," he says.

"You're guessing right."

"Some wine? Champagne? I have a lovely port."

I almost laugh comparing, once again, Josh's home life with mine. "I don't need anything," I say. "I'm driving home." At least, I am if that was beer in Molly's Solo cup.

"Good call, Mackenzie," Rex says, still smiling and somehow inching me away from Josh to a bar that takes up one whole corner of the family room.

I fleetingly wonder how Rex knows my full first name, but then he guides me to a barstool and sits in the one next to me. "My grandson likes you. He's been talking about you for a while."

The announcement surprises me on so many levels I don't know where to start. So I just smile, perplexed that this old guy—I'm no judge of age, but he's got to be well into his sixties—is even attending a high school party, let alone sharing secrets.

"Do you like him?" he asks.

I glance back to Josh, who's already high-fiving and joking around with a few guys I don't know.

"Yes, of course I like him."

"Enough to go out with him?"

I laugh softly. "Are you asking for him?"

"He likes to have my blessing on these things. We're close. You know, his parents are gone."

"I've heard," I say. "I'm sorry." I consider adding that I know he saved Josh's life, but I don't want him to know I've been talking about the family.

He gives me a thoughtful, sad nod. "It was tragic, but I'm just glad that I am healthy and wealthy enough to make Josh comfortable and ensure that he has everything he needs."

"Yeah, I see that he does." I glance around, already a bit anxious to end the conversation. I can't catch Josh's eye and it would be rude to walk away. Plus, something tells me not much gets by Rex Collier.

"It's not easy being an only child," he says on a serious sigh.

"No, it isn't."

"You're an only child." He dips his head and adds, "Now."

Oh, he knows. Not a surprise; Conner's death was big news in Vienna, the loss of a local boy in a tragic, freak accident.

My heart stops and then breaks, as it always does. My throat starts to close in preparation for the fight against tears. Will this response ever go away? It's been almost two years.

"Sadly, that's true," I say.

"How are your parents holding up?"

I appreciate the question because so few people ask about them, but I suppose adults see the loss from their own point of view. "They're getting a divorce," I say stiffly, surprised by my honesty.

"What's the statistic about parents of a dead child? Close to ninety percent divorce?"

I shrug. "It would be nice to beat the odds, though."

He pats my hand and shifts in his seat. "Let's change the subject. I understand you're on that list that does nothing but objectify lovely teenage girls."

I'm grateful for the change of subject and even more so for someone who shares my disdain for the list. "Josh has really told you everything, hasn't he?"

"We're close," he says again. "What number?"

Why dodge it? "Fifth."

"Ah, excellent. High enough to be respectable, low enough not to piss off too many people."

I can't help but laugh at his dead-on assessment. "True."

"You must be thrilled."

Not so dead-on. "I don't think it's such a big deal."

108

"I hear that it is." And judging from this conversation, he hears everything.

More comfortable being honest now, I say, "I don't think being recognized for something that has nothing to do with, you know, an *accomplishment,* is that important."

He raises his glass in approval. "Good girl. You're more worried about getting into college."

"Absolutely. Getting into college is my number one priority right now." Number two would be getting out of this boring conversation with an old man. I kind of want to go back to flirting with his grandson.

"Have you picked out a school?" he asks.

"Well, they have to pick me, but I have a few on my dream list."

"Such as?"

"Columbia," I tell him. Why not? We've already covered death and divorce. "I'd like to study the classics."

His eyes light up. "Impressive. I like a girl with ambition."

"Well, I have to get in first. And get a scholarship," I add glumly. "So we'll see."

"You should try to get the Jarvis. I'd be delighted to give it to a girl for a change."

I angle my head closer, certain I didn't hear him correctly over the party noise. "The what?"

"The Jarvis." When I shake my head, he laughs. "I guess we do a pretty good job of keeping it quiet, because the scholarship is really only for a Vienna High student, which was how Josh's father willed it. Technically, it's the Jarvis Aurelius Collier Memorial Scholarship."

I just stare at him. "Jarvis is, was, your son?"

His eyes mist. "And a very great young man taken far too young."

"I'm sorry."

"But his legacy lives on, right back in Nacht Woods." He angles his head toward the back of the house. "He's buried there, too."

I blink at the statement. I was certain Mrs. Russell had said that Josh's parents died at sea and their bodies were never found.

"Not him, per se," he adds quickly, seeing my response. "But the things that mattered to him. I made a place to honor him."

The conversation is quickly slipping from boring to awkward, so I steal a glance over his shoulder to find Josh.

Rex catches me and inches sideways just enough to block my view. "In any case, Jarvis left a stipulation in his will that every year one junior or senior student from Vienna High can receive a full scholarship to the college of his choice—or hers," he adds with a sly smile. "With no limits on how much that can be worth."

Okay, not boring anymore. "How do I apply?"

He chuckles. "No application necessary, dear. You just have to finish the ropes course Jarvis built in Nacht Woods." With a quick appraisal of my body, he makes a face of approval and lifts his gray brows. "You look fairly athletic."

Not exactly. "I'm more of, you know, a Latin nerd. Any chance there's an ancient classics version of the ropes course?"

"Latin will, in fact, give you quite an unfair advantage. You don't play sports?"

"My mom is kind of overprotective and has an issue with sports waivers. As in she won't sign them." I let out a sigh. "Field trips, too."

He can't hide his disbelief. "Why, that's . . . un-American. Josh is in every sport he can squeeze into his life and far better for it, just like his father was."

"I did do gymnastics until . . ." *Grief and guilt sidelined me.* "A few years ago."

"I hear the wistfulness in your voice, young lady." He leans closer. "You loved it, didn't you?"

For a minute I think he said "him," not "it," and that he means Conner. "Of course."

"I bet you were very good at gymnastics, too."

"I was average at best, but I did love the challenge."

"What happened?"

Conner died. But I just don't want to get into my mother's crazy hang-ups about accidents, so I go with my standard story, which really did happen but it wasn't the thing that made me give up gymnastics. "I fell on a trampoline and my mom decided there were just too many injuries in the sport." In any sport. In the sport of life, in fact. "So thanks for the suggestion, Mr. Collier, but if your scholarship 'application' is a ropes course and you need a parental signature for a minor, it's not happening."

He doesn't answer right away, sipping his drink thoughtfully. "Let me work on that."

"Hey." Josh's hands land on my shoulders. "Quit hittin' on my chick, Rex."

The older man laughs, loud enough to cover my own self-conscious giggle. Did Josh Collier just call me his girl?

As thrilling as that might be—and it is, isn't it?—the idea of getting a full ride to Columbia from his super-rich grandfather's scholarship sends a lot more electricity through my body. How hard could a ropes course be? I can still climb like a monkey.

"She's too smart for you, Josh," Rex teases. At least, I think he's teasing; there's not much humor in his eyes or voice.

"She's a total brainiac," Josh agrees, squeezing my shoulders. "I think that's hot."

"Quite," his grandfather agrees.

The only thing that's hot is my face, which is flaming as they talk about me.

"C'mon, Kenz." Josh urges me out of the seat. "I know Rex is a ladies' man, but I need you to cheer me on in beer pong. See ya, big guy."

As I slide off the barstool, Rex's weathered but strong hand lands on my arm. "Kenzie," he says, "I never met a challenge I couldn't find my way around or over."

I smile at him, not doubting that. "Which is why you love a ropes course."

"My ropes course days are done, but we'll work this out, my dear. No matter what it takes."

I feel my eyebrows go up at the tone and implication.

He just leans closer. *"Exitus acta probat."*

The Latin rolls off his tongue like it's his native language. And I know exactly how to translate his message.

The end justifies the means.

"Sometimes it does," I agree.

"Not sometimes," he counters. "Always."

CHAPTER XII

A little while later, I'm sitting on Josh's lap in the den. The beer pong match is over, a lot of the kids have left, and we're sharing an overstuffed chair in a secluded corner.

I haven't had anything to drink since my one sip of grape vodka, but Molly's borderline tipsy, so I've kept an eye on her all night. She's having way more fun than I thought she would, talking to boys, comfortable with strangers. Still, I feel responsible for her and she left the room at least fifteen minutes ago, so I keep looking for her at the door.

"Hey," Josh says, turning my face to his. "I'm over here."

He's so close I can see the golden tips of his lashes and the different shades of the summer sky in his eyes. I keep waiting for that crush feeling—the one I've had every time I've looked at this guy for the past four years—to wash over me. But it doesn't. I feel giddy and excited to be this close, but not achy or dreamy like I fantasized.

"Wanna go upstairs?" he whispers. "See my room?"

In fact, I don't. "Better not," I say with an apologetic smile. "I don't want Molly to think I left. I should go find her."

"Quit worrying about her. Worry about me." He tugs me deeper into him, leaning his head close to mine. "Worry about kissing me," he says under his breath.

"Should I?"

"Worry or kiss me?" He smiles just as he puts his lips on mine. "What do you think?"

I meant should I go find her, but before I can explain, he's kissing me. His mouth is warm but almost instantly wet as his tongue slips between my teeth. I wasn't quite ready for that, but I angle my head and try not to think too hard about the fact that, except for three short, closed-mouth attempts with Steven McKeever after a study group at the library last year and, of course, that one smooch with Icky Hicky in seventh grade, this is my first kiss.

Certainly my first full-tongue kiss. I close my eyes and try to experience it—still waiting for sensations that don't happen. My stomach isn't fluttering, my heart isn't jumping around, and I really don't like the way beer tastes on his tongue. His hand is rounding my backside, too.

I break away. "I really need to find Molly."

"What are you scared of, Kenzie?"

The echo of Levi Sterling's same exact question plays in my head. *What are you scared of, Mack?* With Levi, I was scared of him. With Josh, I'm scared of . . . nothing.

"I'm not scared." And it's not me talking myself out of fears, either. "I'm not into this right now." I gently push him away. "I don't want to make out when someone could walk in any second," I say.

"Screw 'em." He comes in for another kiss, which I allow, trying really hard again to like it. Fail.

"Josh." I inch him back. "Let me find Molly."

I expect an argument, but get a slow, sweet smile. "I want you to stay tonight."

I almost choke. "Overnight?"

"I told you a lot of these kids will sleep here," he adds. "You don't have to worry. We won't do anything. Just kiss some more."

Molly's mother would never go for it, and my mother? Ha, that's laughable. Plus, I don't want to. "Thanks, but Molly has a curfew, so I better get her. I'll be right back."

To his credit, he easily lets me stand up but doesn't come with me when I head out toward the kitchen. Molly's not there, so I look in the family room, the hall, the living room. The downstairs bathrooms, at least the three that I can find, are open and empty.

As I come around the corner, I'm moving fast enough to nearly collide with someone.

"There you are." It's Chloe Batista, with Amanda and Kylie on either side of her. Second, third, and fourth, I think as I draw back to avoid hitting them.

"What, am I missing another secret club function?"

"You think this is a big joke, Kenzie?" Chloe demands.

"I think . . ." *You don't have enough going on in your life if you take that inane list so seriously.* "I have to find my friend and leave."

"Why?" Amanda asks. "Aren't you going to stay with your new boyfriend?"

"He's not—"

"Yeah, he is," Chloe says. "That's the beauty of the list. Girls

115

who are . . ." She looks me up and down and I brace for the insult. *Ugly. Plain. Nobody.* ". . . *average* can score a hot guy."

I roll my eyes. "It's a freaking list, Chloe," I say, my impatience rising. "It's not magic."

"It's not just a list, Kenzie," she fires back. "And if you think it is, maybe you shouldn't be on it."

"I didn't ask to be on it."

They all share a look; then Amanda angles her head, narrowing her eyes at me. "Chill, you two. Get in there." She nudges me toward an open door, but I hold my ground.

"I don't want—"

Fingers grip my arm so tight I almost cry out. Kylie Leff is grabbing me, staring me down. "In there," she says.

"Why?"

Kylie pushes me. "Just do it, Kenzie."

I stumble into a room that could be a den or a library or, based on the glass walls full of bottles, a wine vault. It's very dark and even darker when the door closes.

"What is going on?" I demand.

"Shhh." They gather around me in a circle, near enough that I can just make out their features in the low lights from behind the wine vaults.

Chloe gets so close I can see each stroke of mascara on her lashes and how her dark eye shadow has formed some creases. But mostly I can see a very, very serious look in her hazel eyes.

"You should never have been on the list," she hisses, unable to let go of our argument.

No shit, Sherlock. "Hey, I didn't control the voting. Or suck off the lacrosse team."

Her eyes remain narrowed as she glares at me. "You don't get it, do you?"

116

Apparently not. "That I don't belong on a list with you pretty girls, is that what you're saying?" A zing of frustration shoots up my spine, popping a little when it hits my head. "I don't deserve the attention of a guy like Josh Collier? You resent me being on your list because it brings down the cachet? Yeah, I get you have issues, but I don't want to be in your stupid club, so why don't you just leave me alone?"

All three of them stare at me. Not looks of remorse or pity or anger or anything like that. Just . . . blank stares. Then Chloe jerks like she's coming after me, but Kylie and Amanda grab her. "Stop it, Chloe. This is more important."

"What is it?" I ask. "I have to find my friend."

Amanda steps closer. "Has anything, you know, dangerous happened to you lately?"

I feel my whole body burn into a hot pool of liquid mercury. "Like what?"

"Like weird close calls?"

Oh, shit. "Like accidents?"

They lean in a little, stealing my air and space.

"Kenzie," Amanda whispers. "Have you almost died in the last few days?"

Yes. Three times. "I've had some . . . weird stuff happen." They share a look that is scarier than any slasher film I've ever seen. "Why?" I ask, my voice cracking.

Chloe's eyes widen. "This is bad."

Horror drains blood from my head. "What? What are you talking about?"

"The curse," Chloe whispers, the words setting goose bumps off like tiny bombs on my arm.

I just stare at her, unable to process what she might mean. "There's a curse?"

"This is the thirtieth year of the list," she whispers, tilting her head like she just revealed the secret of the ages.

I remember the nurse telling me that. "And?"

They exchange another look, but this time Kylie shakes her head hard. "You know what your mother said, Chloe."

"What did she say?" I ask.

Chloe closes her eyes and lets a soft breath out of her nose. "Just be careful, Fifth. I mean, we're probably safe, but . . ."

"But what?" I ask, hating the catch in my voice. "What is this curse? A ghost? Folklore? A campfire story? What the hell are you talking about, Chloe? Have you guys had weird things happen as well?"

"My flatiron fell right off the shelf into my bathtub about ten seconds after I got out," Chloe says.

Oh, Lord.

"My garage door wouldn't go up," Kylie says. "And I was in the car and couldn't get the door to unlock or . . ." She closes her eyes. ". . . turn the damn ignition off. If my sister hadn't come home . . ." She lets out a shudder.

I look at Amanda, who says, "Unless you count tripping on a loose carpet on my stairs, no, but I did get a really weird text the night Olivia died."

I can barely talk. "What did it say?"

"'One down.'"

I let out a whimper and put my hand to my mouth. "In English?"

"Hell, yes, in English. But the weirdest thing of all was the text disappeared about ten minutes after I got it. I can't find it in my deleted texts, nothing."

"You imagined it," Kylie suggested.

No, she didn't.

118

The knock on the door is like a gunshot, making us all shriek and jump.

"Kenzie? You in there?" It's Molly, and I nearly weep with relief.

"Just a sec, Moll."

"I'm ready to go home," Molly replies.

Two of them grab my arm and Chloe gets right in my face. "Don't you tell a soul," she hisses. "Not a living soul. Including your stupid friend."

"She's not stupid," I say quietly.

"Well, she's not one of us," Kylie says.

"Not a soul." Chloe grinds out the words. "Why do you think Olivia is dead?"

I dig for common sense to fight the wave of nausea that comes over me. "Because she got drunk and jumped off a cliff?"

The door handle turns. "Kenzie, come on!"

"She's dead because she talked about the curse."

The *curse*?

Molly pounds harder. "Kenzie!"

Without a word, Amanda steps toward the door and unlocks it, pulling it open until I see Molly.

"I'm coming," I say to her. Then I glance over my shoulder, ready for dark looks from my list sisters, but something else catches my eye: a movement behind them. I blink and make out the shadow of a man slipping into a door on the other side of the room.

Who was that? Rex? Josh? Whoever it was heard this entire conversation. But I won't tell these girls that. They're wack. There's no curse.

I hope.

119

CHAPTER XIII

It turns cold on Sunday night. My hands are stiff and stuffed into my jacket pockets as I walk. The wind chills my face, causing tears to form in the corners of my eyes, and the first true frost of the season reaches into my bones. I'm shivering by the time I get to Starbucks.

All that changes when I step inside. Heated air assaults me and so does the sight of a boy at a corner table, hands wrapped around a coffee, dark hair falling over one eye, no expression on his face as he watches me.

For a second, I can't breathe or remember being cold.

The power of Levi is his eyes. Oh, no, maybe it's that smile. Scratch that, it's the body when he stands up to greet me. Face it, Levi has all kinds of power, and it obviously works on me, or I wouldn't have come tonight. He sent me a reminder text about an hour ago, telling me he really needs help with a certain word problem, but I'm pretty sure I would have shown up even if he hadn't. And not because he's failing math.

So here I am, ready to tutor. Except there's a surprising lack of books, notebooks, practice tests, or anything else that says "tutoring going on here" at his table. I knew this wasn't about math.

Something scary and thrilling twirls around my chest and settles in my belly as I pull out the chair across from him.

"You crying, Mack?" he asks, scrutinizing my face.

I wipe the cold away. "Freezing." I should tell him exactly why I hate the nickname, but I'm not ready to take the conversation there quite yet. Plus, when he says it, the name sounds different from when my brother said it. I like the way it sounds on Levi's lips.

Maybe I just like Levi's lips.

"Here." He slides the coffee across the table when I sit down. "It's really hot."

I glance at the slit in the plastic lid and get another thrill in my stomach at the very idea of putting my lips where his just were. Eyes down, I wrap both hands around the paper sleeve and can't help but sigh with relief at the warmth on my fingers.

"Drink it," he orders. "It's got salted caramel."

Oh my God, that sounds good. I lift the cup and bring it to my mouth, looking up to meet his gaze. He gives me that hint of a half smile tempered with those smoky eyes, a look that's probably stolen virginities, broken hearts, and inspired a few bad poems.

The coffee is delicious—sweet and rich with a surprising tingle of saltiness mixed in. "Mmm. That's great. I should get one."

"We can share." He takes the cup from me, rotates it a bit, and drinks. I can't help but watch his mouth, so full and perfect and incredibly . . . kissable.

And just last night I kissed Josh Collier, who all but asked me to spend the night and be his girlfriend. A nagging sense that I'm doing something wrong is settling all over my insides in a place where I imagine my conscience resides.

This is a tutoring session—so why should I feel like I'm cheating on a guy I don't even like that much? Whoa, that's the first time I've admitted *that* truth, even to myself. I don't like Josh. Does that mean I *do* like . . .

"You're thinking awfully hard," he observes.

"Getting into my tutoring mindset." I nod and glance at the empty table between us. "So, where's your math book?"

"I can't figure it out." He angles his head, scrutinizing me again.

"The word problem?"

"Who you remind me of."

The intimate tone makes me want to lean forward, but I fight the urge and dig for something witty. "Just don't say your mother."

I can tell by his disappearing smile that my humor fell flat. "I don't know what my mother looks like anymore. I haven't seen her since I was about eight."

My heart slips a little. "That's . . . sad."

"Not at all. It's a relief. She's a lunatic."

I look down at the coffee, because what can you say to that?

"She really is," he adds, his tone almost hopeful, as if he wants me to pursue the point.

"My mom's nuts, too." I reach for the coffee, craving another salty sip.

122

"Not like mine."

"My mom won't let me play sports or take a shower when there's a storm or cross the street without a traffic cop," I say with a laugh. "I mean, she's crazy."

"My mom is in a mental institution."

Oh. "Well. You win, then."

That makes him smile. "I always dominate the nutcase mom contests."

He's trying to make light, but I still can't quite get my head around what he said. "I'm sorry," I say. "That must be hard on you and . . ." What was the deal with his father? I have no idea. ". . . the rest of your family."

He lets me dangle, taking the coffee again. After he sips, he leans back, regarding me from under thick black lashes. "It's an actress from those Star Wars movies." He frowns, pointing at me, his finger moving from eye to eye. "It's right in there. Portman."

I look like Natalie Portman to him? "She has brown eyes."

"Shape of the face. That exquisite little chin."

Exquisite? "She's . . . pretty."

"My point exactly." He puts his elbows on the table and drops his chin on his knuckles. "Trust me, it was worse when my mom was around."

What was? I blink at the rapid subject volley, trying to keep up with him. "Do you have ADD or something?"

"Something." He's still staring at me, comparing me to Natalie Portman. "I'm dyslexic."

Oh, again. "You like to drop bombs," I say. "Is that for dramatic effect?"

"I want to be honest and open with you."

I can't help it. I have to know. "Why?"

123

He's not surprised by the question; I think he thrives on directness. A slow smile pulls at his lips. "Because I believe I can trust you."

"You can," I tell him. "Don't other people know about . . . your mom? Your dyslexia?"

He doesn't answer right away, taking the cup and twirling the brown sleeve around as he thinks. "I moved here last year from Pittsburgh."

At the beginning of the spring semester. "I remember." When he arrived at Vienna High, a tremor went through the female population.

"You do?" Now that surprises him.

"Of course I do. You seemed . . ." *Experienced. Dangerous. Hot.* "Older than most of us."

"Held back a few times," he admits with no shame. "I'll be eighteen in four months."

I nod, trying not to show how that affects me. Eighteen seems so much older than my just-turned-sixteen. Mom would explode. And, I have to acknowledge the obvious: he's just about Conner's age. And this boy couldn't possibly be more different from my positive, gregarious, universally adored brother.

"So, you moved here because of your family?"

"It was here or more time in juvie."

I laugh quietly.

"Why are you laughing?"

"Because you're so up front about these things."

He shrugs. "I speak the truth, always."

I like that. "But most kids would either try to hide that or . . . I don't know. I guess I don't hang around kids who've been in juvie, so I really don't know. So what happened?"

"I drag raced."

"That's enough to put you in juvie?"

He shrugs, then closes his eyes. "And wrecked."

"Oh."

"A stolen car."

Ouch. "That was dumb."

"You have no idea."

"Did you get hurt?" I ask.

Color slowly drains from his cheeks. "No, but . . ." He shifts in his seat and blows out a slow breath. "There was a girl in the car with me and she . . . did. She got hurt." He mumbles the last words.

After a beat of silence, he looks directly at me. "She can't walk."

I freeze for a second, then fall back against my chair. "That's horrible."

"Yep. I'm on probation now, and my aunt convinced my officer to let me have a license and live with her. Good thing, since my dad thinks I'm the devil incarnate and my mom doesn't know who I am half the time."

Probation. Juvenile detention. Mental institutions. A paralyzed passenger in a stolen car. Jeez, this guy is trouble—and yet I feel more comfortable with him than with the boy who lives with a millionaire grandfather and tried to make out with me in his billiard room.

"How long are you on probation?" I ask.

"Till I'm eighteen." He looks a little wistful, as if the idea of leaving his aunt doesn't appeal to him. Maybe he's tired of moving around.

"Then where?"

"No clue, Mack." He leans closer. "So, did you have fun?"

The way he jumps topics is like dancing with someone who

125

keeps changing the rhythm—I don't know what to expect. "Fun doing what?"

"At Collier's party."

"How do you know I was there?"

He puts his elbows on the table again, but this time flattens his palms together, looking at me over long, strong, tanned fingers. "Vienna's not that big a place. And there were more Instagram pictures. Hashtag kissing number five."

My cheeks burn again but I refuse to look away from him. "Yeah," I say. "That happened."

He still stares, unnerving me.

"Look, I came here to help you," I say. "If you have problems with math, I can. If you just want to . . . to . . . share coffee? Then . . ." I trail off and wait for him to help me out.

"Then you have a boyfriend already."

"Not technically." Dang, that might have been too fast.

"Just random make-out sessions with good-looking jocks?"

"We didn't make out. Exactly."

He leans forward, surprising me when he snags my hand. "You be careful, Mack."

"I . . ." I want to pull my hand away, I really do, but there's something so incredibly comforting about the feel of his palm and fingers over my knuckles. It's like the coffee: I can't say no. "Why should I be careful? You think Josh Collier's going to break my heart?"

"Not worried about your heart." His voice is rough and low.

"Then what?"

For a moment, he looks far too serious for this semi-flirtatious conversation. Then he shakes his head. "So, about that word problem."

126

I laugh again. "I never know where you're going next."

"Good. It's in Latin."

Frowning, I search his face, which, trust me, is no hardship. "You don't take Latin." Not that many kids take Latin at Vienna High—and Levi is definitely not one of them.

"I need something translated."

"I thought you needed help in math."

He shakes his head. "Latin."

"Then," I have to acknowledge, "I'm your girl."

He gives me a direct look and half smile, squeezing my hand a little. "If only."

Whoa, he's good. Electrical, magnetic, combustible. Levi is a human physics class full of energy I can't resist. But I have to. I slide my hand away. "What's the Latin issue?"

"Why won't you hold my hand, Mack?"

"Why do you insist on calling me that? No one does, you know. It's Kenzie. Or Mackenzie. Not Mack."

"Really? Mack fits you. It's unaffected and straightforward and not quite what you'd expect."

Am I all those things? "I don't like that name."

"Why not?"

Because my brother called me Mack from the day I was born, and sometimes, when I'm going to sleep and the guilt and pain creep up on me, I imagine he's down in that storeroom, his T-shirt caught in the conveyor belt, his head being pulled in a different direction from his body, trapped and alone and dying. Did he call for me? Did he scream, *Hey, Mack, I need help!*

Or did he just . . . *die* trying to retrieve the trinket I'd lost?

"Earth to Mack." Levi waves his hand in front of my face.

"Sorry."

127

"Where were you?"

A bad place. I can't answer, and attempt a shrug.

"My guess is someone special called you that name. Someone who puts a sad look in those baby-blue eyes."

I want to make a joke, be light, even flirt. But he's so damn close to the truth I can barely breathe.

"Your first love?" he asks.

"Don't." My voice cracks with one word and instantly he has my hand again. "What Latin help do you need?"

"You're going to tell me," he says with one of those sly smiles. "It's my secret superpower. People tell me shit."

"Trust me, Levi, you have more than one superpower."

He holds my gaze for what feels like an eternity but is probably just the span of four or five of my crazy-fast heartbeats. And during that time, I feel all the things I didn't feel with Josh last night. The toe-curling, breath-stealing, tummy-fluttering sensations of . . . attraction.

Great. Just great. Couldn't get all gooey over the good-looking jock, could I? No, I have to pick this one, with his record and his background and his scary, sexy eyes.

"You have a pen, Mack?"

I produce one from the cross-body bag I'm wearing. While he grabs a napkin and flips it to the side with no words, I take the shared coffee and sip. It's almost cold now, but I don't care.

I watch how his lashes shadow his cheekbones as he looks down, and study the set of his jaw and the shape of his lips.

I want to kiss him.

All that guilt evaporates, only to be replaced with something worse. Fear. I'm scared of this kid, and so, so drawn to him.

He looks up and catches me, but I don't care. "This is private," he says.

128

"Okay."

"I mean, do *not* repeat what I'm going to show you."

I almost laugh. "And I was just about to tweet it."

"I'm serious." He narrows his eyes and lowers his voice. "*Dead* serious."

"Okay," I say again, just as gravely.

"I need to know exactly what this means." He still doesn't turn the paper over, reaching for my hand. "Exactly. Word for literal word."

"Okay, I'll do my best."

He turns over the paper so I can read:

Nihil Relinquere et Nihil Vestigi

I don't have to think long; these are not unusual words. "It says 'to leave nothing behind and no trace.'"

He frowns. "Google said 'leave nothing and trace nothing.'"

"Google Translate is mentally challenged." I study the words again, double-checking the tense and grammar. "Yes, *nihil* means 'nothing' but *relinquere* is the verb 'to leave behind.'"

"Not 'to leave'?"

"No, it's referencing what's left when you're gone. Also, the second clause is a partitive genitive, so while it directly translates to 'nothing of trace,' it means 'no trace.'"

He frowns, shaking his head.

"You'd have to understand the nuances of the language, but *nihil* is a defective noun."

"Something's wrong with it?"

"*Nihil* doesn't decline like a normal noun; it only has a nominative and accusative. In the first clause, *nihil* is acting as the direct object of the infinitive *relinquere*. . . ." There's more of an explanation—there always is with the accusative case—but he's scratching his head, lost.

"You're sure? It means 'leave nothing behind'—"

"No, 'to leave nothing behind.' It's an order, not just a thing someone does. It's a thing someone wants to do or is ordered to do. Very subtle nuance, but there is a difference."

He nods.

"So what is it? Song lyrics? A poem? Secret code?" On the last guess, I swear he pales.

"I'm doing a favor for a friend," he says after a beat.

That's a weird favor. "Anyone I know?"

"Doubtful." He rolls the paper into a ball. I'm mesmerized by his hands; they might be the most beautiful hands I've ever seen. Blunt-tipped, long, lean, strong, tanned.

After a moment, he slips the napkin ball into his jacket pocket and his gaze moves from me to the window behind me. Once again, I can swear something shifts in his expression and body language. Just like that, he seems . . . taut.

Without thinking, I turn just in time to catch a dark pickup truck pulling out of the lot.

I whip around and look at him. "Do you know who that is?"

"Who *who* is?"

"That truck."

He frowns. "I didn't see a truck." Suddenly, he stands, grabbing the coffee. "I gotta go, Mack. Thanks for the Latin assist."

The abruptness throws me, like everything he says and does, but I stand, too. "Okay." I glance at the parking lot again. I don't like the idea of walking in the dark with that pickup out there. A familiar sensation rolls through me.

Familiar enough that I shake it off. I will *not* be ruled by fear. Yes, I could ask Levi for a ride home, but something stops me. Probably how fast he's moving to get out of here. And if he wanted to give me a ride, wouldn't he offer?

His gaze slips to the window again before he starts to walk away. I slowly sit back down, trying to process this one-eighty change in him. Was it the translation? The truck? Me?

Pausing at the trash receptacle near the door, he tosses in the coffee cup. After a moment's hesitation, he reaches into his pocket and pulls out the balled-up napkin, flipping it into the recycling bin.

He turns and winks. "See ya, Kenzie."

The name—the one I said I wanted him to use—sounds hollow. I guess I liked Mack after all. It's . . . *unaffected and straightforward and not quite what you'd expect.*

Just like him.

I watch him disappear into the darkness. But I don't move, still baffled by everything, including an attraction I don't want to feel. But mooning over some cute guy is not why I'm sitting here, I finally admit.

I'm scared of the blasted truck.

I hate that. I hate it so much I almost take off, but I can't. Finally, my phone rings with a text. When I see Molly's name with a "how's it going" note, I could cry. I text her back and ask her to pick me up, and she promises to be here in ten minutes.

While I wait, I scroll through my Facebook feed, thinking about all these "friends." The number has nearly doubled, but I have to remember there's only one real friend who'd jump off her bed on a Sunday night and give me a ride home.

Everyone is still talking about Saturday's amazing party. A

131

few are posting memories and comments about poor Olivia. Chloe Batista is bragging about how she makes a cool fifty bucks for watering somebody's houseplants while they're on vacation, which is just a tacky thing to post to the world. Josh sent me a private message saying he's thinking about me and that I made a great impression on his grandfather.

I almost laugh at how different my Facebook page looks just days after I landed on the list. How can one thing change people's opinions so fast?

When I see Molly's VW pull in, I get up and walk to the door, but as I get closer to the trash, I simply can't resist. With a glance around at the almost empty Starbucks, I grab the napkin from the top of the recycling bin and stuff it into my pocket.

Nihil Relinquere et Nihil Vestigi

I'm just following the instructions on the napkin.

CHAPTER XIV

It's warm in Molly's car, and I feel relaxed and balanced for the first time since I left my house over an hour ago. "Where can we go on a Sunday night? I'm not in any rush to go home."

She turns up the radio. "Fine with me. Now let's get back to Levi. He asks you to tutor him in math but he really just wanted you to translate something he could have found on Google? Interesting."

"The Google translation was wrong."

She shoots me a look like I'm an idiot. "Don't you see it was just an excuse to go out with you?"

I had to consider that. "I know, right? Otherwise why didn't he just ask me to translate something in school or when I saw him the other day in the parking lot? Why drag me to Starbucks on a Sunday night?"

She rolls her eyes. "What am I going to do with you, Kenzie Summerall? Don't you get it? You are a hot commodity now. Josh Collier wants to be your boyfriend and—"

"He didn't ask me out."

"You kissed him."

"Yeah, but we're just talking. Nothing official."

"Kissing should be official," she says as she turns onto Route 1. "I'd suggest coffee, but you just had some. You hungry?"

"Not really." I look out the window, but I'm not really paying attention until I see a dark truck. Is that the same one? I wonder. I don't have a knack for knowing every vehicle make, model, and year with one glance. Trucks all look exactly alike to me, except for the color. Some have that second back door, some have silver wheels, some are big, some are monstrous. This one looks . . . like the one I've been seeing. I have to know more about it.

"Hey, take the next right past the light, Moll. I want to see something."

"What?"

"I keep seeing that truck everywhere around Cedar Hills," I say, referring to our borough within the city of Vienna. I think about elaborating now, at least about the truck and the weird text or the gas leak. But I still feel as if telling anyone about these bizarre, unrelated, possibly not even real events gives them credence they don't deserve, so I stay quiet.

She'll just think I'm turning into my mother, unhealthy and obsessive.

By the time we get to the road where I saw the truck turn, it's gone. The street is a simple residential neighborhood a lot like mine, only the houses are a little bigger and nicer.

And suddenly, I'm very, very tired of this. "You know, I think I just want to go home."

Without argument, she takes us through some side streets heading back to the part of Cedar Hills where we live, winding around the curves and inclines, talking excitedly about a boy named Brock she met at the party.

"He goes to a prep school in Pittsburgh," she tells me. "So he didn't even know about the Hottie List."

"And you told him?" I ask.

"I might have mentioned it."

"Molly!"

"What? I didn't say I was on it. And I know you think this new run-in with popularity is bogus, but I'm loving it, Kenz. I'm getting a total spillover effect on Facebook. I've accepted about twenty new friends and I'd never have gotten to that party without you being on the list. Thank you, Miss Hottie Pants."

"I . . ." *I see the truck.* I think. "I get it."

"Do you?" Molly asks. "I want you to understand how much this new social status means to me. It doesn't mean I'm using you or anything."

"I know," I say, squinting at the truck parked in front of a house on the corner.

"Why are you so interested in that truck?"

"I almost hit a truck the night of my accident and I swear that same truck nearly mowed me down on Baldrick Road yesterday. I'd love to know who the heck it was. They never even stopped to see if I was alive."

The truck's lights are off and it looks empty. I try to find some kind of identifying feature to memorize. It's got four doors, so it's one of the bigger pickups. A silver bumper. A tow hook on the back. Other than that, it looks like every dark truck in America parked in front of a gray one-story with fancy fieldstone up the sides.

"You don't know who lives there, by any chance?" I ask.

135

"No, but we're in East Ridge, not Cedar Hills, so the people are Richie McRich. Look at the landscaping."

I'm not interested in the trees. "Have *you* ever seen that truck before? I mean, at school, maybe?"

"I don't know." She slows down when we're next to it and I peer inside the empty cab, although the windows are tinted and I can't see a thing. It *could* be the same pickup I saw the night of my accident or the one that almost ran me over on my bike or the one I thought I saw outside Starbucks when Levi suddenly bolted.

Or it *could* be that I am a victim of a wildly overactive imagination and a crazy-protective mother who's made me paranoid.

The house has one light on in the front room, but overall, it's quiet and unremarkable. When we drive past, I turn to get the license plate of the truck—which would be the smartest way to identify it. I memorize the number on the standard-issue blue and yellow Pennsylvania tag.

At the top of the hill, Molly stops at the intersection and points to a house on the corner. "I don't know about that other house, but your pal hottie number two lives there."

"Chloe Batista?"

"That's her Fiesta in the driveway, with the Salt Life bumper sticker." She gives me a wry smile. "Who *does* that?"

"You know, all that surfing in Vienna." I recognize the bright-blue car Chloe paraded when she got it for her sixteenth birthday. "Anyway, she's not my pal."

"Well, she wants you in her Sisters of the List club." There might be a hair of jealousy in Molly's voice, but I totally get that.

"Don't worry, Molly. I'm not going to the dark side."

She laughs, but her heart's not in it. "I'm all about the dark side, if they let me in. It beats hanging out with the band losers on Saturday nights."

"I still think it's bogus that these kids didn't even know my name, or yours, until that list came out."

"The boys knew your name, Kenzie, or you wouldn't have gotten enough votes to make the list."

I just roll my eyes. "I'm starting to hate that freaking list."

"You just need to relax and use it to your advantage, Kenz."

When we reach my house, we make plans to go to school together in the morning, and then I head in to find my mom in the den watching *Dr. Oz* reruns. After some small talk about the weekend—not a word about the party, the kissing, or, oh my God, my first sip of vodka—she starts talking about Olivia. Of course, it's been all over the news.

I tell her I barely knew Olivia and only dumb, drunk kids dive into quarries, and before she can get too deep into a topic I'm already tired of, I escape to my room, close the door, and curl up on my bed.

The next thing I do is pull that napkin out to study Levi's handwriting.

Nihil Relinquere et Nihil Vestigi

Why was my translation so important? Was it just a ploy to have a pseudo-date with me? I'd kind of think that from the way he acted, but then . . . bam. He was gone with the wind.

Or was he gone with the *truck*? I never really saw him get on his motorcycle, which is the only thing I've ever known him to drive. Did he get in that truck?

I open up my laptop to Google the phrase. All that comes up are links to books and articles, and Latin class notes from all different colleges. I get lost for a long time reading, testing my brain, finding a few new words.

This is what I should be doing, I think, aching a little. This is what I *do*. I should be preparing for State and winning the top prize. Instead I'm flirting with bad boys and kissing rich ones.

I consider going downstairs to relaunch the State discussion, which has been dropped completely after the accident last week. Outside I hear a siren, then another, loud and fairly close. But I've found Cicero's *Letters to Atticus*, and I'd rather read that than pay attention to anything. This is my comfort place.

The Latin is beautiful, musical, perfection in every word. I want to hear Cicero himself speak these words. I want to—

My door flies open and Mom is standing there, open-jawed and paper white.

"What's wrong?"

"Another . . . one."

"Another what?"

"Another . . . girl."

I just blink at her, a slow, cold agony already clawing at my heart.

"Another girl what?" Except I know. I know from her face and her voice and, oh, God, the sirens. I just know.

"Dead."

I slowly put my hand to my mouth, a cold sweat stinging my neck. The truck . . . the truck . . . the truck that made Levi Sterling run. "Who is it?"

"I just got a call from Barbara Gaines, whose daughter is married to a paramedic who was in the ambulance. She knows you go to Vienna and wanted to see if you knew her."

"Who? Who died, Mom?" I demand.

"Someone named Chloe."

"Chloe Batista." I croak her name.

"Do you know her?"

"She's . . ." Oh, God. *Second.*

And I'm fifth.

PART II

Non semper ea sunt quae videntur.

Things are seldom what they seem.

CHAPTER XV

We gather around the computer like I imagine people flocked to CNN when news broke in the pre–social network days. Our news comes from Facebook and Twitter, which is far more informative than anything on TV.

But in the social networks of Vienna High, rumors, conjecture, and warnings are flying fast. Fortunately, my mother is content to let me give her highlights from my screen rather than read over my shoulder. Because forget about it if she saw the word *second* or *the list* or, God forbid, my name and *fifth*. If she realized how close to home these posts were hitting, she'd wither and cry.

"What does it say, Kenzie?" Mom asks, crossing her arms and pacing the kitchen, nervous energy electrifying the room. "Are there details? What happened?"

"Nobody has a clue, Mom. It's just teenagers railing about how much they loved Chloe. And rumors." About the list. *The one I'm on.*

"My friend's son-in-law said her dad found her." Mom nearly shakes with horror at this and it's the third time she's mentioned it. She makes a little whimpering sound and drops into the chair across the table from me. "What was she doing at that house?"

"Watering plants." That much I knew from her last post.

"The paramedic told his wife the girl was in some kind of shock." She leans closer and almost reads my computer, but I tip the screen.

"Just let me look, Mom," I tell her, turning the laptop away completely.

"Oh, Lord, that poor family." She drops her head into her hands, and I know this is hard for her, a woman whose greatest fear is an accidental death. This is hard for *me*, a girl who fights that same fear every day . . . and is just two short spots away from being next.

But that's crazy. This has to be a coincidence, right? Or a curse. Or a—

"How well did you know her?" Mom asks.

We were "sisters" on a list. "Barely."

On my phone, I check Instagram, which has blown up with pictures of Chloe all the way back to kindergarten, tagged with #rememberchloe and #ripcb and, oh my God, #secondtodie.

"Who would write that?" I murmur, my insides turning cold.

"Write what?"

I shake my head, and she pushes back from the table to head to the coffee machine.

"You don't need that, Mom," I tell her before she even pulls a K-Cup from the carousel. "It'll keep you up all night."

She gives a soft, derisive snort. "Like that'll be any different from any other night."

I hear her, of course, every night. Fretting. Worrying. Pacing every inch of the first floor. Suffering from dystychiphobia, which Google tells me is a very real fear of accidents.

And during all that insomnia, she never goes upstairs, never. Not to my room for any reason—pretending to give me privacy. But I know she can't bear to go near Conner's room. She just leaves it untouched. Dad's begged her to turn it into something other than a shrine to their dead son, but she refuses.

Even when that refusal cost her Dad.

Frustrated, I don't respond, going back to Facebook to see if there's anything new.

There is: someone has posted a picture of a house surrounded by ambulances and police cars, with the words *Where Chloe died*.

"Oh, here's . . ." I trail off as I click on the photo to enlarge it, my breath suddenly drawn in so deep it feels like my chest is going to explode.

"What?" Mom demands. "They know what happened?"

"No, no." I'm trying to think straight, to be cool, not to give away that . . . "They don't know what happened." But *I* might.

I almost can't look, but I have to, leaning in and squinting at the slivers of fieldstone visible between two ambulances, at the lush landscaping.

"Looks like money." Mom's looking over my shoulder.

Richie McRich. That's what Molly said when we saw this very same house . . . just a few hours ago, with a dark pickup truck parked in front of it. There's no pickup parked there in this picture.

I stare hard at the street and then remember the numbers I got off the truck's license plate.

Oh my God, I can solve this murder.

Except . . . no one has said anything about murder. And I might be the only person in the world who thinks that. Me, with the over-the-top imagination.

Me, who's on the same list and has had three brushes with death in less than a week.

"What's the matter?" Mom asks, studying my expression.

"My friend is dead," I say, hoping the explanation staves off more questions I do not want to answer.

"You just said you barely knew her."

"I mean my classmate. We're like friends. I was just talking to her at a party on—"

"When were you at a party?" she demands, a spark in her gray eyes.

Oh, crap, crap, *crap.* Why did I speak without thinking? Next thing, I'll be confessing about the list. And the fact that Olivia and Chloe were first and second . . . and I'm fifth.

"When?"

I swallow, not a great liar under the best of circumstances. "Molly and I went to a party last night."

"When you slept over?" She leans closer, all that nervous energy directed to one place, one person . . . the one child she has left.

"It was no big deal, Mom, I—"

"Why didn't you tell me?" Her voice rises.

If someone stuck a camera into the Summerall house and watched this fight, they'd figure it was a typical rebellious teenager who lies about what she does and the demanding, distrusting parent who wants control.

But that's not what's going on at all.

I can go two ways here: fight and stomp out of the room, like I did on Thursday night when I wrecked my car, or a gentle, calming talk down from the ledge—that usually works.

But tonight? All bets are off.

"Mom, I swear it was not a big deal. Molly got invited to some boy's house and everyone was just sitting around talking about Olivia. . . ."

Another stupid mistake, reminding her of the other girl who died. She searches my face, as if she can find the crack in my armor. God knows it wouldn't take much. I feel so fragile I could break down right there in front of her.

Any other mom, any other life, and I would. I'd tell her about the close calls and the nurse and the truck and the low-grade, inexplicable fear that everything has just taken a turn for the worse.

But she'd fall over dead with worry right in front of me. And, honestly, I can't have another death in the family on my conscience.

"Mom." I stand up and reach for her shoulders; she's been shorter than me for over a year, and that alone makes me a tad protective of her. "I'm sixteen. You can trust me. I don't drink." Except that tiny sip of vodka with my list sisters—the list with two dead members. "I don't mess around with boys." Except I did make out with Josh Collier. "And I don't lie to you."

Except about everything tonight.

Her features soften a little. "I am not the least bit concerned about any of those things," she says.

"You don't have anything to worry about." More lies.

"I have everything to worry about." She manages a sad smile. "That's what I do."

147

I pull her closer, grateful this conversation, which usually makes me ache with suffocation, isn't turning that way tonight. Probably because this time . . . she might be right.

I squeeze her shoulders and give her a rare hug. "I have to be normal," I say, as much to myself as to her. "I cannot live in fear because this happened."

I feel her nod in agreement and turn my head to look at the Facebook screen, my eyes falling on the latest post in all caps.

CHLOE DIED OF ANAPHYLACTIC SHOCK!!!

I inch Mom away to read the rest, not in caps. "She ate something with peanuts in it," I say as we both turn to the computer.

"Was she allergic?" Mom asks.

I can see Chloe's face at the party, the grape vodka in her hand. *Thank God I'm allergic to peanuts and not grapes.*

"I think so."

Mom shakes her head. "At her age, with a potentially fatal allergy? She should know not to eat something unless she's sure of what's in it."

Yes, she should. I dig for relief. This was a real accident, unless . . .

Unless someone forced her to eat food that would kill her. Then it wouldn't be an accident . . . it would only look like one.

148

CHAPTER XVI

No surprise, Vienna High School is at a virtual standstill on Monday morning. When we left on Friday, Olivia Thayne and Chloe Batista were alive. Now, in two separate, awful, fatal accidents, they're gone. And the halls are on fire with speculation.

There's a curse.

There's a killer.

There's a very bizarre coincidence.

While the prevailing winds blew toward the last guess, there were enough curse and killer conspiracy theories that I felt the stares of all my classmates. The strongest connection between Olivia and Chloe—the Hottie List and their order on it—became the focus.

In Latin class, I'm barely listening to Mr. Irving telling us that grief counselors are available at the office for anyone who is having trouble coping. I feel a few eyes on me and know what people are thinking, so I look out the window to the parking lot.

Even Irving gives me a glance, his usually crisp, cold features turning soft as he adjusts his horn-rims. I hate that teachers know, that everyone knows. I look at my desk, avoiding the pity or worry or whatever it is.

I turn back to the window just in time to see a Vienna police cruiser pull into the front lot, followed almost immediately by another. My imagination goes right to a place I don't want to go: another accident, another death.

But these guys are moving slowly, gathering in a small group and talking, one on the phone. No one's hustling like there's been another incident. Another car pulls up and parks illegally, and two men and a woman get out and join the others.

Grief counselors?

No, they're too familiar with the officers. Detectives, I guess. Or whatever you call plainclothes police. My stomach knots up and so do my fists as I watch them slowly make their way to the front of the school, out of my line of vision.

Police are good. If there's a crime, the police will solve it.

They must be here to talk about Olivia and Chloe. I'm not a big fan of those procedural shows on TV and haven't a clue how these things work, but they can't just dismiss two kids dying in freak accidents in one weekend, can they? They have to talk to people . . . which means it's only a matter of time until they hear about the list. And then they'll want to talk to everyone on it.

The other girls can tell them about their strange near-miss accidents, like Kylie being stuck in the garage with her car ignition on, and I can tell them about the truck I saw in front of the house where Chloe died. They can't ignore that.

150

Will my mother have to be there? If not, I'll tell them about the accident on Route 1, with my brake-fluid line broken, like my dad said. And the gas leak and—

"Do you, Kenzie?" Mr. Irving's question pulls me out of my thought spiral. I stare at him, waiting for a hint on how to answer.

But there's no clue, just that soft sympathy on his face, and I remember that we're talking grief, not Latin. "Do you want to go to the office, Kenzie?" He holds out a hall pass. "Probably not a bad idea for you to at least meet the grief counselors."

Probably not a bad idea for me to get the heck out of this classroom. I scoop up my bag—we hadn't even bothered to take out books—and snag the pass. "I'm going to be a while," I tell him.

Irving nods. "Take your time, Kenzie."

"I wasn't close friends with them," I say under my breath, as though I need to offer him some relief. Or maybe that's not what he's worried about. Maybe he knows about the list and thinks I'll be dead, too, and won't get to State and pull Vienna High a first place.

"Everyone's affected," he says gently.

Everyone on that list is what he means. I slip out into the hall with absolutely no intention of going to the office to have my grief counseled or to talk to the police—not until I know they won't alert my mother. She'd die.

I'm just about to hide in the bathroom when I see the posse of police leave the office and step into the hall, with Principal Beckmeyer right in their midst. He looks a little redder than usual—and he's always pink and sweaty—talking to one of the officers and pointing in the other direction. From the office door, the dean steps toward them. I hang back, watching them, wondering what their plan is.

After a moment, they break into two groups, the dean taking two of the cops and two of the plainclothes guys one way, and Beckmeyer heading toward me with the rest.

On instinct, I slip into the bathroom, not willing to get my pass checked by the principal and some cops. The girls' room is empty, and I wait behind the door long enough to hear them go by; then I step back out to see them head toward the atrium that feeds into the cafeteria and media center.

Staying back as far as I can, I follow them to the wide center hall, where giant skylights bathe everything in a natural light, making the atrium a cheery gathering place no matter the time of day. Rimmed by bright-blue lockers and peppered with long tables where kids can eat or study, this hall is the center of Vienna High. We have pep rallies and assemblies here when it's too cold to go outside, and the place always echoes with laughter and talking and life.

Today it's silent but for the heavy footsteps of the cop brigade. It's early, but the smells of fries and pizza are starting to roll out of the cafeteria as we get closer to first lunch. There are a few kids in small study groups, but no one's working. They're whispering in hushed tones, and then everyone is silent as they stare at the arrivals.

The police and Principal Beckmeyer head toward the media center, and I can't follow them without getting on their radar. I have a feeling I'll be on it sooner or later anyway, when they get wind of the list. I drop onto one of the benches and let my backpack hit the floor with a thud.

I refuse to meet the eyes of the few kids in the atrium—

I don't even know them except for one who was in driver's ed with me last year—so I reach down and grab my phone from the side pocket of my backpack. What did people do before they could fake text to not look like an idiot?

One touch of my screen and I realize I don't have to fake anything. I've missed three texts, the first from Josh.

Want to skip 4th per and take a ride? Need to talk.

I stare at the words for a second, trying to decide just how they make me feel. Good, I guess. I mean, Josh really seems to like me. I don't know why that surprises me so much, but it does. Maybe because he's been the object of my crush for so long that it just seemed incomprehensible that he'd ever notice me. I don't want it to be because of the list, but hey, if that's what put me on his radar, then fine.

But I can't fight the facts anymore. I feel absolutely nothing for him. I mean, he's cute, obviously. And he's cool and popular and, oh my God, if his grandfather could really do something about a scholarship for me, then I ought to be nice to him, but shouldn't I feel all buzzy inside? Shouldn't I want to text Molly with a cyberscream? But all I do is click to the next text, from Dena Herbert.

Holy shit, are you scared?

Dena. Sixth on the list. If what we might be scared of had any merit, then I should be exponentially more terrified than Dena. After all, I'll be dead before she is.

But I'm jumping to crazy conclusions too soon.

No one pushed Olivia off that cliff or held her underwater. The official word was that her foot got trapped between two rocks and by the time they got to her, she was dead. And Chloe had a food allergy that could—and *did*—kill her. She shouldn't have raided the fridge while watering her neighbor's plants. The truck could turn out to belong to a next-door neighbor. We didn't know everything yet, so that must be why the po—

"Hey."

I jump a foot in the air as two girls sit down, one on either side, trapping me. I look from Amanda to Kylie and back again, feeling very much like I'm in the middle of a cheerleader sandwich.

"You scared the crap out of me," I say, slamming my hand over my hammering heart.

"Then you're as smart as they say you are." On my left, Amanda turns to straddle the bench and face me. "We need to be scared."

They look at each other and Kylie nods, giving permission to Amanda to speak.

"We need to have an emergency meeting of the Sisters of the List," she whispers. "As soon as possible."

Under any other circumstances—like, you know, if two people weren't *dead*—I'd laugh in their pretty faces. The Sisters of the List business is too stupid for words.

"In secret," Kylie adds.

I whip around to look at her, taking in her heavily made-up amber eyes and bright-green slut-liner, as Molly calls the inside-the-eye pencil. It doesn't look slutty on Kylie, though; it looks stunning. And it does nothing to hide her abject fear.

Amanda grabs my arm and makes me turn to her. She doesn't cake on the makeup, but she doesn't have to. Blond, blue-eyed,

154

and blessed with every bone-structure gift, Amanda Wilson totally belongs on the Hottie List.

I'm ready to fire off a response when the media center doors open and Principal Beckmeyer steps out, a frown on his ruddy face. Behind him, the two uniformed cops come into sight, their arms posed as if they have someone between them, but Beckmeyer's six-foot-two blimp-shaped body is blocking my view.

"What's going on?" Amanda asks, repositioning herself to get a better view.

"Are they arresting someone?" a kid from another table asks.

Two more students stand up, cell phones already out to take pictures. The quiet of the atrium is replaced by the echo of rising voices.

When Beckmeyer steps aside, I hear the collective gasp, and only then see who is being escorted by the police.

My heart squeezes and nearly stops as I lock gazes with Levi Sterling.

He lifts his chin imperceptibly, a secret nod directed right at me, but then he's hidden as they surround him and walk out. In my hand, my cell vibrates and I look down, remembering that I'd had three text messages and I'd only read two.

I ignore a new one from Molly and flip back to see what Levi sent to me while I was in Latin class.

Mack, I need your help.

CHAPTER XVII

The noise level rises in the atrium as some kids pour out of the media center and everyone naturally gathers around them to find out what happened. Of course, we join the fray to hear what we can.

"They totally surrounded him at a table."

"Beckmeyer was about to explode."

"They read him his rights."

"They did not, dickhead. He wasn't even cuffed."

"Man, he didn't flinch. Sterling is one tough dude."

I try to block it all out, still processing what I know about Levi, when a new girl joins the conversation.

"He used to date Chloe," she says, bringing the group to silence. *And he also used to date Olivia,* but I keep that to myself.

"Really?" Amanda says. "I never heard that rumor."

"Well, they had a thing."

"Define 'thing,'" someone else challenges.

"Yeah, with Chloe a thing could be a hand job in the locker room," one of the boys says, making them all snort. As soon as they see the vile looks they're getting from the girls, they go silent.

"She's dead," Amanda says sternly, then turns to Kylie. "It's time."

They back away from the table and Amanda's hand lands on my shoulder. "Let's go, *sister.*"

I can feel everyone's eyes on us, but no one says anything. I don't want a scene, so I walk out with them, although I'd prefer to stay and hear more about what happened to Levi.

"This way," Kylie says, indicating a stairwell that leads to the subfloor, which is what the basement of Vienna High has been called since the beginning of time.

"Down here?" I ask, hesitating.

No one goes into the subfloor, at least no one who isn't a janitor or some other staff person. Years ago, it was part of the high school, but after a complete remodeling sometime in the 1990s, the subfloor was turned into storage and utility rooms, and the old labs were abandoned when the new science and technology wing was finished.

When we reach the bottom of the stairs, Kylie pushes a fire door into the hallway, which is so dark it takes a second for my eyes to adjust. With no natural light and cuts in every budget, which I assume includes the electricity bill, the corridor is airless and shadowed.

"Chem lab two," Kylie says, pointing forward.

"Have you been down here before?"

They exchange a look. "The cheerleading initiation program includes a little, uh, scavenger hunt," Kylie explains.

"Also known as hazing," Amanda adds.

I can't help but make a face. "Why? Why would anyone put themselves through that?"

"To prove your worth," Kylie says.

"Doesn't your ability to do a split and wear those inane ribbons in your hair prove your worth?"

Amanda shakes her head, giving me a smile that doesn't reach her eyes. "Some people just don't get it."

"Cheerleading?"

"Friendship. Connection. Forever sisterhood."

"Oh, please," I say, disgusted with this waste of time and still longing to know what is going on with Levi. "That just makes you a conformist, a joiner, and a person who needs a full support system."

"So what do you belong to?" Kylie asks me.

Latin club. I hesitate to fully announce my geekdom. But what the hell? It is who I am.

I'm saved by the sight of Dena Herbert and Candace Yardley rushing toward us. Dena's in jeans and sneakers but Candace is in full-on designer wear, with a short black skirt and wedge heels that clack against the linoleum in an exaggerated beat.

Ashleigh, Bree, and Shannon are right behind, rushing to catch up.

"Did you guys hear about Levi Sterling?" Dena asks when they reach us.

"He must have killed them both," Candace says without flinching, but then, I doubt she's ever flinched in her life.

"But if I know Levi," Dena adds, "he screwed them first."

I blink at her, not sure I heard her right. "What?"

158

"Levi's a ladies' man," she explains. "And maybe a lady-killer."

The others throw her a look, but I slow my step and frown. "Do you have any idea how serious it is to say something like that?"

"Dena." Kylie grabs her arm to tug her forward. "Nobody killed Chloe or Olivia."

The words flood me with relief. Not just because there's someone with a voice of reason, but because I want her to be right. She has to be right.

"And you know this how?" Dena challenges.

"Chloe told me."

"From the grave?" one of the girls behind me asks with a snort.

"She told me the day Olivia died," Kylie answers, holding up a hand to stop all eight of us.

"Why didn't you tell us that?" Dena's voice rises in frustration.

Kylie ignores the question. "In here."

The words *Chemistry Two* are faded on the frosted-glass panel, the wood frame as old school as, well, this old school. Kylie opens the door and leads us into a very dimly lit lab, with empty cabinets against the wall and six large black-topped tables in the middle.

It smells faintly of dust and bleach, and a film of dirt covers almost everything.

When we file in, voices rise with comments and questions and extremely uncomfortable giggles, until Amanda locks the door and the click snaps us all into silence. We stand there for an awkward beat; then Kylie waves us into a small circle.

"Get in order," Kylie says, gesturing at us. Like sheep, we comply, three through ten, but Dena and I share a look of amusement. Like me, she's not a girl I'd have pegged for the Hottie List. She's got a 'fro and isn't bone skinny, but her smile is infectious and people really like her.

I'm glad she's next to me.

"Sisters of the List," Kylie says in a perfectly serious baritone. "The worst has happened."

Sighing, Dena shifts her feet, her sneakers sticking to the old linoleum. "Seriously, Kylie?"

A rumble rolls through the girls, part laughter, part embarrassment, but Kylie hushes us with a look.

"I'm quite serious, and you would be, too, if you were third." Her golden-brown eyes spark. "That is . . . next to die."

Stone silence is the only answer, except for a pathetic whimper from Shannon. Next to her, Bree bites her lip to keep from laughing.

"You think it's funny, Bree?" Amanda demands. "'Cause when Shannon's dead, you won't be laughing so hard, number eight."

All the smiles are wiped away, especially mine. I look around and don't see too many honors students in the group; Candace is in some of my classes and Ashleigh is pretty smart, but the rest? I might have to be the brains of the operation.

"You better tell us everything," I say to Kylie. "It's only fair that we know what you know so we can figure out what to do about it."

"Thank you," Dena exhales.

Kylie steps in a little closer and looks from side to side, like

160

one of the Vienna High janitors might be lurking in a corner and listening to eight crazy chicks in an abandoned basement lab.

"Chloe's mom, as you know, is list legacy."

Candace lets out a grunt. "Sorority talk makes me want to puke."

Kylie ignores her. "She knows . . ." She drags out her dramatic pause long enough to irritate. "A lot."

"A lot about what?" I ask.

Kylie and Amanda look at each other, silently communicating their agreement. Then, in perfect unison, they whisper, "The curse."

There's a second of quiet, then a chorus of female voices, high-pitched enough that I think the old glass door's going to shatter. Kylie shushes them but not before a few demand, "What the hell are you talking about?"

"You can't really believe in a curse," I say.

Kylie lifts a shoulder as if to say yes, she can. "It's not a matter of *believing*, Kenzie. Two girls are dead by freak accidents."

"Or not," I say.

"This is what happens," she says, her voice low. "This is how it works."

Seven sets of horrified eyes are the only answer to that.

"There's a curse on the list," Kylie whispers. "Chloe told us everything Saturday night."

"And are you going to tell us?" Dena asks.

"As much as we can—"

A chorus of arguments rises, and Kylie holds out her hand until we're quiet again.

"Amanda and I were sworn to secrecy."

"Well, screw secrecy," Dena mutters to a round of agreement.

"We can't. That's part of the history of the curse. She shouldn't have told us." The pain in her eyes intensifies. "If she hadn't, maybe she'd still be alive."

"What?" I practically spit the word. "This is ridiculous. There are cops arresting kids and two girls are dead and you think there's some kind of ancient curse?" I feel like my head's going to explode.

"It's not ancient," Amanda says. "It started with the list in 1984."

"And girls have been dying ever since then? And, like, no one noticed?" I can't keep the disbelief out of my voice. "This isn't a campfire game, you guys. This isn't some sorority hazing joke."

Kylie takes a step forward and levels me with one hell of a frightening look. "Don't you think I know that? I'm third. I'm *next*."

"Then you should talk to the police and get help."

There's a catch in Kylie's voice as she says, "That's the last thing I want to do. That's why all these girls have died."

"What?" The question comes from several other girls, but I'm still staring at her, processing this.

"Who's died besides Olivia and Chloe?" I demand. "All the seniors from last year are fine. And no one died when we were freshmen." Except . . . I shake off the thought. I will not let Conner's death into this conversation. They'll turn it into some sign from the list gods or something.

"Trust me," I continue. "If teenage girls were getting killed on a regular basis and they all were on the same list, don't you think *60 Minutes* or *Dateline* would be in here in a heartbeat sniffing a story?"

"It doesn't work like that," Kylie says. "It's not always teenage girls who die. Sometimes grown women who've been on the list have accidents. Sometimes it happens when they're in college. Some years no one dies. But every time, it's an *accident*—always accidents, and always girls, or women, who've been on the list."

"Accidents happen to other people, too," I say softly.

But she and Amanda are having none of it, shaking their heads.

"And no one has investigated this?" I ask, incredulity rocking me to the core.

"There's nothing to investigate, Kenzie," Amanda insists. "There's no *murder*. There's no crime. There's no *killer* when it's an accident."

Just like Conner. No one had investigated his death; it was ruled an accident. No one had ever asked why he'd gone to the storeroom and no one had ever found my necklace and added two and two together to get . . . guilt. Who knows better than I do that sometimes there is guilt even when there is no crime?

"Every single person who's ever died after she's been on the list was killed in an accident," Kylie tells us. "Not one has ever been murdered. *Ever*. No foul play, no investigation, no open case. Accidents."

"How do you know that?" Shannon asks.

"I just do," Kylie says, relying on a favorite answer of teenage girls who actually know nothing.

Candace makes a sound as though she's thinking the same thing. "How much of this did Chloe know before she died?"

"A lot," Kylie says. "And she shouldn't have told us or she might still be alive."

"Does the curse always kill in order?" Bree asks, earning a disgusted sigh from Dena.

"This has never happened before." Amanda crosses her arms and looks at me. "But this is the thirtieth year."

So we've heard. "And that means what?" I ask, tamping down every imaginable emotion and frustration at this insanity.

"It means this year might be different," Kylie answers. "This year might be *everyone* on the list."

"We're all going to die?" Ashleigh shrieks.

"Or it might not," Amanda says. "You know what Chloe said."

"What did she say?" About six of us ask in perfect unison.

Kylie waves us all in closer, putting her arms around Amanda and Candace, forming a huddle. We all follow suit, even though Dena and I share a look that tells me she thinks this is as dumb as I do.

"Sisters of the List," Kylie says breathlessly. "We have to appease . . . the keeper of the curse."

No one says anything for a moment; then Shannon inches in closer, frowning. "What does *appease* mean?" she whispers.

I shoot her a look, my patience waning. "It means this is sheer idiocy," I say, jerking out of the huddle. "You can't mess around with BS like this when people are dead."

"No shit, Sherlock," Kylie hisses.

"Who the hell is the keeper of the list?" Dena wants to know.

Another shared look, but Kylie shakes her head. "She didn't tell us."

Amanda agrees. "No one knows who . . . *or what* . . . it is. Just that it has to be appeased."

More questions and comments, but Shannon stomps her foot. "Will someone please tell me what that effing word means?"

"*Appease* means . . ." Kylie hesitates. "'To pay off.'"

"Not exactly," I correct. "It means 'to make peace.' *Pais* is *peace* in Latin."

"So is there, like, a war?" Shannon asks. "Like vampires versus zombies?"

I puff out an impatient breath.

"It's more like blackmail, Shannon," Kylie says. "We have to pay so we don't die."

"How much?"

"Pay in some way," Amanda explains.

All around, eyes widen and cheeks pale. Except mine, because this ranks with the stupidest, most preposterous conversations I've ever had. "Or we could go upstairs and talk to the cops about the weird things that have happened to us." I look at Dena. "Have any close calls lately? Any almost accidents?"

She frowns, then her eyes pop wide. "My cat chewed my charger wire and I got shocked."

"Really?" Bree steps closer. "That's weird, because a power line fell on our roof the other night and my dad said if any of us had been touching anything electric, we'd have died."

Kylie lets out a soft groan and looks around. "Anyone else?"

Candace pales and looks at Ashleigh. "Tell them."

"We were stuck on the railroad tracks in my car yesterday. The car stalled and . . ." She closes her eyes. "We just got off, like, five seconds before a train came."

"Holy shit," Bree murmurs.

165

"I told you guys," Kylie says.

Amanda looks around and sighs. "We may have to make an offering."

"Like at church?" Shannon asks in a shaky whisper.

"Like a sacrifice," Kylie adds, looking at Amanda. It's clear these two know a lot more than they're telling us. Not that anything they know makes a damn bit of sense, but everyone in the room is riveted.

"What kind of sacrifice?" someone asks.

Kylie closes her eyes. "A blood sacrifice."

Chaos erupts around me, but I don't move. Once again, Kylie calms the others down.

"Oh, brother." Dena pulls away, disgust on her face. "This is totally bogus. I have class and I'm out of—"

"You can't leave!" Amanda shouts. "We have to have a plan and a vow of silence and a chain to stay in constant contact. Mostly we need more information. Unfortunately, the only person we can think to ask is Chloe's mom, but how can we?"

"We have to!" Shannon insists, her voice rising.

"No!" I bark the order, imagining Mrs. Batista. I don't know her; I've never met her. But I know what a mother is like after she's lost a child. "We can't ask her anything right now. But I know someone we can talk to."

"No," Kylie says. "We can't tell anyone. If you tell anyone, you're next."

"Not even the police?" I ask.

Amanda and Kylie suck in simultaneous gasps. "You might as well write your will tonight, Kenzie," Kylie says.

I open my mouth to answer, but nothing comes out. What if she's right? We need help. I glance down at my hand and have my answer. Someone who told me I might need "protection." Will Nurse Fedder be normal or believe us? But I'm not willing to get into a fight over who I can talk to right now, so I stay quiet.

"Listen, I'll call the next meeting," Kylie says.

"Well, what do we do until then?" Shannon asks, a distinct note of panic in her voice.

Kylie gives her a mirthless smile. "Be really careful."

CHAPTER XVIII

have a moment of panic when I learn Nurse Fedder isn't in her office, but then I see her behind a glass-walled conference room, huddled around a table with a few other adults and two girls I don't recognize.

But I know grief counseling when I see it.

The parent volunteer at the desk gives me a pitying look when I ask for the nurse. "Can you wait? She and the counselors can probably see you in a few minutes. There's no one else in front of you."

I don't want to talk to the counselors, but I know there won't be any other way to get to Nurse Fedder today. After about fifteen minutes, they all come out.

Nurse Fedder spots me immediately. "Kenzie, how's your finger?"

"Healing. Can I talk to you?"

One of the counselors, an older man, steps forward. "You can talk to all of us. I'm Dr. Horowitz, a psychologist."

I shake my head and gesture to the nurse. "I just want to talk to Nurse Fedder."

"Don't be put off by the profession," the doctor says. "We can just talk. And this is Pastor Eugene." He indicates another man.

"Hello, dear," the pastor says, his voice so gentle and kind I'm almost tempted. But I doubt my questions about a curse would go over big with a pastor.

"Please?" I ask Nurse Fedder.

"I know this young lady." She reaches for my arm. "We'll talk in the clinic."

The shrink looks like he's about to argue, but another student comes in looking for counseling and helps me out. I follow Nurse Fedder down the short corridor to the same room where she'd bandaged my hand.

She closes the door and turns to me, as pale as I must have been the last time I was in here.

"This is bad," she says simply.

Whoa. Wasn't expecting that. "Yes, it is," I agree.

"I've been waiting for one of you to show up."

I assume she means one of the girls from the list. "We were too busy having a coven in an empty lab downstairs."

Her expression flickers. "A coven?"

"Talking about curses and stuff . . ." I eye her carefully, praying for her to look at me like I'm crazy. Like Kylie and Amanda are totally wacked out and there is nothing remotely true about this.

Instead she nods. "This could be a bad year," she says solemnly.

My weak knees bend and I sink into the patient cot. "What are you talking about?"

169

She glances at the door like someone might barge in. "We can't talk here."

"Why not?" I demand, despising the note of panic that hitches my voice. Why isn't she just waving this off as nonsense? Has everyone who's ever been on that list been brainwashed or something?

She sits next to me and closes her clammy hands over mine. "Most of the time, actually almost all the time, the girls on the list are . . . fine."

"Fine." I whisper the word. "What about the rest of the time?"

She closes her eyes and blows out a slow, noisy sigh. "There have been accidents."

So I've heard. Frustration and fear mix into a black ball of nausea in my stomach. I want to know more . . . but I kind of want to run away and never hear that word again.

"Are you sure they're accidents? Not . . ." *Murder.* "Intentional?"

"They're fatal. Never anything but bad luck or, more accurately, cursed luck."

"Nurse Fedder." I am fighting for calm, trying to ignore the quivering of terror and irritation in my body. "I don't believe in the supernatural. I don't believe in a curse."

Her smile is wry. "No one comes into this believing. But after a while . . . There's no denying that the hand of something very powerful is on this list. Something insidious and unpredictable, something that thrives on the unexpected and never leaves a trace of crime in its wake, only the stink of a curse."

How could someone so smart—trained in medicine and, one would assume, science—fall for this crap?

"Nurse Fedder—"

"Christine," she corrects. "Call me Christine."

"What I'm calling you is crazy." I don't care what I sound like. "I don't believe in curses or supernatural garbage or any insidious hands that . . . whatever you said. I don't buy any of that."

She gives a shrug that says it all: what I think matters not one bit.

"I think these deaths might be . . ." *Murder.* Levi's face flashes before me. If someone is accused, it'll be him. "Not accidents."

"They're not," she agrees readily. "But if you think someone killed anyone who's ever been on the list, think again. Not one death has ever been anything but a freak accident. No crime, no evidence of murder, no other person involved. Believe me, we've investigated."

"We? You mean other women who've been on the list?"

She nods. "We hired a private investigator who found absolutely no shred of evidence that any death was anything but accidental. Of course, there were two suicides."

I just blink at her. "How many girls have died who've been on that list?"

"Counting Olivia and Chloe? A total of eleven."

"Eleven?" I flinch in shock.

"That's not that many," she says.

"By whose math? It sounds like a buttload to me. How can this not be in the news? Eleven women with this list in common are dead and—"

"Eleven over thirty years, Kenzie? Before yesterday, it was only one every three years."

I practically sputter in response. "Which still qualifies as the handiwork of a serial killer."

There's a spark of something like hope in the nurse's eyes; it fades as she shakes her head. "There's no serial killer, Kenzie. No one forced Chloe to eat something that killed her."

In my mind's eye, I see the pickup truck. "You don't know that."

"They found Olivia's leg trapped between two rocks."

"That's what they say. What if someone put her there?"

"A scuba diver? Underwater and waiting for her? They have the full police report and evidence. None of the boys were in the water, no one else was even wet. She jumped—"

"Or was pushed."

She shakes her head. "No. It's on camera. One of the boys taped the whole thing on his phone. I've talked to the police and they have the proof that she jumped of her own accord and went so deep her foot got trapped between two rocks. Just very bad luck."

I puff out a breath, frustrated. "You know murder can be made to look like an accident."

"No one put Sylvia Rushing's scarf between elevator doors in a hotel in Cincinnati, strangling her when the doors closed. No one knocked Susan Cordaine off a ladder while she was stringing Christmas lights on her front lawn, breaking her neck."

I can't do anything but stare at her. My brother died from a broken neck.

"Trust me, Kenzie. A killer would be more . . . appealing. A killer could be stopped. A killer would be a great improvement over worrying about a tree falling on you and killing you on the street like—"

"Roberta Livingston." I remember that accident, of course. Mom obsessed about it for days. It happened about a year ago not far from here, and she was a Vienna High graduate. A huge branch of a willow tree just cracked off and killed her right on the street with multiple witnesses. That wasn't murder, and that wasn't suicide.

So, that was . . . a curse? "How did the others die? When?"

She shakes her head like she doesn't want to tell me or, possibly, refuses to tell me. "Is there a list somewhere?" I demand. "With every name? I want to talk to the others. I want to look at these eleven 'accidents.' For God's sake, hasn't someone told the police? A reporter? Something to stop this?"

She stands and puts her hands on my shoulders as if that will stop the rising alarm in my voice. "If you say a word, you're bound to be next. That's part of the curse."

Or a way to keep us all quiet. "No." I shake out of her grip. "I don't believe that. I can't."

"We know how to stop it, Kenzie. My year never lost anyone, not once. And none of us have ever talked outside the group. If I learn anything to help you, I'll contact you."

Oh, for crying out loud. "How? By voodoo? Through the clouds? In time for me to escape a falling tree?"

Her fingertips tighten and pull me a little closer. "I know you're scared, Kenzie. But just remember not to trust a soul. Don't even think about telling someone outside the list."

I let her ease me into a comforting hug because, hell, I need one right now.

173

CHAPTER XIX

After leaving the nurse's office, I cruise by my locker and find Josh leaning against it, nodding and murmuring "'Sup?" to passersby but holding my gaze as I approach.

"Hey, Fifth."

I want to smack him for calling me that, but he reaches out his hand to me and I take it, letting him pull me in closer. "Where have you been?"

"Nurse's office."

He frowns. "Why'd you go there?"

I search his face for a second, considering telling him more. Everything, in fact. But Nurse Fedder's words are still fresh. "Grief counseling."

"Are you okay?"

"No." The admission is out before I can stop myself. "I'm not okay. How can anyone be okay?"

He lifts my hand to his heart. "You can be okay because you're with me."

I appreciate the sentiment, corny and cocky as it may be, but it doesn't comfort me. It makes me want to laugh. "You sure don't lack for ego, do you?"

"Because I'm sexy and I know it?" he sings, giving his shoulders a playful shimmy.

I'm still smiling at him, maybe—just maybe—starting to feel that sensation I've been waiting for. He's funny, he's cute, and, holy hell, he likes me. And, added bonus, he hasn't been escorted out of school by the police today. Why am I fighting it so much? Why am I thinking about the wrong boy?

"Seriously, babe," he says, fleetingly making me prefer Fifth in the nickname department. "I didn't realize you were such good friends with Chloe."

"I wasn't." To be honest, I didn't even like her. But that doesn't make this any easier. "It's still sad."

"School's a wreck," he agrees. "Nobody's doing anything. Me and Ty are cutting out. Did you get my text?"

I nod.

"Well? Wanna come?"

The idea of cutting class is so foreign to me I almost laugh again. "I don't . . ." Wait a second. Why not? Who's going to know, today? I've always wanted to just walk out of school and not care, to go have fun and laugh and hang out with kids who don't worry about declensions or trig identities or passing the AP exams. And God knows I could use a change of scenery.

"Okay. Where to?"

"Let's just drive." He gestures toward my locker. "Ditch your books and we'll go. Ty's in the parking lot already."

A few minutes later, I'm sitting in Josh's Audi, inhaling the smell of leather and listening to really annoying rap music.

Tyler Griffith, another football player, is slouched in the back, earbuds in, his attention firmly on his phone.

Josh keeps one hand on the gearshift, tapping the other on the steering wheel as we pull out of the parking lot, the image of a young man in control, cool and calm. That helps me—a lot. With each passing minute, I consider the possibility of sharing the whole curse business with him.

Ty isn't paying attention, but will Josh think I'm a nutcase and tell everyone, and the other girls will want to kill me? What if there's something to the secrecy? What if telling someone about the curse brings it to fruition?

Stop it, Kenzie. You're too smart for that crap.

"So what's everyone saying about this?" I ask, hoping to get information instead of giving it.

"Other than that the Sterling dick was arrested?"

Ire shoots through me at the assumption. "He wasn't arrested, was he? I heard they just took him in for questioning."

"Whatever. If anyone is capable of murder, it's that kid."

"Murder? Who said anything about murder?"

"Like, everybody. And Sterling's a complete bag of douchery, if you ask me."

No, he's a kid with dyslexia whose mother is in a mental institution, and he carries a bunch of guilt in his back pocket because of an accident that paralyzed a girl. And he disappeared on me half an hour before another girl was found dead.

"Being a douche bag doesn't make him a murderer."

"Haven't you heard he tried to kill some chick in his old town?"

"I don't think he tried to kill her, but—"

176

He turns hard onto the main drag, his jaw set a little. "Kenzie, you know he was at the quarry, right?" He says it like the statement is proof positive that Levi pushed Olivia off the cliff.

"Did you know the whole incident is on tape?"

He shoots me a look. "Doesn't mean Sterling didn't give her a nudge off camera."

I don't know why I have to defend Levi, but I do. With everything in me. "Last time I checked, this was America, where you're innocent until proven guilty."

"Bullshit. If someone killed those chicks, he's the one, and you better hope like hell they lock him up."

I turn and look out the window, watching a strip mall roll by. "What if no one killed them?" I say.

"Then we have one hell of a weird coincidence at Vienna High this weekend."

I can't argue with that. "What if . . . I mean, I heard people saying there's a curse." I slide him a look to get his reaction. It's a slow, sly smile.

"Cool." The word comes from the back, startling me because I'd kind of forgotten about Ty.

"Cool?" I ask, turning to look at him. "What is cool about that?"

"I totally dig all that paranormal shit." Ty doesn't take his earbuds out, so I have to assume he's heard the entire conversation. "A curse? Man, that's just cool."

Speaking of douche bags. I manage not to roll my eyes as I look away. "I personally don't think it's anything but creepy. And bogus."

Josh takes his hand off the gearshift and transfers it to my

177

leg, his palm warm even through my jeans. "You don't know," he says. "Maybe the list *is* cursed. Like there's a price you have to pay for being so hot."

I have to work to keep the disgust out of my voice. "That might be the stupidest thing I have ever heard. And not even funny, because I'm *on* that list."

"Thanks to me."

"I know you voted for me," I say, not sure if Josh is really expecting me to thank him or not. I look to the window, my eye on an interstate sign as he slides into the right lane. "I can't believe I got any votes at all, let alone one from you and enough to make the list."

"More than enough," Tyler says.

I turn around to stare at him. "How do you know?"

He looks up from his phone, but not at me. He catches Josh's eye in the rearview and they exchange a silent message, Josh's expression clearly a warning.

"Did you count votes?" I ask Tyler.

I see Josh give the tiniest shake of his head and some fire shoots through me. "Did you?" I ask Josh. A guilty look passes between the two of them, followed by silence.

"Josh," I say. "Do you guys know who tallied the votes?"

"It's a secret, Kenzie. We can't say."

More secrets? "Or what?"

Another exchanged look, and this time Tyler kind of laughs nervously. And neither of them says a word, which just tightens my stomach with all kinds of aggravation.

"I think, given that two girls from the list have died, you owe me an answer, Josh."

He doesn't respond, easing onto the ramp to I-70. "Where

are we going?" I ask. I didn't plan to get this far out of Cedar Hills, let alone leave the town of Vienna.

"I'm thirsty," Josh replies. "Let's get some brewski." He juts his chin at a highway sign that says it's nineteen miles to Wheeling, West Virginia. "Gotta love the rednecks in Dubya-V-A," he says. "Never look twice at a fake ID."

"Do you really know how the votes are tallied?" I ask again. "Do you know if it's . . . legit?"

"Fifth, you do not give yourself enough credit. Of course it's legit. You are top ten, and you"—he squeezes my leg—"are in for the ride of your life."

Sliding around a van to get in the left lane, he slams on the accelerator, taking my breath away. "Hey!"

"Relax." He gives the steering wheel a pound and turns up the music. "This machine was made for speed. Why take forty minutes to get our beverages when I can get us there in twenty?"

"Please, slow down." I pull at my seat belt, a low-grade panic rising with the speed of the car.

He responds by flooring it, revving the expensive engine, and whipping around a slower car.

"Look, I don't care about the voting," I lie, aware that every vein in my body is pulsing. "And I don't want to drink, so—"

"We do," Tyler says, proving again that he's hearing everything we say, despite the earbuds.

"Then get something at your house. Your grandfather's hardly strict about you drinking at home."

"Just chill, Kenzie. This is what we do."

But it isn't what *I* do. What made me think this was a good idea? I don't cut class with two football players I hardly know and get booze from across the state line.

I inhale slowly, forcing myself to do exactly as he says: *chill*. But questions plague me. I go to the one that bothers me the most.

"How many boys count the votes?"

Josh laughs softly. "Damn, woman, you're relentless." He adds a devilish smile that has probably gotten him through most sticky situations in his life that involved a female on the opposing side. "After we get our refreshments, I'll tell you."

Ty leans forward. "But then he'll have to kill you."

At my gasp and look of horror, Josh cracks up. "He's teasing, Fifth." But he can't wipe the smile from his face as he taps a button on the steering wheel to make the music so loud no one can think or talk. The whole car vibrates with bass, or maybe that's my insides. My stomach is doing cartwheels, my heart is jackhammering, and my head is screaming *Get the hell out of here.*

But we just keep going faster.

"Josh." He ignores me, drumming the steering wheel to the beat, so I grab his arm. "I really want to go back to school."

Throwing me a look, he changes lanes—far left now—without even glancing in the rearview mirror, accelerating enough for me to feel glued to my seat. Blood pulses even louder in my ears and I turn to Tyler for help, but he's oblivious. I can see enough that the needle is well clear of seventy. It feels like eighty. Ninety. Oh, *God.*

This wouldn't even technically be an accident. He's doing this *on purpose*. Chills explode all over me, at war with the heat of terror that's making me sweat.

"Josh . . ." My voice cracks. What the hell was I thinking getting in this car? I wasn't thinking—not at all. I should have thought about the possibility of an accident. Me, of all people. I just forgot.

I breathe slowly and look out the window at a rush of browns and red autumn oaks, surely the fastest I've ever witnessed scenery passing when not in an airplane.

Everything blurs with the first sting of tears, and I curl my toes hard to fight the fear bubbling up inside me.

Dystychiphobia. Maybe I have it as badly as my mother.

We're flying now, but the car's so smooth it's impossible to gauge our speed. I look anyway, leaning to the side to make it obvious I want to know how fast we're going.

"Just passed three digits, babe," Josh says with a broad grin, weaving around much, *much* slower cars.

"Hell yeah!" Tyler hollers, slamming his hand on the back of Josh's seat. "Stomp that thing, dude!"

I manage a ragged breath. "Please, please, slow down."

He just laughs. "You can trust this car."

But can I trust the driver? Panic wends through me, wrapping my chest in bands of pain, a wholly different kind of suffocation from what I feel with my mother.

"Dubya-V-A!" Tyler calls out over the loud music. "We have crossed into beerland, my good man."

"Screw beer," Josh says. "My girl drinks the good stuff, right, Kenz?"

I can barely talk. My knuckles are white on the seat and I'm staring straight ahead.

"Hey, come on." He taps my arm, making me gasp.

"Watch what you're doing," I warn.

"It's cool." But he doesn't slow down. "This is fun, Kenzie."

Fun. *Fun?* I feel something snap in my head when I turn to

181

him. "How is this fun? Two girls have died in the last forty-eight hours from accidents—two girls I'm on a list with—and you're driving a hundred?"

"And ten!" He leans over. "Kiss me."

"Watch the road!"

He glances at it for a split second, then back at me. "Kiss me!" he hollers over the deafening music.

Anything to make him look back at the road. I lean over and give him a peck, and instantly his hand curls around my head, pulling me harder into his mouth. Our teeth crack and I can barely hold in my scream as I feel the car accelerate and veer to the left, then the right, the wheel being controlled by a man paying absolutely no attention to the road.

"Give 'er tongue!" Tyler hoots, clapping his hands.

Nausea and horror collide in my chest, but Josh has a death grip on my head, smashing our mouths together. We're careening all over the highway and all I hear is one long, endless wail of a truck's horn as Josh jerks away. We both whip around to face front, inches—no, a centimeter—from sideswiping an eighteen-wheeler in the next lane.

Josh flings the wheel, jerking the whole car to the left, inches from an SUV. I let out the scream I've been holding in, automatically covering my face and eyes and bracing for certain death.

"Son of a bitch!" he cries, then rights the car and gives the truck driver the finger.

Tyler whoops and slaps the back of Josh's seat. "Hell yeah, man! That's what I'm talkin' about!"

My pulse is hammering so hard I can barely hear over the rush of blood in my head. "What are you doing?" I shriek at him. "Trying to kill us?"

Josh throws his head back and howls. "I'm invincible, baby!"

I glare at him, stunned by his stupidity and the thought that I ever imagined this idiot was attractive. "No one is invincible," I say softly.

He doesn't hear me. He and Tyler are reliving the thrill of their brush with death. But he's slowed down to a relatively reasonable eighty miles an hour while I will this joyride to be over.

My heart finally starts to settle as he glides onto an exit ramp, still going way too fast, but I do believe a car this well made can handle the turn. Holding on to that hope for dear life, I brace into the curve. In less than a minute, we're pulling into a gas station with a convenience store called Kipler's that looks like it was built around the turn of the century . . . the last century.

"Come with me," Josh says, turning off the ignition.

Out of the corner of my eye, I see a woman walking away from the side of the building, giving me an idea.

"I need to go to the bathroom," I say.

He guffaws again. "I scared the piss out of her, Ty."

Fueled by how much I hate that he thinks that's funny, I grab my door handle and try to get out, fumbling with the latch.

"It's locked," Josh says.

"Let me out," I reply through gritted teeth.

"You need to remember, Kenzie, I have the control."

My whole being clutches as I narrow my eyes at him. Anger won't work with this guy, nor will tears. I need to be creative. "I'm gonna puke all over your brand-new Audi in about five seconds."

He mumbles a curse, and the lock clicks open. I thrust my

whole body at the door, somehow having the smarts to grab my purse and tear off in the direction the woman came from, praying I don't need a key. A rusted, graffiti-covered metal door sails open when I yank the handle, the pitch-black inside only slightly less frightening than that heartless prick who drove me here.

Inside, I pat the wall frantically, looking for a light. I find one, but the bulb emits about as much light as a cell phone, leaving the room little more than shadows. I slide the lock and look around to see the floor is wet, the rust-stained sink has no hot-water handle, and the toilet might not have been flushed in the last few weeks.

I retch a little and twist the faucet to run cool water over my hands. What should I do? Get back in that car with them? Drive back another twenty miles on the hairy edge of certain death, with Josh sipping a beer?

I pull out my phone and stare at it, debating who I could call for help. Absolutely not my mother. My dad, who might be more understanding, is at work and couldn't leave. Molly? No, she's in class and won't answer. One of the girls on the list? At least they'd get why I'm scared to death.

While I'm staring at it, my phone lights up, startling me. I suck in a breath at the name of the incoming caller, more in disbelief than anything.

Levi Sterling.

Without hesitation, I answer, praying he's help and not just the devil's other hand.

CHAPTER XX

"Kenzie, I have to talk to you." His voice is soft, clear, and comforting. I press the phone harder to my ear, the putrid bathroom disappearing around me.

"What's the matter?"

"We just need to talk. I have to . . . *you* have to know the truth. Before you hear anything that says otherwise."

I'm stunned by how much the words—and the way he says them—affect me.

"What happened today?" I ask. "Did you . . ." *Get arrested?* I don't even want to put that into words. Plus, how could he be calling me? Surely I'm not his one phone call. Or am I? "Did you talk to the police?"

"Yeah, for a few minutes." I hear him let out a sigh and I feel relieved. "Kenzie, I barely knew Chloe. I have no idea why they'd question me."

I believe him. Deep in my gut, in a place I trust, I believe

185

him. Doesn't make it right or smart, but it's what I feel. "What did they want to know?"

"If I knew where she was that night, and where I was. I told them I was with you, at Starbucks, so they might want to talk to you next."

Oh, Lord. That will make my mother so happy. "You were with me . . . for a while."

"I went home after I left you."

Is he lying? Or can I trust him? "Did you see that truck?" I ask.

"What truck?"

"The one in the parking lot at Starbucks. Did you see it?" If he lies, then I know he's a liar. Because I am dead certain he saw that truck and left because of it. To meet the driver or . . .

"Yeah, I saw it." His voice is low and so honest.

"Why did you lie about it?"

"Because . . ."

I brace on the metal door, the vile closeness of the bathroom penetrating my whole being as I wait for him to complete the explanation. When he doesn't, I say, "I saw that truck at the house—"

"Stop, Kenzie. Don't say another word."

"Why?"

"Just . . . don't. Not on the phone. Not to anyone. Where are you?"

I cringe before answering, not even considering a lie. "Right outside of Wheeling at a place called Kipler's."

He snorts. "This whole mess drive you to drink?"

"How'd you know?"

"Everybody buys beer there."

"Look, Levi. I need help," I admit. "The kids I'm with are . . ." *Trying to kill me.* "Nuts."

"I'll come and get you."

His instant answer and desire to help washes me with an unspeakable happiness. But what about Josh . . . who is probably shotgunning a Budweiser right now.

A loud thud on the door makes me jump back. "Hey, Fifth, you okay?"

"Are you with Josh Collier?" Levi asks.

"Yes." I answer them both.

I hear one of them swear, but my heart is pounding so hard I'm not sure if it was Josh or Levi.

"Don't move," Levi says. "I'll be there in half an hour, tops." The phone beeps with the disconnection before I can even agree to that. He'll pick me up on a *motorcycle*?

"Kenzie, what the hell?" Josh bangs again. "You puking?"

I close my eyes. What's worse? A kid drinking beer and driving a hundred miles an hour in a sixty-thousand-dollar car or one who cares about me on a motorcycle?

Neither option is exactly thrilling right now, but I go with my gut.

"Josh, I'm getting a ride home," I say. "You can go."

He's silent for two, three, four heartbeats and I don't move, waiting for the argument.

"You sure?"

"I just need to be alone for a while," I tell him. "A friend is getting me, so you and Ty go party. I'll be fine."

He jiggles the handle. "Open up. Lemme see you."

I don't move. "Really, I don't want you to."

"Babe, I've seen a barfing chick before."

"I'm not barfing. I'm . . ." *Oh, damn it, just leave me.* "It's girl stuff."

"Oh." After a long silence, he says, "You need something from the store? I can get it."

The suggestion surprises me and suddenly makes me doubt my decision to wait for Levi. Maybe Josh was just showing off in the car. Maybe he was trying to impress me and feels bad about making me sick. Or maybe he is an accident waiting to happen.

I have to go with my instinct on this. "Really, Josh, I'm cool. You guys go."

A good fifteen seconds go by; then I hear him tap the door. "I don't like leaving you like this, Kenz. Come on out."

I reach for the door handle and slowly open the door. He's about a foot away, concern on his face, a beer can in his hand. He doesn't look scary or wild or like he'd cause an accident, and I'm torn with doubt about my decision.

"Listen, I'm sorry about the driving." He actually sounds like he means it.

I nod. "It's okay. I'm just going to get a soda and wait for my friend."

"Come on, I'll take you inside and buy it for you." He reaches out his hand, the gesture conciliatory and sweet. I take it.

"Thanks for understanding."

He smiles at me while we walk around the building to the front of the store. "Who says I understand? Women baffle me."

Inside, I grab a Coke from the cooler and he gives the clerk some money and turns to me. "You sure you want to wait for your friend?"

"I'm sure," I tell him, popping the can. "Go have fun."

He strokes my cheek, pushing back my hair. "You really do deserve to be on that list, Kenzie."

I can't pinpoint what I see in his blue eyes. Regret? Confusion? Maybe he just feels like crap for driving like a lunatic and scaring the hell out of me.

"Thanks," I mumble.

He leans down and brushes my mouth with his, a halfhearted kiss that leaves my lips cold. After a second, he leaves, heading out to the car with enough bounce in his step that I don't think he really regrets stranding me in a dump in West Virginia.

His tires squeal on the way out, tossing up some gravel, and I'm instantly convinced that I made the right decision. Just as I start to sip the Coke, the clerk slams his hand down and scowls.

"Hey, you know that guy? Is he coming back?"

"No, why?" Did he leave his phone or wallet? I walk closer to the cash register.

"This." He holds up a coin. "I'm not an idiot and this is America! I don't take foreign money. What the hell do I do with this?"

"Oh, I'm sorry." Embarrassed, I dig into my bag to get a quarter to give him.

He snorts and flips me the other coin, which bounces off the counter and lands on the floor. I bend over to pick it up, noticing instantly how shiny and yellow it is, almost like . . . No, even rich kids like Josh Collier don't carry real gold.

It's heavy and thick, unlike any coin I've ever seen. I tilt it to the sunlight to see what country it's from.

No country. Unless ancient Rome counts. I stare at the words on the coin.

NIHIL RELINQUERE ET NIHIL VESTIGI

The same phrase Levi had me translate for him.

To leave nothing behind and no trace.

But Josh just left something behind, and I have only one question: why?

Levi made it in under half an hour—I shudder to think how fast he drove his little red Kawasaki. Even though he brought me a helmet, I was hesitant to start the ride home, so now we are standing on the side of the convenience store next to the parked bike. The coin Josh left behind is warm from being passed back and forth between us as everything—absolutely everything, from the first accident to the gas leak to the last wild ride—pours out of me as fast as I can talk.

Screw curses; I need another brain on this.

As he listens, Levi studies the coin. The Latin words are wrapped around an ornate scroll that says *NR*, decorated with a laurel wreath like an ancient Olympic champion would have worn. He hasn't explained how these happen to be the same words he asked me to translate, but he will. He has to.

Little about my story really surprises him. Until I tell him about the curse. Then he's torn between being incredulous and fighting not to laugh out loud.

"They really think there's a curse? Like a voodoo curse?" He shakes his head, the laughter in his voice fading as he looks at my expression. "Do you?"

"No, but . . ." I sigh. "Every death is a freak accident."

"There's no such thing as an accident," he says ominously, flipping the coin in his fingers. "Damn, this thing is heavy."

"Real gold is," I say. "I can't believe Josh carries it around like pocket change. And then leaves it by accident."

He looks up, his eyes saying what his mouth just did: *There's no such thing as an accident.*

"You think he left it here on purpose?" I ask. The possibility had crossed my mind, but it made so little sense I'd disregarded it. Now I think maybe Josh had a reason to leave this coin.

Levi just shakes his head, and my frustration grows.

"Where have you seen those words and why did you ask me to translate them?" I'm tired of waiting for this explanation.

"He must have made it pretty far to have this."

Far . . . how? "What are you talking about?"

For a long moment, he doesn't answer. "Mack," he finally says. "What I'm about to tell you"—he takes my hand, pressing the coin between our palms—"you can't tell anyone. I mean it. I'm not kidding."

"This theme is repeating itself today."

"This time you have to follow the rule. It's a matter of life and death."

I give him a solemn nod. "I swear." And I mean it.

"There's a source . . . of money." He looks at the coin. "A place full of coins like this."

"Like buried treasure?" I fight the urge to laugh. "Only slightly more ridiculous than a voodoo curse."

"It's not ridiculous and it's not really buried, but it is treasure. One person every year gets it in the form of a fat, juicy, secret scholarship."

I gasp. "The one named after Josh's dad?"

He jerks back like I've burned him. "How do you know about that?"

"I don't think it's so secret," I tell him. "I met Josh's grandfather at his party the other night and he offered me a chance to apply. Only I'd have to finish some kind of obstacle course he has set up. Is that what you're talking about?"

"He told you that? I don't believe it."

"Why, is it some big secret?"

He raises his dark brows. "Have you ever heard this scholarship mentioned? Read about it in the papers? Know anyone who ever got it?"

He's right, I haven't. "But aren't some scholarships private like that? Especially when they're given by an individual?"

"Yeah, but this one—"

The screech of tires steals our attention, making us both spin to see a vehicle careening into the parking lot at about sixty miles an hour. For a second, I can't breathe. I stare at the pickup truck, stunned into speechlessness.

Levi's gaze follows mine. "Holy shit."

"No kidding." The driver's side is away from us, the windows tinted too black to see in, and I can't see the plate.

Levi instantly yanks me away, behind the cover of the building, and when the truck parks, he gets in front of me.

"Don't move. Don't talk."

Blood is rushing through my confused brain, pounding and vibrating in terror. I don't even know why I'm so afraid, or why we're hiding, but instinct says he's right.

"Who is that?" I demand.

"Truth is, I don't know."

We hear the slam of a truck door, the squeak of an ancient front entrance, and the bell announcing a new customer inside.

Is it the same truck I saw on Route 1 when I spun out? The

one that almost hit my bike? The one I saw in front of the house where Chloe was killed? Or another coincidence?

"Stay here," Levi says, taking a few steps to the side of the building to look around.

"Do you know who it is? Can you see him? Read the license plate?"

"No, no, and no. But we're not taking any chances." Turning to his bike, he grabs the other helmet. "We're outta here."

Without a moment's hesitation, I pull on the helmet and climb behind him on the bike, wrapping my arms around his waist. He walks the bike forward, closer to the road, before starting the engine and attracting any attention. Then we take off, going the other way so we don't pass the front of the store, but that means I can't check the plate on the back of the truck.

As he turns onto the road, I cling harder, my breath stolen by the thrill and speed.

"If that is the same guy, what is he doing here?" I call into the wind and Levi's ear.

He shakes his head, revving the engine and then turning in to a gas station less than a quarter-mile away. Pulling the bike behind the pumps, we're blocked but can still see the truck parked in Kipler's lot. It's too far away for us to make out a face, but we're hiding and looking anyway.

"This has to do with me," I say, my thoughts focused on that one undeniable truth.

"You don't know that. You don't know it's the same F-150."

Is that what that truck is? I squint harder. "If it is the same truck and the same guy I've been running into, then this is no coincidence." Good Lord, he's following me?

Levi puts his hand on my knee, giving it a squeeze and

leaning back so that our helmets touch. "You don't know that it's the same guy."

But deep inside, I do. "You should have gone into Kipler's and gotten a picture of him so we could see if we know him."

He shakes his head.

"I want to know who he is and what he's doing here."

"I can't let him see me," he says.

"Why not? Would he recognize you?"

After a long silence, he nods his chin toward the store. "He's leaving."

I look, but all I can see is a guy in a hoodie walking briskly to the pickup truck, his face down, looking at a phone, no package in his hands.

All of a sudden the man looks up. His head jerks around and he stares right at us—or right at the pumps hiding us. I gasp as he looks back at his phone, then the gas station.

"What the hell?" Levi whispers.

In a flash, the guy jumps into his truck.

"Hang on," Levi says.

"Did he see us? How is that possible? Wha—" I swallow the word as the engine revs and we go flying out of the gas station. I stifle a scream by pressing my face into Levi's back, inhaling leather and gas.

My whole body tilts left, then right, the acceleration zipping through me like I'm on a roller coaster. Oh, how I wish I were.

I manage to lift my head, still not breathing, squeezing Levi with all my strength, and I can't look anywhere but down. I see the asphalt. . . . It's so damn close. Inches. We are inches from being slathered all over that.

I close my eyes and fight the urge to scream as we fly up the ramp to the highway, weaving in and out of traffic at a frightening speed, my whole body vibrating with the engine between my legs.

I can taste the terror, metallic and hot in my mouth. Why is this happening?

The truck. The truck and the driver *who knows where I am* when I'm somewhere even I never knew I'd be today. Somewhere miles and miles from Vienna.

Fear rolls through me as I angle my head to look over Levi's shoulder into one of the rear-facing mirrors. Way in the distance, I see a black pickup truck hauling ass right at us.

Levi sees him, too, and whips around a semi, dirt from the giant tires spitting in our faces, the sound of the monstrous engine even louder than the one I'm sitting on.

Another wild bank to the other side and we're in front of the semi, and the rearview mirror is filled with a metal grille and the word *Peterbilt* in green.

I stare at the logo, watching it get smaller as we pick up speed and fly down I-70. I don't want to think about how fast we're going. I don't want to think about that truck. I sure as hell don't want to think about how easily this could all be . . . another accident.

"Levi." I croak his name and it gets thrown away in the wind. I have no control, so I hold on and hope and pray and finally let my body roll into each turn.

He's tense, leaning forward, concentrating on keeping us alive and surprising me by flying down an off-ramp, turning right at the bottom, and zooming past a Stuckey's and a Dairy Queen before winding up a steep hill.

With all the courage I have, I turn and look over my shoulder just in time to see the black truck fly across the overpass, skipping our exit and continuing on the highway.

"You lost him," I call out.

He nods but keeps going, maybe a tad slower, but I'm too numb at this point to be able to tell. He zips left, farther up the hill along a fire path, then down a road so gutted it's mostly dirt, and finally pulls over at the edge of a wooded area.

When he turns the bike off, it does nothing to stop the full-body quivering that has control over me. I try to speak but I can't, still clinging to his arm as he climbs off and roughly removes his helmet, dark eyes blazing.

"Give it to me," he insists.

"Give wha—"

"The coin! Give me the damn coin!"

With trembling hands, I reach into my jacket pocket and close my finger around the coin I've forgotten all about. "Why?" I manage to ask as I pull it out.

He doesn't answer, but grabs it from my hands and stares at the thing like it's the devil himself. With two hands he picks at the edges, his expression darkening with frustration as he bites it and swears under his breath.

"What are you doing?"

"Don't you see, Mackenzie? He's tracking us with this thing!"

"Then throw it away. Toss it off a cliff. Drive over it and ruin it."

"No." He gives it one more good squeeze, then looks at me. "If we do that, we lose him and we don't know anything more than we know right now."

He's absolutely right. A wave of gratitude rolls over me, the first thing I've felt that isn't fear in what seems like hours, but I can't tell him. He's doing a three-sixty, scanning the area. "We have to do this right. We have to see if he comes back for it and where he takes it."

"How?"

He peers out toward the highway. "We have to be fast. The minute he realizes where we are, he's coming back."

At the thought, I steady myself on the bike. "What's your plan?"

"I have no idea. I'm making it up as I go along." He gives a half smile. "But I'm sure it'll be good."

CHAPTER XXI

The plan, it so happens, is brilliant. We ride back to the I-70 off-ramp, where Levi hides the coin in some brush as if it fell out of a pocket. Then we head to the parking lot behind Stuckey's to get a direct view of the ramp. The sweet, rich aroma of coffee wafts from the restaurant as we wait on the bike, still wearing our helmets.

Worry curls through me, drawing me closer to Levi, my arms secure around his waist, my chin on his shoulder. It feels good, like I was meant to be here. But the moment of security doesn't stop the many, many questions that plague me.

"You better start explaining," I say simply. "Starting with why that coin bears the same words you asked me to translate the other night."

He adjusts his feet and the seat under him so he can divide his attention between the ramp and me. "That ropes course in the woods?" he says. "It's not like anything you've ever seen."

I'm not sure what that could possibly have to do with the coin or the Latin phrase, but I trust he's going to tell me. "Have you done the course?" I ask.

"Some of it. I was invited, but I didn't get to the next level."

I frown, somehow not seeing this boy as one who'd merit an invitation from Rex Collier. "Who invited you? When?"

"I have no idea. A few weeks ago, I got this anonymous invitation to do the ropes course. At first I thought it was some stupid Vienna High jock thing and I ignored it. Then the invitations got more . . . inviting." He rubs his two fingers together in the universal gesture for cash. "Kind of hard to ignore an envelope when it lands on your doorstep with a picture of Ben Franklin in it."

"Someone just gave you a hundred dollars to do the ropes course? Did you?"

He snorts. "Hell yeah. This thing needs gas, you know, and Mickey D's doesn't hire kids with probation officers."

"What happened?"

A blue car takes the ramp, diverting our attention for a second as it travels on.

"Nothing happened," he says when the car is gone. "In fact, it was like any high school party that Josh throws. Tons of idiots getting loaded and climbing trees and zip-lining like they're George of the Jungle."

"Like Josh and his football friends?"

He shakes his head. "No, kids I didn't recognize. No one talked to me and not everyone was taking it seriously, but some did. Some followed the course. Which is marked . . ." He slides me a meaningful look. "With instructions in another language."

"Latin, by any chance?"

"By every chance."

"Is that why you asked me for the translation?"

"One of the reasons, yeah. I wanted to know what that meant . . . *nihil* whatever."

"'Leave nothing behind and no trace.'" I nod toward the bushes. "Besides being on that coin, where did you see it?"

"The phrase is stamped or burned or even painted in a couple of places along the course," he says. "But everything's in weird, ancient languages, including the instructions on each platform for getting from obstacle to obstacle."

"That adds to the difficulty quotient."

"Especially for a guy who struggles with English, let alone Latin," he agrees. "I quit after a while because it got to be a stupid risk. No one gets very far."

"What happens if someone does?" I ask, imagining just how athletic and intelligent you'd have to be to attack that challenge.

"I imagine they get the scholarship, but I've never heard of anyone getting it. Maybe they just get one of those gold coins."

With tracking devices in them. "But someone might have finished the course?"

He shrugs. "I guess. I haven't been around Vienna long enough to hear about anyone getting the scholarship. Have you?"

"I told you I'd never heard of it. So what did you do when you quit the course, just walk away?" I ask. "Did you ever hear from whoever invited you again?"

"Once," he says after a beat. "Somebody put a note in my locker to go to the senior lot and find . . ." He adds a meaningful look. "A black F-150 pickup, presumably the one we're waiting for. Anyway, when I got to the parking lot, I saw that truck—or one that looks exactly like it—windows down, no one in sight. On the dash was an envelope with my name on it."

"And another Benjamin Franklin?"

This time he gives me a sardonic smile. "Ten of 'em."

"A thousand dollars?" I choke on the words. "To do the ropes course again?"

He shakes his head, his eyes as dark as a night sky, filled with regret and something a little scarier. "To go to the Keystone Quarry. The same night Olivia Thayne was killed."

Holy, holy hell. "And you went."

"Not until I got a text from you."

"That I didn't send." Then who did? "Any other times?"

"Yeah. One more that I ignored."

"To go where?"

"A house." He grimaces. "The house where Chloe Batista died."

I inhale so sharply I almost cough. "The night she was killed?"

He nods. "But I ignored it and the money because I didn't want to miss a chance to see you."

"But someone invited you to go to both places where the girls were killed?"

"Died," he corrects, but I just look away. Did they die in horrible accidents or were they helped along?

"And you saw the truck in the lot when we were having coffee," I say.

He nods again. "I got a little freaked out by that, thinking I was being followed. So I left, hoping that if he was on my tail, he'd follow me and leave you out of anything."

"Did he?"

He shakes his head. "Never saw the truck again. But you did."

At the house where Chloe was killed. "And I got the plates. Which we have to give to the police."

A dark truck comes down the ramp, and we're both silent, but I feel his whole body relax. "That's a Tundra. Different truck." He turns back to me. "We're not giving anything to the police, Kenzie."

"*What?* Two girls are dead."

"Exactly."

I don't follow, and then I do. "Do you think they'll accuse you?"

"I think that if they stop thinking these deaths are accidents, then I'm their number one suspect."

"But you're innocent!" I insist. "And girls on this list are dying. And everything we know is—"

"A bunch of coincidence and conjecture to the police," he says, staring at the ramp as if he can will our truck to come back. "Kids like me make perfect fall guys, Kenzie. And I think that's why I've been paid to be in the wrong place at the— There he is."

The truck pulls off at the bottom of the ramp, the driver's side away from us. For a few minutes it just sits there. Then the same guy we saw parked at Kipler's gets out, his jacket hood still up over his head. We're even farther away than we were before, and it's impossible to see any details of his appearance. He goes directly to the bushes and bends over where we left the coin.

"I was right," Levi murmurs. "It's a tracking device."

After a minute, the driver gets back in the truck, turns around in the Dairy Queen parking lot, and gets on the ramp in the direction he came from.

"Let's go," Levi whispers, starting the engine. "This time we're following him."

I'm not quite as terrified on the ride home toward Vienna, since Levi doesn't seem to want to break the speed limit or kill us. Relaxing into his back with my arms comfortably wrapped around him and my thighs pressed against his, I actually breathe steadily and lean into the turns.

A few of them are fun. Or maybe that's just being this close to Levi Sterling. All around me, the golds and russets of the trees and the brisk autumn scents are intensified, each sensation at war with the confusing questions in my head. Questions focused on Josh Collier.

Why did he have that coin? Did he leave it on purpose? Did he take me out to the middle of nowhere for a reason? Is he involved with the guy in the truck? Is the guy some kind of recruiter for his grandfather's ropes course challenge?

With those questions on my mind, I'm not completely stunned when I see where the black F-150 is leading us . . . to the easternmost edge of Nacht Woods. Levi widens the distance between us and the truck, and we finally lose track of it when it turns into what looks like a slight clearing in the woods, not exactly a legit road.

He weaves the bike around and we follow the perimeter of the forest, most of it rimmed with a stony creek, evergreens, and brush so dense it would be impossible to penetrate. But periodically, there are fire roads and breaks in the trees, and it looks like if you go deep enough, there might be a way through the woods.

After a few minutes, we come to a road that eventually leads to the Collier house.

"I don't want to see Josh," I say to Levi.

He nods and we head back east where the truck has gone. Finally, he stops the bike and braces us with his feet. "This is more or less the beginning of the ropes course," he says.

"Can I see it?"

He angles his head to get a look at me. "You want to go in there?"

"I want to read some of the Latin instructions. And to find out how hard it would be to do the course."

He considers this for a minute, and then agrees. "Let me stash the bike and I'll show you the first challenge. It's not far."

After we hide the bike, Levi pops the seat up and pulls out a navy bandana that he ties to a tree. "You can get pretty lost in here."

He takes my hand and we work our way through some thick trees before the forest clears. In October, there are just enough leaves on the tall oaks and sycamores that the gray skies are almost completely blocked. The ground is soft, mostly dried leaves that crunch underfoot, the scent of pine and earth almost overwhelming.

"The start of the course is down this way," Levi says, his whisper barely audible over the creek water rushing near us.

I look around and imagine the utter blackness of this place at night. "No lights, I take it."

He laughs softly. "That's another caveat of the course. It has to be done between midnight and three."

Whoa, that Rex is a sadist. "Hasn't the guy ever heard of an essay? There's got to be an easier way to get a scholarship."

A few feet away something scurries through the brush, making me hesitate and pull closer to Levi. He's strong, warm, and knows where he's going, which is small comfort.

"Okay, look up there," he says, pointing to a space about twenty-five feet wide between tall white birch trees. "That's the line."

I squint and look up to the treetops, some a good forty feet high. "Line of what?"

"A zip line. See? Between those two trees."

A wire so thin it could be considered a thread links the trees, and I peer closer to see very small platforms built on thick telephone poles that blend into the trees. "You mean you ride that?"

"Yep."

"In a safety harness?"

He laughs again as though charmed by my naïvety. "You clip a rope and hang on."

Holy cow. "How do you get up there?"

"Climb. And follow the instructions. Here." He takes me around the tree and lifts the gray bark like he's peeling back skin. The words are burned into the trunk.

AUT VIAM INVENIAM AUT FACIAM

"Literally, that translates to 'I'll find a way or make one,'" I tell him, "but it's sort of the motto for the person who doesn't quit. How did you translate this when you did the course?"

"I didn't, but I could tell that the way was up." He points upward and my neck practically cracks as I follow a series of two-by-fours, each about six inches long, nailed into the tree.

About halfway up, the thickest branch reaches over to the telephone pole, where there are more "steps" up to a platform. That piece of wood is about two feet wide, with no railing, no safety line, no chance a human in her right mind would climb that.

At least, not this human.

"This is how it starts," he explains. "You climb up to the top, grab a rope, and connect it to the line and zip to the next platform. You need upper-body strength and a pair of titanium balls."

Neither of which I have.

"And," he continues, "when you get up there, you don't know which line to take, since there are two or three or even more. One takes you farther into the course, the other two dead-end on the ground and you have to start over. Or quit."

Which is what I would probably do. "How far did you get?"

"I made it through about three platforms, then—" He freezes, frowning. "Did you hear that?"

"What?"

"Shh." He touches my lips with his fingers, peering around with narrow-eyed intensity. An engine in the distance. We're fairly far from the road, but it sounds like . . .

The truck? "Let's hide," he says.

Using one hand, he pushes branches aside to get us through a thicket, the sound of our ragged breaths and footsteps on soft ground filling my ears.

We round a hill, avoiding any chance of high ground, and are passing more broken, bare trees when Levi stops so suddenly I crash into him. Without a word, he holds me still and we both listen. The engine is definitely in the distance now and headed the other way—but we're deeper in the woods and lost.

"We need to get cover," he whispers. "Long enough to use a GPS to get out of here."

I spot a steep drop off a small cliff and we work our way there and peer over the edge. It's about a twelve-foot drop down an embankment, but it's protected and hidden at the bottom.

"Let me help you." He crouches and I follow, turning and slowly letting my whole body drop over the cliff. Holding on to him, I dangle, but it's only about five feet to the ground when I let go.

A second later, he scrambles down and drops the same way.

The sound of the engine might have disappeared, but I still feel vulnerable knowing we're not alone in the woods, so I nestle deeper into the brush to hide.

Levi pulls out his phone and starts stabbing a GPS program and I lean back into the mound of earth, a chill snaking over me like fear.

No, that's an actual chill. Like a draft. Curious, I turn around and push through thick branches of a bush until I realize we're right in front of what looks like a small cave.

"Can you get satellite from in there?" I ask. "We'd be hidden."

"Let me try."

Branches scrape my face, but we muscle our way into the opening and right away, I feel safer.

As I get my bearings, the light of Levi's phone allows me to look around, revealing that we're definitely in a cave, which isn't unusual in Nacht Woods. But this one has unnaturally smooth walls and a sense of, I don't know, *hominess* to it.

My eyes catch something on the cave wall—a drawing? How cool would that be? "Levi, shine your phone over here."

He does, and we see letters that have been carved into the stone.

"It must be part of the ropes course," he says.

I don't answer, my brain already in translate mode as I read:

ARS EST CELARE ARTEM.

"Meaning . . . 'It is art to conceal art,'" I say. "What the heck does that mean? Are all the clues this arcane?"

"Who knows? I couldn't read them. Look." He tilts the light toward the bottom of the wall. "It's signed."

"Jarvis," we read together.

I blow out a breath, my head humming as I try to snap together puzzle pieces that just won't fit even though I know they somehow do. "Jarvis Collier," I whisper, and this time the chill is real. "Rex Collier told me he buried some stuff of his son's out in these woods."

"Nice, we're in a grave," Levi says dryly, his attention back on the phone.

"Not a grave, technically. Jarvis's body was never found, but Rex must have made a shrine or something."

"Either way, a grave."

I turn to Levi, an idea brewing. "I wonder if this is, like, the end of the ropes course. If you find your way here, you're finished—you've gotten to the final destination?"

He looks up from his phone. "Possibly." He peeks around a large boulder near the wall. "This is a passageway?" he says, throwing me a questioning look.

"My answer is yes."

He lifts an eyebrow. "Mack, I wouldn't take you for such an adventurer."

"Color me curious. I'll take any advantage if I have to do that course."

His look of pure skepticism is accompanied by a low snort. "You're not going to do that course."

"For a scholarship to Columbia? If I have the advantage of being able to translate the clues and know how it ends?" I give him a nudge. "C'mon, let's just see where it goes."

He takes my hand and we inch into a dark stone corridor, barely high enough for us to stand. His phone gives us just enough light to see.

There's a sense that we're going downhill, though the slope is so gradual it's hard to be sure. As we descend, it's impossible not to notice that the walls have a finished feel and the path under our feet is made of fitted stone. This is not nature's cave: someone deliberately created this passageway.

This is some "burial ground" for a few "things" that belonged to Jarvis. But then, rich people are eccentric.

The corridor turns again, sharply, and I catch the shadow of more words carved into the wall. "Shine the light," I say, lifting our joined hands to indicate the wall.

MULTI SUNT VOCATI, PAUCI VERO ELECTI.

"'Many are called, but few are chosen,'" I read.

"I know that quote," Levi says. "It's from the Bible. Matthew."

It's my turn to look skeptical. "Wouldn't take you for a Bible reader, Levi."

"My aunt is born again," he explains. "That quote's

209

embroidered into a pillow on our sofa." He shakes his head. "Why would someone carve that in a cave?"

"I don't know." We take a few tentative steps forward. "To recreate the catacombs of Rome? Maybe Jarvis was one of those classical freaks. There's a whole subculture that tries to reenact Roman times. Like Civil War battles, only this is Nero and the gladiators."

Before Levi answers, we abruptly reach a dead end. The whole thing stops with three stone walls. I'm kind of surprised by how disappointed I am. "Guess that's it."

"I don't think so." Levi kneels down to examine the bottom of one of the walls. "Look."

I crouch next to him as he shines the phone light on another carving along the very bottom, the words tiny:

EX UMBRA IN SOLEM

"What's it say?" he asks when I don't immediately translate.

"Well, literally, it means 'From shade to sunlight.' But most of these expressions are more idiomatic than literal. My guess is that it figuratively refers to bringing things out in the open or revealing a secret."

"I bet it opens, then," he says, pushing on the wall.

I can't help but laugh. "A secret door, like in the movies?"

He flattens his hands and shoves, the sound of stone scraping stone making him freeze and me take in a breath.

"*Just* like in the movies." His smile is smug as I scramble to my feet to peek through the door.

Neither of us says a word.

This is no cave or grave. This is nothing anyone would ever dream would be underground in a forest.

"What is this place?" he says, but I still can't answer as I take it all in.

The room is huge, the size of a basketball court, with a high ceiling and shadows in every corner cast by dim light from ornate wall sconces that are clearly running on electricity. The focal point is a large round table with elaborately carved high-back chairs that give the place a medieval-castle feel. The table is freakishly shiny—good God, is it made of gold?

But it's the walls that pull my attention. They are covered with tapestries and artwork and framed manuscripts and carved busts. Everything is museum quality—everything is *real*.

Roman swords, glass boxes of leather-bound manuscripts, weavings and paintings and something that looks like the wide leather belt of a gladiator.

My classics training kicks in when I see a carving I recognize from an art history video I had to study before Regionals. That's Mithras, an ancient Roman god. All I remember is that they worshiped him in underground temples, which eventually became part of the catacombs.

"Mack, look."

Levi's behind me, staring at the center of the table. I join him to read the raised letters.

NIHIL RELINQUERE ET NIHIL VESTIGI

CHAPTER XXII

*H*ours later, long after Levi and I made our way out—like, hauled ass at warp speed because the place was creepy as hell—I am still thinking about all I saw and experienced.

We said goodbye, and now I'm lying on my bed, staring at the ceiling after dinner with Mom, working it all out. Or not, as the case may be. I'm fixated on one terrifying thought I don't want to have: the guy in the truck, who was following me or Josh or that coin, has something to do with Olivia's and Chloe's accidents.

If they were accidents.

And if he has something to do with them, then that coin and that eerie place might, too. Maybe I should do that ropes course, if only to find out more about—

"Hey."

I jump a foot at the voice, rolling over and blinking at Molly in my bedroom doorway. "Holy crap, you scared me."

She doesn't move, searching my face. "I texted you, like, seventeen times."

Four, actually. And I just couldn't deal with being normal around Molly since being normal around Mom had taken it out of me tonight. I dig for a smile and wave her in. "Sorry. I was out all day—"

"With Josh."

I nod slowly, not sure how she knows that. "Yeah, for a while."

"And Tyler Griffith."

"He was there." I sit up and frown, not sure why Molly sounds so weird. "Are you okay?" I ask.

She stops a few feet from my bed. "Are you?"

Not really, but I'm not ready to admit that to her. "Fine. What's up with you?"

"What's up with *you*?" she fires back.

"Molly." My heart races as I take in the anger and uncertainty on her face. Could she know . . . anything? "Are you mad at me?"

She widens her eyes and gives me a "get real" look. Definitely mad.

"What did I do?"

"Kenzie, you skipped school with Josh Collier and Tyler Griffith, two of the hottest—and coolest—guys I may ever know. And *you didn't invite me*."

I almost laugh, but of course I don't. If only she knew just how dangerous and not fun that little adventure turned out to be. "It was no big deal," I lie. Because it was a big deal and I am not about to tell her that.

"No big deal?" Her voice rises. "I'll tell you what is a big deal. The deal we had. You get cool and popular and start hanging out with kids who are at the top of the food chain and you bring me along. Remember? Coattails? Train? Best friends?"

She finally flops onto the bed and lets out a sigh.

"Molly, I'm sorry, it really wasn't that much fun."

"Oh, right. Driving around—during school—in Josh's million-dollar Audi isn't fun."

"It wasn't," I assure her. "He drives like a freaking lunatic."

She doesn't seem appeased. "But Tyler Griffith? He's so hot. I could have double-dated."

"He's a jerk," I say. "I really had no idea he could be such a major douche-bag."

Deflated, she gets more comfortable on the bed. "Where'd you go?"

"Wheeling."

"West Virginia?" Her eyes pop. "Why?"

"They wanted booze."

"Did you drink?"

I shake my head, my mind whirring. How much should I tell her? The story is long and complicated and kind of unbelievable. The truck, the chase, the coin. *Levi.* The idea of sharing it seems overwhelming, and I don't want to.

"So what did you do?" she presses, getting closer. "Did you make out with Josh? Is he your boyfriend now?"

"No." I can't keep the hint of disgust from my voice.

"Don't you like him? He's so cute."

"Cute isn't everything, but he has his moments."

"I hear he's having some kids over to his house tonight." She gives me a hopeful look and then gestures toward her clothes, which I only now notice are pretty cute for a school night at home. "Can we go?"

I frown and shake my head. "I don't know anything about this. How do you?"

As soon as I ask the question, I regret it. Her eyes look hurt. "God, Kenzie, you're not the only one with Facebook friends. I got some spillover from your newfound popularity, remember?"

"I haven't been on Facebook since I got home."

"You think we can go?"

"To Josh's house?" That might be the last place on earth I want to go. "My mom would never let me." And for once, I'm grateful.

"Just tell her you're coming over to my house."

"I don't want to go," I say honestly. "I have a ton of home-work, and—"

My phone buzzes with a text. Instinct tells me it's Levi, who I've been texting on and off all evening. When I don't pick it up right away, she reaches for the phone. "Here—"

I grab it from her, not ready for a lecture about the dangers of Levi Sterling.

"Sorry!" She opens her hand and dramatically lets go. "It's not like I haven't read your texts before." She angles her head and adds a meaningful look. "Before the list."

"Stop it, Molly. Nothing's changed."

"Yeah, right."

"It hasn't."

"Then who just texted you?"

I flip the phone over and read the name. "It's . . ."

"Amanda Wilson," she says out loud, reading over my shoulder. "Is she your new BFF now?"

"Oh, for crying out loud, Molly." I touch the screen to read the text. "I barely know her."

Emergency meeting of the Sisters of the List TONIGHT.

"The Sisters of the List?" Molly almost gags on the phrase. "Who *says* that?"

Our favorite joke question sounds real, and pained. "I told you, it's just a . . . thing."

"Is that seriously what you call yourselves now?" she demands. "A sister with girls like Amanda Wilson and Kylie Leff?"

"Five minutes ago you wanted to go to a party with them," I shoot back, irritated and wishing I could just text Amanda without being drilled.

"Kenzie." Her voice lifts in a little whine. "Why are you doing this?"

"Why are *you* doing this?" I demand. The phone buzzes again with another text. I force myself to look at Molly and not the message. I can't remember the last time we had a fight. Sixth grade? Seventh? But why is she acting like a baby? "I'm not allowed to have other friends?"

"You promised you'd bring me along." She crosses her arms, a challenge in the eyes that rarely look at me in any way but with friendship. "You promised."

"I know, but I'm not going anywhere tonight." Another text comes in and I lose the battle, touching the screen to see this one is from Dena.

Want me to pick you up? I can be there in 10 min.

Of course, Molly reads it. "Dena Herbert?" she asks.

I nod, tapping Reply. "I'm not going anywhere tonight," I say again, more forcefully this time.

216

"Even if I go with you?"

I look up from the phone without having typed a text. "Molly, I don't want to go."

"You don't want to go with me," she says.

"That's not true. I don't want to go out tonight."

"Because I'm not a *Sister of the List*." She mocks the name, and with good reason. But her hurt and anger and jealousy aren't funny right now. I just look down at the phone as another text comes in, this one from Bree Walker.

Candace almost died tonight. We have to meet!
DO NOT TELL ANYONE OR YOU COULD BE NEXT.

Instinctively, I angle the phone away from Molly, staring at the words.

"I saw that," she says softly.

"You did?" *Candace almost died?* My throat closes with fear. I have to know what happened.

"I saw 'do not tell anyone' in caps." She pushes off the bed. "I suppose that includes your BFF."

"Molly, come on. This is . . ." Bigger, worse, and scarier than she could ever understand. "This is . . ." A matter of life and death.

"I know what this is," she says, backing away. "This is you blowing me off so you can hang with much cooler girls."

I shake off all the fear that's gripping me and give Molly my full attention. "This is not something you can understand easily."

She coughs and says, "Oh my God," rolling her eyes. "Of course, only the *Sisters of the List* can understand."

"I mean it, Molly. I'll explain it to you later, but now I . . ." *Can't tell anyone or I might be next.*

217

Not that I believe that for one minute, but I can't completely disregard the warning.

"Whatever, Kenzie. Do what you have to do. I'm going home."

"Molly, please, if I could take you, I would. I swear I would."

She turns on her way out, a world of pain in her expression. "Then why don't you?"

Because what if she got hurt? What if she was somehow in danger? What if I was responsible for that? An old familiar ache takes hold. "Because I can't," I say simply as the text buzzes again. I ignore it, looking hard at Molly, praying she somehow understands and forgives me.

"Better get your phone, sister," she says, turning back to the door.

"Molly, please."

But she doesn't hesitate, leaving without another word. I stay still for a moment, then pick up the phone to read the text from Dena.

Pick you up in 10?

I type one word in response: *Yes.*

Mom buys that I'm going outside to ride back to Molly's house with her so we can do homework together. First I pray Mom doesn't come outside to wait with me; then I pray that Molly doesn't come running back to make up after I'm gone. Because that would turn my mother into a screaming, police-contacting lunatic who doesn't know where I am.

But Molly was pretty mad and I doubt she's coming back

tonight, so I take the chance and hop into Dena's ancient Subaru that smells vaguely like gym clothes and Gatorade. She's dressed in sweats, and tells me she just left volleyball practice. But she still manages to look pretty.

"What happened to Candace?" I ask.

"She damn near drowned in her bathtub. Wait till you see her hair."

"Oh my God," I mutter, turning in the seat to face her. "What happened to her hair?"

"Her mom had to chop it off to save her life. She was in her mom's Jacuzzi taking a bath and her hair got sucked into the bubbly thing and it pulled her under. If her mother hadn't walked into the bathroom . . ." She closes her eyes and blows out a shaky breath. "We are all in such trouble, Kenzie. We have to do something. We have to stop this."

"Why don't we go to the cops?"

"Because they don't investigate *curses that cause unavoidable accidents.* And before you say anything, yes, I'm buying into it."

"Oh, Dena." I'm disappointed to lose my only ally on the "curses are ridiculous" side of the issue. "There's no such thing," I say, but even I can hear the doubt in my voice. Could there be a curse?

"Oh, yeah? Then tell me how come all this weird shit is happening to us? No one was in the bathroom holding Candace under. No one made my cat chew a wire that damn near electrocuted me. No one stuffed peanuts into Chloe's allergic mouth."

"You don't know that."

She fires a look at me. "Do you?"

"I don't . . . Maybe." I look out the window, half expecting

219

to see the truck. In the distance behind us, I see headlights, much too small and close together to be a truck's. "Where are we going, anyway?"

"Shannon's dead grandmother's trailer."

"That sounds lovely."

"Don't knock a good inheritance." She veers onto a highway that heads toward Pittsburgh. "Most grandmas leave you their knitting collections when they kick. Shannon got her very own trailer in the country that she can move into when she's eighteen. Until then, we go there to party sometimes."

"This is hardly a party," I say dryly.

We drive in silence and I try to memorize where we're going, a slow, low burn of worry building in me. Periodically, I look behind us and every once in a while I see headlights, but they are way in the distance.

We cross a bridge, cut through a rural area, and eventually turn off onto a narrow road that looks like it leads into utter darkness. "Where are we going?"

"Here." She pulls into a long dirt drive tucked between huge oak trees and the car jolts, kicking up gravel, until the lights finally shine on an ancient double-wide surrounded by nothing but dirt, grass, and a few abandoned appliances.

The three other cars parked there look completely out of place, yet familiar. I recognize Amanda's silver SUV and Candace's bright-green cube-shaped thing as we park and walk to the dimly lit mobile home.

The night is silent, and cool. Beyond the trailer are a wooded area and some fields. I rub my jacket-covered arms against the chill and follow Dena.

Inside, the girls are gathered in a rattily furnished living

220

area, a few on a plaid sofa, some on the floor. They are all staring at something on the coffee table, but a few look up to greet me.

"Maybe Kenzie can help," Kylie says. "Aren't you, like, some kind of freak with foreign languages?"

My chest tightens a little and I lean to the right to see around Amanda's head to what's on the table. "Just Latin," I say.

"This looks like Latin." Amanda scoops something up and holds out her hand, the shiny gold making me gasp.

"Where did you get that?" I exclaim. I grab for it, but Amanda yanks it away.

"You've seen this before?"

Today, as a matter of fact. "Please, Amanda. Let me look at it. It could have a tracking device and someone could be on his way here right this minute to kill us."

Seven sets of horrified eyes stare at me as Amanda slowly opens her hand and relinquishes the coin.

It's exactly like the one Josh left at Kipler's. "Where did you get this?"

"I found it in my bathroom," Candace says from the sofa. I look at her for the first time and barely recognize her with shorn hair. I can't help but recoil in surprise. Her thick, waist-length hair looks like someone hacked it off two inches from her head.

She gives me a hard stare, like she doesn't give a crap about her locks. She's alive.

"Holy shit!" Dena lunges at the coin. "I found one like that, too. Right on the floor where my cat chewed the cord."

"Do you have it?"

She shakes her head. "I thought it was my dad's because he

221

just got back from a business trip in Europe. It's probably still sitting in the junk drawer in our kitchen."

I look around. "Anyone else find something like this?"

"Maybe," Bree says, standing to get a better look. "I heard my parents talking about finding something gold after that power line fell into our house. I didn't pay any attention, but they were fighting over where it came from. My dad accused my mom of buying it at the flea market even though she said she wasn't going there anymore, but she swore she didn't. I just ignore them when they fight."

"Maybe it's the mark of a curse," Kylie says.

"Or a calling card," Candace suggests.

I give her a nod. "That makes sense, except for two things. One, the inscription means 'to leave nothing behind and no trace,' but that would mean someone left something behind. Two, worse than that . . ." I lift the coin to the dim light and try to imagine a chip or something inside. "It can track where you are."

"Holy hell," Shannon mutters, standing up. "I'm out of here."

"Wait a minute," Amanda says. "How do you know this?"

I search a few faces and debate what's safe and smart to tell them. All of their lives are at stake—and mine. I can no longer doubt that this coin—which showed up after these freak accidents—is somehow related to the deaths of two girls on the list and the near misses of several others.

"I know it because I was followed by someone when I had a coin like that today in my hand. I was—"

"Shit!" Dena jumps back from the window, eyes wide. "Someone's coming."

A collective shriek rises from the group.

"Let's hide!"

"Run!"

"Kill the son of a bitch." Candace stands, fearless, fixing Shannon with a hard look. "Surely your grandmother kept a gun in this redneck hellhole."

"Hey!" Shannon's eyes pop. "What are you—"

"Not now!" Dena gives her a good shove. "There's a freaking car out there."

We all freeze for a second as Shannon slams a fist to her mouth. "Oh my God, I don't want to die!"

"Then don't." I look around to find something to arm us, spying a faded, speckled mirror in a frame over the sofa. "Two of you, grab that mirror!"

Amanda and Kylie leap to action, kneeling on the sofa to work in tandem to take it down.

"Get behind the door so you can smash it on his head if he walks in. Turn the lights off!"

"What if he's a ghost?" Shannon asks.

I don't bother with a response to her shocking stupidity. "Are there knives here, Shannon? Anything in the kitchen?"

"I'll look," Dena says, darting into the galley kitchen and whipping open drawers and cabinets. "Coffee mugs," she hollers.

"Give one to each of us," I order. "We'll throw them at him. No knives?"

Dena's handing out mugs to Bree and Ashleigh, while Candace yanks open a cabinet and finds a cast-iron skillet just as someone kills the lights. "I'm good," she says.

The slam of a car door freezes us all.

"Shit," someone murmurs.

"Quiet!" I say in a hushed whisper. "Get into position to attack the minute the door opens."

They scramble and I give Amanda and Kylie a push into the right place, near the door. Taking Candace's hand, I pull her next to me.

"I'll kill him," she says under her breath.

"I have no doubt."

We hear footsteps, light and fast. Inside we are totally silent and still, and I'm surprised I can't hear eight thumping hearts. Someone breathes softly. Someone—Shannon, I think— whimpers a little. And we all jump when there's a hard, sharp bang on the door.

He's knocking?

No one moves, the air hot and thick and tense with our fear. Could he have a gun? A knife of his own? No way he's armed with skillets and cups.

Very slowly, the handle moves. Candace takes a single step forward, raising the pan. Amanda and Kylie move, too, lifting the heavy mirror.

"Wait till he's inside," I whisper softly. "We have one chance."

I brace myself as the latch clicks open, certain I'll see the hooded man who drove the truck. I train my eyes at the six-foot height where his head will be. The wood snaps as the door creaks open. I grip my mug, ready to fling and smash and—

"Kenzie?"

What? "Don't!" I scream as I see the mirror fall and Candace lunge. All I can do is leap forward without thinking, tackling Molly to the ground with a thud, covering her body with mine.

Chaos erupts and something hits my head as I roll us both out of the doorway, screaming, "Stop! Don't hurt her!"

I'm aware of lights going on and Molly fighting with everything she's got and another cup whizzing by my head.

"Stop, she's my friend!" I holler again. "She's okay! Don't kill her!"

After a few heartbeats, we're surrounded by girls yelling and questions flying, and finally I trust them enough to let Molly go.

"What are you doing here?" I demand, but I already know, remembering the close-together headlights behind Dena and me on our way here: Molly's VW.

She's barely able to make it to her knees, shaking as hard as I am, her gaze darting around the circle surrounding us. "What the hell's going on here?"

After a beat, Dena steps forward, lifting her mug like a toast. "Private party," she says coolly.

Molly's eyes widen and shift to me. "Kenzie?" There's nothing but disbelief in her voice. "Why did you attack me?"

"Molly, I—"

"Hazing ritual." Amanda reaches to help Molly up. "And, sorry, *chica,* but you're not in the group."

Molly's jaw drops. "What are you—"

Candace gets right in her face, lifting the skillet. "It's time for you to leave."

"You guys," I say, getting next to Molly. "We can trust her. She's my friend."

Every one of them looks at me like they could kill me, too.

"We don't trust anyone," Kylie says.

Molly shudders and looks at me. "Is this what that list has turned you into?"

My shoulders sink. I feel sad for her gross misconception, but know that if I tell her anything, these girls will not react well. They're scared, they're dangerous, and Molly's in the wrong place at the wrong time.

"You better leave, Molly," I say simply.

The hurt in her eyes is ten times worse than it was when she left my bedroom. "Why are you doing this?" she whispers.

"You don't understand," I say, knowing it sounds lame. And so damn mean.

"Yeah." She sniffs. "I do. That list changed you, and I . . . I . . ." She looks around from one to the other. "I don't like who you've become."

"Good." Candace gives her a little shove. "'Cause we don't like you. *Adiós, amiga.*"

Molly gives me one more pleading look, and in the space of two seconds that look turns to ice. "Bye, Kenzie." She pivots and heads back to her car. I feel a physical pull to follow her, to explain everything, to assure her that she is and always will be my best friend.

I take one step, but Candace grips my elbow. "Don't even think about it, Fifth."

I let Molly go.

CHAPTER XXIII

We left the trailer, ditched the coin about a mile away, and went to Amanda's house, where I told them the story of what had happened that day with Josh and Levi. I got a mixed reaction; not all the girls were ready to let go of the curse theory, and some of them rose to Josh's defense. They all wanted to blame Levi for everything bad that had happened in town.

The next day, Molly doesn't show to pick me up, so Mom has to drive me to school. The first place I go when I get there is the media center. I am certain that I once saw a whole section containing all the old Vienna High yearbooks. I have to find out more about Jarvis Collier and his weird collection of ancient Roman artifacts . . . which could include coins left as a killer's calling card.

There are very few kids in the media center this early, and Mrs. Huffnegger, the librarian, is reading her computer screen intently enough that she doesn't notice me. The reference area is abandoned, and I walk between the stacks to find the year-books.

They date back to 1943, when it was simply Vienna School, a brick building that housed twelve grades for the kids of the farmers who lived in rural western Pennsylvania, long before my town became a populated, popular suburb of Pittsburgh. But I'm not interested in history that ancient. I go straight to the middle and pull out yearbooks from the early eighties, guessing that's where I'll find Jarvis Collier.

I do, as a junior in 1984. Immediately I'm struck by how much he looks like Josh. I can't help scanning the black-and-white photos of this junior class, studying the girls with big, big hair, lots of winged bangs, and plenty of shoulder pads.

The fashions don't interest me, though. Somewhere on these pages are pictures of the first hotties, women who are now in their forties. Are they all still alive? Were any of them friends with Jarvis?

In the 1985 yearbook, I find Jarvis again, this time as a senior, so I learn more about him, including the fact that he was president of the Latin club, among other academic and athletic pursuits.

While I read, I slide down the side of the stacks until I'm sitting on the floor, my gaze landing on his senior quote.

QUALIS PATER TALIS FILIUS.
LIKE FATHER, LIKE SON.

He does look like his father, I muse, and his son looks—
"Hey."

I jump a foot at the sound of a voice, flipping the book closed over my hand as I look up guiltily. His son is standing directly in front of me.

228

"Josh."

"What are you doing back here?"

Digging up dirt on your father. "Studying." I press the top of the yearbook but that just smushes my hand between the pages and the hard cover. "How'd you find me?"

"Huffnegger told me you were here."

The heat in my cheeks slides lower and settles in my chest, where it starts to burn. He's lying. Mrs. Huffnegger never even saw me. A fleeting thought crosses my mind: do I have a coin on me somewhere I'm not aware of? Has one been slipped into the lining of my backpack?

I make a mental note to check as he crouches down to the floor where I'm sitting. "So, you got home okay?"

I just nod.

He reaches to my face, caressing a hair off my cheek, and I instinctively inch back, looking down, noticing that the other yearbook is open next to me, his father's face staring right up.

"Kenz," he says softly. "I'm really sorry."

"'Sokay," I say, looking away from the book because I don't want him to follow my gaze.

"It's not okay." He relaxes and lets his backside hit the floor next to mine. "I acted like a shit."

"No, no." I finally look up at him. I have to hold his attention—talk, flirt, whatever, but I can't let him look at the book that's open one inch from my leg. "You just wanted to have a good time and I was a drag."

"You are so not a drag, Fifth." He leans a little closer. "Can I make it up to you?"

I kind of shrug and shake my head, giving him a shy smile. Anything but have his eyes move one foot over and spot his

229

dad, whose picture looks so much like Josh they could be twins. "It's no problem, really."

He touches my face again and, for some reason, it's all I can do not to recoil.

"Come over to my house tonight," he says.

Not a chance. "I'm busy . . . studying."

He rolls his eyes. "You don't have to study and everybody knows it. We're having a list party."

Through superhuman effort, I manage not to blink in shock and disbelief. "A list party?" No one told *me* about it.

"Just some friends and, of course, the girls on the Hottie List."

Why wouldn't one of them text me about this? After all I told them last night? I search for a response that won't give away my thoughts. "Nobody calls it that anymore, Josh."

"Hey, it's legacy at Vienna High. You should love being on it."

I look at him like he's lost his mind because, well, he has. "Two girls on that list are dead, Josh."

"They had bad accidents, but we can't stop living, babe."

With a small shudder, I look down again, stealing a glance at his father's face.

"You don't like when I call you that, either."

"Just Kenzie," I say. "Because I'm not your girlfriend."

"Could be," he says without a second's hesitation, moving a little closer and tunneling his hand under my hair possessively. "I'd like you to be."

I can barely breathe. "Josh, I . . ."

"Think about it, okay?" He leans so close he puts his mouth against my ear. "I really like you, Kenzie. Come tonight and we'll make it official."

How could I not go tonight? I could find something out, or learn more about the coins—even Jarvis. And all the girls will be there, as vulnerable as possible. But do I want to put myself in a dangerous situation?

"I don't know," I say vaguely. "I really have to study."

He glances down at the book on my lap and my heart absolutely freezes. My one hand is splayed over the cover, hiding the year but not what it is. Only an idiot would not ask why I'm reading thirty-year-old yearbooks. Maybe he's an idiot. *Please be an idiot.*

"What are you doing studying old yearbooks?"

He's anything but. "I'm just . . ." Empty. Totally without anything that could be a plausible explanation. "Looking back at . . ."

He smiles. "Previous hotties."

That'll work. In fact, it's like he handed me an answer. "Just curious what became of some of those girls."

His expression softens with sympathy. "You're worried about the curse, aren't you?"

"Sort of, yeah."

"Then you have to come tonight."

"Why?"

He cozies up next to me, his hand on my back. "Listen, Kenz, a bunch of us have been talking and we know there's something . . . serious going down with this year's list."

I try to back away but he's holding me close, his voice nothing but an intimate, airy whisper, appropriate for the library, a little too personal for me. "I'll say."

"And that's why we're getting together tonight. Gonna put an end to this shit before anybody else . . . gets hurt."

Does he feel the chills that are dancing on the nape of my neck? "How?" I ask.

He doesn't answer for a minute, but somehow manages to get closer. "I can't tell you now because walls have ears, you know?"

"I need to know," I tell him. "Otherwise I'm not coming."

He plants a kiss on my temple, holding me tight, then moves his lips right over my ear again. "Someone's gotta take the fall."

I jerk back. "What does that mean?" Images of unprotected platforms thirty feet in the air flash in my head. "Who?"

"We don't know who yet, but it'll be the right person. I have some ideas."

"Someone else is going to die?" I practically shriek and he slams his hand over my mouth.

"Shhh! No one else is going to die." His eyes are bright blue, reminding me of the gas flame that flickers when I turn on the stove.

Or someone else turns on the stove when I'm upstairs.

"But I have to take control of this situation, or what kind of guy would I be?" he asks, clearly a rhetorical question. "What kind of *boyfriend* would I be if I didn't protect you and put a stop to this?"

"What are you going to do?"

"We're going to have a meeting, all the guys and girls who are involved. We need to put the blame where it belongs, and then, once we do, the rest of you girls will be safe."

"What are you going to do?"

"Kenzie." He cocks his head to the right. "I put the freaking list together, I can do whatever I want."

The burn in my chest is like a five-alarm fire now, so wild

it actually hurts with each out-of-control heartbeat. "*You* put it together?"

"With some help. Listen, babe." He slides his hand back under my hair, holding my head a little tightly. "I'm going to do what I have to for my girl." He kisses my hair again, then adjusts my face so I can't look anywhere but at him. "Be there at ten tonight. And wear sneakers or boots."

"Why?"

He smiles. "We're going into the woods."

Before I can react, he pushes up and pulls me with him, and the yearbook I've been clutching falls open to the page I've practically marked by holding my hand in the spine all this time.

Of course, he leans over and squints at it. "That's my dad."

"Really?" I do a magnificent job of acting surprised.

He looks hard at me and I brace for the accusations and questions. But his face relaxes into an easy smile. "Looking up my dad, huh?"

I just stare at him.

He plants another kiss on my head. "I knew you liked me a lot."

Thank God he has a massive ego. He steps back and points a finger at me. "Ten tonight. I want you there, Kenzie. Promise me you'll be there. Promise."

"I . . ."

"Oh, and by the way," he adds while I'm thinking. "My grandfather is setting up a special course for you to do the ropes. He said he's been looking into your grades and references and he's dying to give you that scholarship, so he's gonna make it easy for you. I know he'd like to see you, too."

What was that? An invitation . . . or blackmail to get me there? I just nod. "Okay."

And that's enough to make him grin and walk out, leaving me feeling really, really sick.

"I have to go."

Levi stares at me and somehow I'm able to look beyond the dreamy eyes and exquisite lips to brace for his response. "Over my dead body."

Exactly what I expected. "Under the circumstances, I think that's a terrible answer," I tell him.

We're lying side by side on a grass hill where we've spent all of our lunch period and half of my AP Lit class. It's warm today and we both took our jackets off to relax under rare blue skies.

I don't even care about school anymore, which is probably the most unnatural thing about everything going on. I'm a regular class-cutter these days. When I saw Levi in the hall and he suggested we leave, I didn't even think about it, happy to hop on his motorcycle and get out of Vienna High.

"You don't have to go," he says. "Dena can tell you what they're planning, if she really goes."

"She'll go. All the girls on the list said yes to the invitation."

"Not a single one had the good sense to think that maybe it's not safe?"

"Most of them are still certain there's a curse. Dena and Candace are the only sensible ones, and Dena wants to party and Candace wants to kick someone's ass for ruining her hair."

"What about Molly?" he asks.

I close my eyes, remembering her silence when we were at our lockers at the same time, and how she walked away without eye contact. "She's mad at me," I say, having already told him what happened the night before.

He gives me a sympathetic pat on the shoulder. "You'll work it out with her," he says. "And we'll figure this out."

"How?" I ask, still not sure what "this" is.

"For starters, I searched the Internet for information on some of the art you listed."

I'd given him the names of any pieces I remembered from the vault in the woods and he'd promised to find out anything he could about them.

"None of the things on that list are listed anywhere as stolen," he says. "All of them were sold to private collectors."

"Maybe some private collector hides them underground so they don't get stolen," I suggest. "If Rex Collier is the collector, it makes sense, because his house is not exactly secure with all those parties he lets Josh have."

He blows out a breath and looks up at the sky before turning to me.

"If I get wrapped up in anything illegal, I'm not going to get a second chance. I'll be back in juvie or even prison if I do one stupid thing wrong."

"Then don't do anything wrong."

He gives me a slow smile. "Would kissing you be wrong?"

Something melts inside me, the urge to kiss him so strong it takes my breath away. "I've wanted that for a while," I admit.

He leans over and gives me a tentative kiss, then threads his fingers through mine, bringing our joined hands up to press his lips against my knuckles. "Don't go to that party, Mack."

"I have to," I tell him. "I have to know what the connection is with the Colliers and that guy in the truck."

He falls back against the grass, frustrated. "Then I'm going, too."

"Um, hate to say this, but I don't think you're invited."

"Who needs an invitation?" he scoffs. "I know my way around those woods. I know how to climb a platform and watch. And you just keep texting me and let me know where you are every minute."

More melting inside. By now I'm mush. "That's very heroic, but—"

"No buts," he says.

"But—"

He stops me with a kiss, and this time it's sure and certain and not soft at all. This kiss has a purpose. In a few seconds, he rolls around again and pulls me closer, deepening our contact. I just keep my eyes closed and ride the crest of the wave, enjoying every second, every strangled breath, every touch of his tongue.

I finally sigh into his mouth and open my eyes, half expecting the world to be spinning since I'm so dizzy. "Josh asked me to be his girlfriend today."

He laughs and I can feel his breath. "And you're telling me this why?"

"So you know I don't want to be his girlfriend." I close my eyes and reach up to touch his hair. Oh my God, I could touch this hair forever. "I want to be yours."

He kisses me again, then trails a few down my neck, making me want to scream. "You already are," he whispers.

"I am?"

"You think I'm going to fly through the jungle to save just any girl?"

"Good," I say, still grinning.

"But you have to make me a promise, Mack."

I nod, waiting.

"Don't do anything stupid. Don't go anywhere alone. Don't try a zip line or drink something someone hands you. And for God's sake, tell that moron you're not going to be his girl-friend."

I curl closer and kiss him first this time. "Done and done."

CHAPTER XXIV

Everything works in my favor for leaving the house that night, including Mom's decision to take Dad up on his offer of dinner and a movie. He asked us both to go, and I know why: tomorrow is the anniversary of Conner's death, and Dad wants to help Mom handle what will surely be a bad day.

It's really best that I don't go, so I use a Latin tutoring job as an excuse, and a few minutes after Mom leaves, Dena picks me up.

When I get in her car, we share a quick hello, and I feel the pressure building up inside my chest. Taking out my phone, I read Levi's last text.

I'm here, waiting.

That should calm me, but it doesn't. Where is he? What's he doing? How does he know where to go? Teenagers are pretty adept at carrying on a conversation with one person and texting another at the same time, but I'm paralyzed.

"You okay?" Dena asks as we head across town.

"Just . . . you know."

"I *know*." She drags out the word. "This whole thing sucks."

I try to get comfortable but the seat belt is pressing on my chest. Along with guilt and fear and worry. "I'm not sure what this is going to accomplish tonight."

"We have to put a stop to this curse, Kenzie."

I just look out the window while she chatters about rumors and curses and all manner of BS that is floating around school. I barely answer, almost relieved when we reach Josh's estate. There aren't nearly as many cars as there were at the last party, but there are some kids gathered in the long drive. As we get out, Josh ambles over to me, his letter jacket hanging open, his expression serious.

"Hey, babe."

I can't fight that nickname and, hell, it's better than Fifth. I give him a smile and shoulder deeper into my own jacket, my hand closing around my cell phone like it's my lifeline. Because, well, it is.

"Everybody's here now," he says to the group, putting an arm around me. "Grab a beer and let's go."

I do a quick head count of the other seven girls on the list, inching away from Josh's side to get closer to Kylie. When I reach her, she smiles warmly.

"Glad you came, Kenzie."

"I still don't know why I'm here."

She angles her head. "There has to be a plan to stop this. I've talked to some list legacies. And Josh and the boys are going to help us. We'll talk out in the woods.

"Why?" I can't keep the frustration out of my voice. "Why

239

do we have to go back there? I don't understand why we can't just sit in someone's living room and have a normal conversation and not some kind of—of—witches' council."

"Are you afraid, Kenzie?" The deep, masculine voice comes from behind me and shocks the shit out of me. I spin and come face to face—well, face to chest—with Rex Collier.

My first thought is what is this old man doing out here with these drinking teenagers? Doesn't he have anything better to do? "Hi, Mr. Collier."

"Are you afraid, Kenzie?" he says again, stepping a little closer.

"I'm not a fan of the woods at night," I admit, trying for a laugh but coming off kind of dorky.

He gives me a patronizing smile and puts a hand on my shoulder. "Come with me." He adds some pressure and urges me away from the group.

I glance toward Josh, who's busy with his hand in a cooler; none of the other kids seem to notice me.

"This way," Rex insists, steering me farther back. My feet are like lead, and I almost trip from my determination not to follow him.

He laughs softly. "I have that paperwork we discussed for you."

I draw a blank. "Paperwork?"

"For the scholarship. I have a special option for you."

"Josh told me, but . . ." I'm still scared spitless. "I don't think I'm going to do that course, Mr. Collier."

"Don't you want to go to Columbia?"

Of course I do, but do I want a scholarship *that* badly? "I don't want to miss the party," I say.

"You won't. Josh!" he calls. "I'm going to give Kenzie the papers I told you about. Wait for her, please."

Josh raises a beer can to his grandfather in acknowledgment and Rex gives me a "Feel better now?" look as he nudges me down the walk to an open front door. "I'll just keep you a moment, but I think you'll be very happy with what I came up with for you. A very personalized course with special instructions."

My steps are slow, but he's determined.

"You won't need that pesky parental form signed at all," he adds.

"How can you do that?" And, moreover, why? I take one more glance over my shoulder to see most of the kids—about twelve in all—heading in a pack across the lawn toward the darkness of the woods. Josh is with them, next to Tyler Griffith.

"Wait," I say, freezing in place. "Josh is leaving." I do not want to be alone in that house with this man. Every instinct of mine is blazing with that certainty.

He smiles, but his patience is obviously wearing thin. "Just wait here, Kenzie. I'll get the papers."

He jogs up the stone steps and leaves the door wide open while he disappears into the house. Maybe I *am* overreacting. I stand for a minute alone, feeling super awkward.

Out of habit, I pull my phone out of my pocket to check for texts and realize that I've totally broken the promise I made to Levi. I press his last text and quickly thumb a response.

Not with the group going into woods yet. Still at house.
G-father getting me something. Alone right now.

Then I stare at the phone after I hit Send and will him to reply, which he does, almost instantly.

241

Is the garage door open?
See if there are any *trucks* in there.

Good thinking, Levi. I type back a quick *K* and walk toward the driveway again. There are five double garage doors and the one at the far end has been left open. With a quick glance over my shoulder, I jog across the driveway to peek into the garage. It's dark, so I click the flashlight app on my phone and shine the beam on an empty bay, the walls just rows of closed cabinets, the whole place impeccably clean. I take one step deeper into the garage and look down the row, past Josh's Audi, a small sports car, and a big white SUV.

No black truck in here.

All of a sudden, I'm blinded. A light so bright it actually hurts shines directly into my eyes, making me throw my arms over my face and back away, my heart exploding with hot, holy terror.

"Looking for someone?"

I suck in a loud breath at the low, menacing voice coming from deep inside the garage. The light is relentless, an assault of white that makes me turn and stumble toward the open door.

"Kenzie!" It's Rex, calling from the front porch. "Where did you go?"

I open my mouth but nothing comes out. I spin away from the light, but I still can't see anything else, even when I close my eyes.

"Kenzie!"

"I'm here," I call, the older man suddenly a safety net instead of a threat. "By the garage." I run a few feet across the

242

driveway, chancing a glance back at the open garage bay. Everything is dark.

At least, I think it is. My eyes are wrecked. Squeezing them open and closed, I frantically try to clear my vision, and little by little, I can see again.

"I thought you ran away," Rex says, a chuckle in his voice as he meets me halfway along the walkway.

"I just . . . went to . . ." Finally, I can see him. Looking quite kindly and old, his face more lined than I recalled, his shoulders ever so slightly slumped.

He isn't scary, this old man. What's scary was in the garage.

"Mr. Collier," I say, breathless. "There's someone in your garage."

He lifts both brows. "One of Josh's friends?"

"No." Was it? "I don't think so. Someone older." That voice was no teenager's. It was low, booming, demanding. Terrifying. "Maybe an . . . intruder?"

He draws up his chest in a deep breath, the dark brows furrowing. "Then we better kill him."

My eyes pop.

"Come on, Kenzie." He puts his hand on my shoulder again. "I'll show you how it's done."

I stand stone still, shocked. "I'll wait here while you check."

"And miss this?" He reaches behind his back with his right hand, holding my gaze for a second, then suddenly whips out a shiny knife that glints in the light.

I draw back. "Oh my God."

He angles it so I can see the deadly point. "She's a beauty, huh?"

"She's . . ." Got a carved white handle and a tiny gold ring on the end. I've seen that knife before, but where? "Sharp."

In the underground museum! It was on the wall with the other weapons. I saw it, I know I did. "Why don't we just call the police?" I suggest.

"Oh, child, what am I going to do with you?" He has papers in his other hand, which he uses to gesture me forward. "Let's go."

"He has a really bright light and he'll shine it on your face," I warn.

His laugh is the condescending chuckle a wise adult would give to a naïve little kid. "A bright light, huh? Well, we can beat him at his own game."

Getting ahead of me, he reaches the open garage and walks in fearlessly. Staying a few feet behind him, I realize my hands are both pressed to my mouth, stifling a scream I know is going to come out. What can he do with a knife in the—

Light floods everything. The driveway, the garage, the whole world seems lit up by a million watts.

"He can't blind me now," Rex says with a chuckle.

He must have hit a switch that turned everything on, inside and out. Dozens of spotlights pour light all over the lawns and highlight the trees; the whole house is as bright as if it were noon.

Only a little less terrified, I walk closer to the open garage, but just as I do, all the other garage doors start rumbling up in unison. I turn to the cars, feeling completely exposed, fully expecting to see . . . someone. Someone who just spoke to me.

But there's no man, just Rex Collier marching up and down

the shiny gray flooring, around expensive cars, the massive garage lit up like a football stadium. There's not a shadow or a place to hide.

"It's deserted," he says, leaning over to look in the sports car, then opening the doors of the SUV and leaving them that way for me to examine.

"Could he have . . . gotten away?" I ask.

At the only door into the house, Rex pauses and jiggles the knob. "Locked tight." And there are no windows, and not a cabinet big enough for a man to hide in. "Look in the cars if you like."

As if to underscore that, he pops the trunk on Josh's Audi and peers in. "No one."

I hear it in his voice, then: disbelief. Maybe a little amusement. Some condescension. "I think we're safe, Kenzie."

"How could he . . . ?" Exasperation washes over me.

"Maybe it was your imagination?" he suggests.

The hot denial rises up, but I swallow it. He isn't going to believe me. "Maybe," I croak, stepping back into the driveway because, even with the lights on, I don't want to be in that garage. He had to be in there somewhere. I didn't imagine that light or that voice.

Instantly, it's dark again. I take a second to adjust my eyes, blinking at the sound of footsteps. For a second I can't see Rex, and I imagine someone else is coming toward me, but I recognize the size of his shadow as he approaches.

Only then do I realize he turned out *every* light. Even the tiny white lights that line the driveway and the dim coach lights on the side of the garage. The only glimmer of light is a slim, slim moon.

"Here you go," he says, holding out a piece of paper. "This is what you need for the scholarship."

I reach for the paper and as I do, I notice the ring on his finger, so close I can see it even in the dark. It's as large as a sports championship ring, with a bright-red stone. As he angles his hand to give me the paper, I catch a glimpse of the carving in the stone, letters in a distinctive script.

NIHIL RELINQUERE

Just as I look up in shock, he backs away so I can't see his face and turns from me.

"Mr. Collier?"

He keeps walking into the darkness of the garage.

"Mr. Collier!"

Very slowly he turns around, just as my eyes are adjusting and my vision is clear. And I see his face, the sight stealing my breath and my sanity. That's not Rex Collier—this man is much, much younger. He looks like Rex and he looks like Josh, but . . .

"You'll want to read that paperwork carefully, Kenzie," he says.

I stare at him, speechless.

"All you have to do is follow the rules and finish the course."

I try to speak but all that comes out is a croak. How is this possible? How can I be standing here talking to Jarvis Collier? He's dead!

"They're all wrong, you know."

I just try to breathe. "Who?" I manage to ask.

"The people who say you don't look like Conner. You have exactly the same expression when you're in shock."

I inch back, my legs wobbling. *Conner?*

"Of course, he talked quite a bit more than you. Right up to the very end."

For a moment, I actually feel like I'm slipping sideways, like the whole world has tilted and everything I'm standing on is falling away.

"They're waiting for you in the woods, Kenzie." He turns and disappears into the shadows.

CHAPTER XXV

Wind sings in my ears as I tear into the inky blackness of the forest, forcing my legs to move as fast as they can. I can't think yet. I can't absorb or understand what I just saw—or heard—until I'm somewhere safe.

I need Levi.

That realization spurs me on. I ignore the scrape of pine needles on my cheeks and the sharp pain in my ankle when I trip on a rock and manage to right myself without falling. I slow down only to steal one look over my shoulder at the house, now as dark as the rest of the night.

Did he follow me?

What just happened? Did I talk to a ghost? No, I'm not Shannon. I don't believe in ghosts or curses. That man was alive and that man was . . . Jarvis Collier.

Who died at sea years ago . . . but *talked to my brother.*

Or was that just some kind of joke? Some test of my will? Some . . .

Right up to the very end.

Fear wraps around me like icy arms. I don't see any movement in the shadows, no man—or ghost or zombie or whatever that was—chasing me.

Oh my God, what if Conner's death wasn't an accident? And it wasn't my fault?

I trip again and stumble as I run deeper into the woods, blinking as my vision adjusts to the lack of light. The clouds are heavy now, blocking even the pinpoints of stars, so there's not a chance of me navigating my way out of here if I get lost.

I need Levi.

I remember my lifeline again, slowing my steps long enough to dig into my pocket for my—

Shit! It's gone. My phone is not in either pocket! I stop completely now, frantically sticking my hands into my jacket, slapping my jeans, my hopes draining. My phone is gone.

How will I reach him?

I spin around, hearing the crack of a branch . . . somewhere. I don't know where. It's too dark to get my bearings. I know enough to nestle deeper against a tree trunk and stand very, very still until I can figure out what to do next.

Who was that man?

Of course, I know who it was, but I can't accept it. I don't believe in ghosts any more than I believe in curses, but I know Jarvis is dead. Or is he?

They never found his body.

I shake my head, forcing anything out that won't help me strategize how to escape and be safe. I listen to the sounds of nature, suddenly all so threatening.

Is that a possum wandering about . . . or a killer on my heels?

Is that the hum of crickets and cicadas . . . or the catch of a gun safety?

Is that the breeze fluttering the leaves . . . or the steady breathing of someone taking aim?

I can barely hear against the hammering blood in my head, but I try anyway. I can't see anything; all I have is my sense of hearing.

And smell. I sniff, turning toward a sudden strong and acrid scent that I know. It smells like the field behind school or a car in the back of the junior lot. It smells like pot.

Hallelujah, I found them. I follow my nose toward the pungent scent, working my way more slowly now through the trees. I try to swallow against my bone-dry throat and it makes me want to cough, so I cover my mouth and just let my eyes sting until it passes.

The first low strain of voices reaches my ears, barely audible. They're whispering. A laugh, then the *shush* of someone hushing them.

Silence for a while, and the pot smell is dissipating, so I move more slowly, hugging some oaks, still looking over my shoulder in case Jarvis Collier makes an appearance.

I hear that laugh again. Dena. I gather up a breath to make a run toward the sound just as I hear something behind me, definitely alive, definitely human. My whole being tenses, waiting for the *whoosh* of a knife, the crack of a gun, the end of my life.

Nothing.

I tiptoe forward, listening for the threat but waiting for Dena's laugh. Or just a whiff of pot to guide me in the right direction. I get both and I know I have them, but then I hear another voice, coming from my far left, a completely different direction.

Female laughter on my right, male voices on my left.

If they've separated for some reason, I want to be with the girls. Can I tell them who I saw . . . what he said? Shannon will go full tilt with her ghost theory.

I hear a voice, deep and authoritative, about a hundred feet away. I can't make out the words, but I instantly recognize Josh's tenor and inflection. Okay, not Levi, but at this point, phoneless and desperate, Josh is my only hope for safety.

Should I tell him about . . . his father?

I take a few more tentative steps, cringing when I crack a small branch underfoot. I freeze for a second, waiting; then I move toward his voice.

". . . that little prick is our only hope."

I stop dead and listen. What did he just say?

"They're working on it," someone else says. "He's been paid, lured, and followed. We'll get him soon enough."

What the heck is he talking about?

At least two other voices reply in low rumbles I can't catch. I hear what sounds like Tyler with his baritone, *dude*-peppered language. I'm still walking very slowly, only slightly less concerned about the threat behind me, but fully intrigued by this conversation.

"So it's decided." I don't recognize that voice, but then I didn't recognize some of the guys who were in the driveway. "I have the car covered," someone else says.

"I have the note in place." Yet another voice.

"All we have to do is make sure he's arrested as a murderer for any one of these accidents, and they'll stop."

251

My knees weaken. Levi? They're going to blame these deaths on him?

"You *think* they'll stop," one of the boys says.

"They'll stop," Josh insists. "That's how the curse works."

He believes in the curse, too?

"Hey, you guys!" A female voice cuts through the night, and I instantly step back into shadows when a cell phone shines a beam not ten feet in front of me. "Where did you go?"

It's Shannon; I recognize her singsong voice. "We've killed the blunt without you. Hey, what's going on?"

They don't answer right away.

"You guys?" The aroma of weed wafts toward me along with her giggle. "And guess what else we've killed?"

"Shut the hell up, Shannon!" Josh says in a harsh voice. "And turn that thing off."

"Why?" But she does snap off the light.

I hear one of the male voices again, and another snorts. "Jeez, she's annoying. Wish she was higher on the list."

A couple of males laugh in response to that. I grab the tree trunk, trying—and failing—to take it all in. I don't know what they're talking about, but I do know this: I have to find Levi.

No, I have to *help* Levi and I don't have a phone.

Josh's voice echoes in my ears and I back up while I listen to the two groups converging. I slide behind a bush, ducking low and working back the way I came, as silent as possible.

I hear laughter and talking and the normal sounds of a—

A hand clamps over my mouth so hard I jolt like I've been burned, and another wraps around my chest, revealing my phone.

If I were the fainting type, I would have.

"Kind of hard to stay in touch when you drop your phone."

Levi's voice is like sweet, hot caramel all the way down to my soul, making me feel so safe in spite of the way he's holding me. "We have to climb."

I shudder, trying to turn to face him.

"We have to hide, Mackenzie. They're after me."

I nod, dimly aware of the boys and Shannon talking and messing around about thirty feet away. He's still covering my mouth but I sense that his hand is more protective than predatory.

"Wait until they're gone," he says.

After a few seconds, they continue back to where the girls are, their voices growing distant. I can feel Levi's heartbeat slamming into my back and tuck deeper into the warmth of his body. I have to tell him about Jarvis, but not now. Not yet.

When we're alone, he slowly takes his hand off my mouth and I turn, desperately needing to see his face, needing to be completely reassured by his presence, needing to see the confidence and certainty in those jet-black eyes.

I see all that and more, the impact making me wrap my arms around him and take hold. He clutches me back, as if he senses he has to right then. But not for long. Before I even begin to feel secure enough, he pulls us both about ten feet away to a thick tree.

No, not a tree. It's an old telephone pole, with homemade ladder rungs. He boosts me up without a word and my fingers grab the nearest two-by-four, clinging with all I have. The first few steps are easy, but my arms quickly start to burn.

The sound of a motorized vehicle breaks through the silence of the forest, a loud rumble vibrating the whole pole I'm clinging to.

"Hurry!" he orders, giving my backside another push.

Forget burning. Forget pain or height or the possibility of falling hard. I have to move. Clenching my teeth, I hoist myself higher, straining every muscle as I shift my foot back and forth to find the next rung.

In the distance, I see two blinding lights from a four-wheeler rolling across what must be a dirt path in the woods. And then a single beam, as bright and wide as a klieg light, shoots through the forest just ten or fifteen feet from our pole. And it moves slowly, searching us out.

I hear a girl scream—not bloodcurdling, but playful. I think. I hope.

And I finally feel the thick wooden platform. It juts out over my head, so I'll actually have to bow my back, reach for it, and swing up to the top.

"You can do it," Levi whispers. "Once we're up there, we're safe."

Not exactly, but safer. Bending backward, I close my fingers over the wood. *I can do this*, I say to myself. *I have to do this.*

The spotlight crosses over the base of our pole. That's all I need to grab and swing and heave myself up to the platform, rolling onto the wood toward the center. Before I so much as sit up, Levi follows, rolling right into me.

"Stay low," he orders. "Flat as you can."

We both smash ourselves onto the wood, side by side, our ragged breaths deafening. In the distance, the sound of the others drifts toward us, coming from the direction of the house. I turn my head to look over the treetops and I can see the roof and second floor of Josh's mansion.

Lights are coming on around the house and lawn, not like the show Rex put on for me when he went into the garage, but like someone is home. The party must have moved back there.

Does Josh wonder where I am? Does Rex? Does . . . *Jarvis*?

The roar of the four-wheeler rumbles closer now, almost under us. The light is moving slowly, in a circular pattern. Searching for us. At one point it shines right up to the platform and only the planks of wood nailed together hide us.

But they do hide us, and after a few minutes, whoever is in that four-wheeler continues his search in the rest of the woods. We stay perfectly still, turning only our faces to each other.

"They want to hurt you," I whisper.

"I heard."

"They want to pin the accidents on you. They think it will stop the curse."

He nods.

"I won't let them."

Closing his eyes, he inches his face forward so that our foreheads touch. "I won't let them hurt you, either, Mack."

"Oh, and there's one other thing," I say, tipping my head so I can see his reaction. "I'm pretty sure I saw Jarvis Collier."

His eyes widen.

The woods are quiet now, the four-wheeler far enough away that we don't hear the engine, and the kids are back at the house.

"We can't stay out here all night," I finally say.

"It's safer than anywhere else."

That's not true. "Can we get to your bike?"

"Yeah."

"Then I know where to go," I tell him. "The safest place I know to spend the night. And you have the added benefit of another witness."

"Where's that?"

"My home. And you're staying there all night."

CHAPTER XXVI

I'm grateful we're on a motorcycle, because I don't want to talk on the way home. I want to replay everything, every word, every image that is burned into my brain.

But I fail; all I can do is remember one face, one sentence, one life-changing piece of information.

Of course, he talked quite a bit more than you. Right up to the very end.

Over and over the words play in my head until we're pulling into my driveway. I'm relieved that the house is dark and there's no sign of Mom's car, but she'd texted me that she was still with Dad. That's good because she probably wouldn't be thrilled that I brought Levi home—on a motorcycle, no less.

"So tell me everything this guy said to you," Levi says as he pulls out a kitchen chair.

"He talked about . . . my brother."

"What?"

I didn't reply right away, knowing that if I share anything with Levi, I have to share everything.

I take a shaky breath. "Jarvis . . . or whoever that man was . . ."

"Yeah?"

"He knew my brother."

He waits for me to continue, but I'm still battling how much I want to reveal. I've never told anyone my role in Conner's death, but I've carried the weight of it for two years, and it's getting heavier by the day. But what if that accident wasn't my fault? What if it wasn't even an accident?

I reach for Levi's hand and tug him toward the stairs, something inexplicable drawing me to that room where we never go. "You didn't live in Vienna two years ago," I say softly. "So you didn't know my brother." I add a smile. "He called me Mack."

Levi angles his head in a silent apology for using the nickname. "I've heard about him," he says, coming with me. "I've heard he was a force to be reckoned with."

That makes me smile. "He was that and more." We climb the stairs. "Did you hear how he died?"

"An accident at a store where he worked?"

I'm not surprised he knows that much; it had been huge news at the time and was still talked about. I come to a stop at the top of the stairs, feeling unnatural next to Conner's door. Normally, I breeze right by it and go into my room.

"I've always thought it was an accident." I look up at him and hold his gaze.

I feel his hand on my shoulder, comforting and strong. On

257

a low, slow exhale, I turn the handle and push the door, the paint sticking a little in the jamb.

For a moment, I don't breathe, but then I do, inhaling the musty, stale smell of a room that hasn't been used in two years. It's very dark, but my eyes adjust quickly, taking in the Pittsburgh Steelers comforter on the double bed, the books piled up on the desk—some textbooks I'm using now for AP Calc and Latin.

There's a bookshelf—or five—of trophies. From his days playing Pop Warner as a five-year-old to the year Vienna won the division when Conner was a sophomore, he collected hardware. I'm drawn to the shelf, the physical memories of games I watched from the stands. Why didn't I pay attention? Why was I so bored?

"Busy guy." Levi's voice surprises me; I'd forgotten him for a moment because in here, there was only Conner. Tall, loud, funny, talkative, beloved by everyone, even me—even when I wanted to hate him because I'd never be him.

"Yeah," I whisper. "He was something."

"Must have been quite a shadow to live under."

"Yes and no. It could be overwhelming, but he was also really encouraging. Every single day when we'd get to school, whether we were on the bus in elementary school or in the car in high school, he'd say goodbye to me the same way. 'Go get 'em, Mack.' And that made me believe I could. Like I could do *anything*."

He smiles. "That's a good brother."

I sink onto the bed, emotions bouncing around my chest and off these walls. "It makes me feel even more guilty."

Levi turns from the bookshelf to give me a questioning look. "Why would you feel guilty?"

It's time, a little voice whispers in my head. "I've always thought I was responsible for—for his accident."

"Why?"

I pick at a black thread on the bed and run my fingers over the diamond design on the Steeler logo. "Because he wouldn't have gone down into that basement if I hadn't dropped my necklace on the conveyor belt." The words feel harsh and foreign. Words I've thought a thousand, maybe a million times in the past two years. Words I'd never dared to speak out loud.

Levi doesn't move, waiting for more, giving me space.

I inhale and exhale, the sound loud in the silent room. "He had to work and I didn't want to be home alone," I say, taking the story back a bit. "I whined and complained and he dragged me to the store, where I was supposed to be doing homework, but I was bored. In the back room, I found this conveyor belt they used to take stock from the basement up to the main floor." My voice cracks and Levi takes a step closer, but I hold up my hand.

I need to get this out. I need to tell him. "I was playing with my necklace and dangling it over the conveyor belt and I dropped it." I close my eyes. "Maybe on purpose because I wanted to go down to the basement to see what was down there."

I take a second, swiping my hand through my hair, closing my eyes to see the gold M with tiny diamond chips—fourteen of them—swinging back and forth over the belt. M for Mackenzie.

"I loved that necklace," I whisper, touching my neck as though I might somehow find it still hanging there. But the necklace was long gone . . . like my brother. "Mom gave it to me for my fourteenth birthday."

259

"Kenzie . . ."

I don't open my eyes to see the sympathy in his. I don't want sympathy. I don't deserve it. "I dropped the necklace on purpose, certain it would just get carried down to the basement and we could go down together and get it. But he wouldn't let me come. He made me stay in the back room and . . ." I drop my head into my hands, the pain of the admission too much for a second.

"Kenzie . . ."

"He went down there and I guess he had to dig behind the conveyor belt to get it. He must have bent over the belt to reach for my necklace and his shirt got caught and . . ." My voice fades into a sob as grief and guilt gang up on my heart and squeeze. "If I hadn't done that, he'd be *alive*."

"Kenzie." I feel Levi's weight on the bed next to me. "You're forgetting something," he says softly.

"That's just the problem. I *can't* forget anything. I can't forget that necklace or that decision or that moment or that long, long wait until I had to find someone and then . . ." The screaming. The sirens. The look on Mom's face when she got there. The look that has never—

"You're forgetting what that guy said to you. And the accidents that have happened. Maybe you're not responsible."

I grab that hope, wanting to cling to it, but it's dashed with what I've learned. "Only girls on the list have those accidents."

"Are you sure?"

Not of anything. He touches the light switch and bathes the room in brightness, making me blink. "What are you doing?" I ask.

"Let's look around."

"Why?"

"Has this room ever been cleaned out?" he asks.

I shake my head. "My mom refuses to touch a thing. My dad has threatened to come in here with boxes and trash bags, but that always ends up in a screaming match. It's why they separated."

With the light on, the room is less ominous and sad. There's a strange life to all these awards and trophies and books, a lingering energy that emanated from Conner. No wonder Mom didn't want to take it all down and turn it into a guest room or something. Conner was still alive in here.

I stand up and walk to the shelves again, then to his desk. Behind me, I'm aware that Levi has opened the closet door. I'm not ready to touch Conner's clothes quite yet. But I pull out the desk chair and run my finger along the thick powder of dust surrounding his big calendar blotter.

It's opened to the month of October, the year he died. I stare at the eighteenth, but the day is blank. Most of the other dates have notes in them—Conner was insanely organized, with homework due dates, his work and football practice schedules jotted in. The name *Alexa M* on the Saturday after he died.

He hadn't had a date with Alexa Monroe that night; he had a funeral instead.

Swallowing that morbid thought, I run my finger along the side of the blotter, drinking in the notes on Conner's calendar. Behind me, I hear hangers moving over the rack, unsure what Levi thinks he'll find in the closet.

I read Conner's writing.

History exam
Pick up paycheck

Debate team mtg. 8:00 a.m.
AP Language essay due
Practice 4:30–7:00
Game at St. Edward's
NRNV course

"Kenzie."

I barely hear him say my name because my eyes have just moved back to October seventeenth, frowning at the entry on that page: *NRNV course.* What class was that?

"Look at this."

I want to turn to him, but I'm staring at those letters. What was NRNV? A school group? A team he was on? Why do those letters feel like they should mean something?

Levi's hand lands on my shoulder. "This was in his letter-jacket pocket."

I finally look at what he's set on the desk in front of me. It's a paper folded in thirds with a thick, broken wax seal. I frown at it, the wax seal such a foreign thing to see.

"Look closely," he orders.

I do, lifting the paper so I can see the half seal in the light and read the letters that remain: *et Nihil Vestigi.*

"It's only half a motto," he whispers. "But we know the part that's missing."

Nihil Relinquere et Nihil Vestigi.

My heart drops as a puzzle piece snaps into place. *NRNV.* "Oh my God, Levi." I look up at him. "Conner did the ropes course the night before he died."

I flip open the paper and let out a soft grunt. It looks like a freaking Latin exam.

My phone dings in my pocket but we both ignore it, our attention on the paper.

"What does it say?" Levi asks.

"It'll take some time to translate."

The phone dings with another text, immediately followed by another.

"You better see who that is," he says.

I reach into my jacket pocket to get the phone, but my hands brush a folded piece of paper—the one Jarvis Collier gave me. I pull it and my phone out at the same time, absently unlocking the phone with one hand while I flip open the folded paper with the other.

And see the same Latin words. The same phrases that Levi found in Conner's pocket, the same numbers, the same everything. In fact, the sheet I have is an exact replica of Conner's.

"Oh my God, Levi, do you see that?" I look up at him but he's not reading either paper. The color has drained from his face and his dark eyes are burning in horror.

I follow his gaze to the phone, my blood turning ice cold as I read the words that show up over and over in the last three texts.

Amanda . . . Kylie . . . car . . . bridge . . . dead.

PART III

Mors tu vita mea.

You must die so that I may live.

CHAPTER XXVII

Levi slept in the basement and slipped out before Mom got up this morning. I left early enough not to have to tell her any of the bits and pieces I learned overnight.

A few blocks from my house, Levi picks me up on his bike and rides me to school, but Vienna High is like a ghost town. At least half the student population is out, taking any excuse—like the deaths of two more girls on the infamous Hottie List—to cut class. He pulls into the junior lot but doesn't get off the bike after he parks.

"Aren't you going to school?" I ask.

"I have something else to do." The tone in his voice snags my attention as I climb off and remove my helmet.

"What?"

He takes off his helmet, too, his mussed hair making my hand ache to smooth it. "Just some stuff."

The vague response hurts and when I look away to hide the

impact, he touches my chin, turning my face back to his. "I have to go find out what's going on."

"How? What are you going to do?"

It's his turn to look away. "I'm just going to talk to a few people. Maybe look around the woods."

"Without me?"

He chokes out a wry, mirthless laugh. "Yes, without you. Don't you realize how unsafe you are right now? You should have stayed home."

"Home is the number one place for accidents to happen," I say, quoting my mother. "I'm better off in school."

But the truth is, I'm not better off anywhere. I'm next. And we both know it.

"This has to end, Kenzie," he says softly.

"Are you going to talk to the police?"

He shakes his head. "I can't, and I don't think it will help anyway. Maybe tomorrow, but I have to—there's someone I have to talk to."

"Who?" I demand, but he stays maddeningly quiet. "Josh? Rex? *Jarvis?*"

"Just give me a few hours, okay? And watch your back. And your front. And whoever is next to you."

I step closer to him. "I want that to be you."

He brushes some hair off my face, his fingers warm. "It is and it will be." Then he kisses me long enough for me to hold on to that promise as I head into school.

The few kids who are in the halls openly stare at me, some with sympathy, some with curiosity, all with sadness. I ignore them and go to the locker bay, which is quiet and empty when I get there. While I'm facing the still-closed door, I hear soft footsteps behind me.

As much as I want to spin around and see who it is, I don't want any more looks that say *You're next, Fifth.*

"Kenzie?"

At the sound of Molly's voice, I pivot, meeting her sad gaze. She looks so wrecked I almost collapse on the spot. "Molly," I whisper, my voice cracking.

She hesitates and searches my face, her eyes swollen and red. I know she's been crying. Wordlessly, she walks over and folds me in a hug.

"I'm sorry." We say the words at exactly the same time, in the same voice. Any other time, we'd laugh. But today, we just hug tighter. I don't know if she's sorry we had such a horrible fight or that Amanda and Kylie have died or what, but I don't care. I just hold on to her.

"You okay?" she finally asks, pulling away.

I shudder as I shrug a nonanswer.

"What happened?" she asks.

"I don't know any more than you probably do," I say.

"They committed suicide? Why?"

I don't believe that for a minute, but the rumor mill says the police found a double-suicide note taped to the end of Seneca Bridge, which is a good twenty miles from Vienna. Amanda's car had been deliberately driven over the bridge, and both she and Kylie had drowned. The doors were locked and they were still in their seat belts, though none of this had been officially released. It all came from a friend of a friend of a friend who knew somebody in the Vienna Police Department.

"I saw them a couple of hours before," I tell her. "They were fine."

"Another private party?" she asks, unable to keep the bitter note out of her voice.

"Molly—"

"I'm sorry. I shouldn't have said that. I'm really sorry about that."

"*You're* sorry?" I grab her arms again. "Molly, that was so awful, and there's so much you don't understand."

"Clearly."

I squeeze a little, a thousand ways to say this playing in my mind. "I think there's a—"

"Curse? I've heard about it."

"I'm not buying the curse theory," I say. "But the believers insist that your number's up if you tell anyone what I'm about to tell you."

"Then don't," she says, inching away. "Kenzie, if anything happened to you, I'd—"

"Hey!"

We both startle at the sound, fired by Candace, who's standing ten feet away with her hands on her hips, her butchered black hair still as shocking as the first time I saw it. Behind her is Dena, who looks like she hasn't slept at all.

"You better zip your lips, Summerall," Candace says. "Unless you want to be next."

Instinctively I get even closer to Molly, refusing to shut her out the way I did before. "I trust Molly," I say quietly. "She's my best friend."

Candace takes a few steps closer, ignoring Molly and focusing on me. "You want to know the last thing Amanda Wilson did before she and Kylie took off last night?"

I just stare at her. I'm not sure I want to know, but I have to.

"She texted her freaking cousin and asked if she and Kylie could go stay with her for a few days. And she told her cousin *why*."

"And you think that's why her car went off Seneca Bridge?" I ask. "'Cause I'd bet my life it's not."

"You're betting your life talking to her," Dena says, coming up to join us. She throws a dismissive look at Molly. "Better leave, Kenzie's best friend."

"No." I grab Molly's hand and cling to it. "She stays with me. We're a package deal."

Candace crosses her arms. "Just like Amanda and Kylie."

Molly gasps, but I dismiss the comment with a wave. "What do you want?"

"I want to talk to you," Candace says. "Alone." She gets my elbow and pulls me a few feet away from Molly. "Listen, we have to meet tonight. At the trailer."

"Why?"

"Because it's the only place we're safe. No one knows about that trailer, and we can talk freely about what to do and not worry about someone killing us."

I shake my head. "I don't know."

"Suit yourself. Stay home and risk an accident. Or come, but don't bring anyone." She gets closer to my face. "And I mean anyone."

She walks away, and Dena follows, slowing down to whisper, "Kenzie, please don't tell anyone else."

"She hasn't told me anything," Molly says. "So you can quit freaking out."

Dena slumps with a sigh of gratitude.

"But if I do," I say, "I don't think that has anything to do with what's happening."

"It might," Dena says in a harsh whisper. "Don't take any chances, Kenzie. You're next. And I'm right after you."

I want to reassure her, but I can't, swallowing hollow words. I just nod and when she leaves, I turn to Molly.

"Don't," she says, cutting me off when I open my mouth. "Don't tell me anything that will jeopardize your life."

"Telling you isn't going to put me in danger. Anyway, I'm in enough already."

"Kenzie, you're scaring me."

She should be scared. We all should be. "Please understand that this has nothing to do with our friendship and I'm not ditching you for these girls."

"I know that." She reaches out and pulls me into a hug. "Please be careful."

"I will, I promise." But I'm not sure I can be careful enough.

I head into Latin hoping Mr. Irving can be my savior. He won't know what he's doing, of course, but I need to get some help translating the page of Latin I got from Jarvis—if that was Jarvis—that matched the paper Levi found in Conner's jacket pocket.

It has to hold some kind of answer for me.

When I hand it to Mr. Irving, he gives me a sympathetic smile. "Preparing for State already, Kenzie? That's a good way to get your mind off things."

I nod and go with the explanation he's handed me. "I found this on the Internet in a forum about testing, and I thought it might help me."

A glimmer of hope crosses his face. "You can go? Did you get the parental consent form signed? The competition's in less than a month."

"Not yet, but . . ." I point to the paper. "Can you give me some help here?"

"Sure." He pulls reading glasses from his pocket and perches on the empty desk next to mine, frowning at the page and glancing at the few notes of translation I've already made. The Latin is over my head, though, written in a way that doesn't make sense to me. I hope that's not the case with Mr. Irving.

"Is this a game?" he asks. "Riddles or something?"

Maybe. "I'm not exactly sure." I point to a section where I was really lost. "I understand the actual words, but it's those subtle modern meanings that throw me. Like that one. *Hodie mihi, cras tibi.*' I know that translates literally to 'today to me, tomorrow to you,' but what's the figurative translation?"

"That, Kenzie, reflects the inevitability of change and normally is used to remind a reader of their mortality."

Mortality. That doesn't sound good. "And what about '*Extinctus amabitur idem*'?"

"Quite famous, actually," he says. "That's some lovely insight from the *Epistles* by Horace, which you'll read in Latin Four."

If I'm still alive by then. "But what does it mean, Mr. Irving?"

"It means the same man will be loved after he's dead. Or underground, which is the way some would interpret that."

"Underground?"

"Buried." He gives me another gentle look. "Are you sure you want to wallow in such morbid stuff today, Kenzie?"

I don't answer as a few kids come into the classroom and Mr. Irving takes another look at the paper. "Can I keep this and work on it for a while? It's fascinating."

I left the other copy at home in Conner's room so I'm hesitant to give this one away. "I really need to study it."

He smiles. "I should have ten more students like you, Kenzie. Look, I'm not lecturing today, no one is in the mood. I'm just going to put on a movie about the history of Ephesus, so I'll make a few notes on this while it runs. How does that sound?"

As long as he doesn't figure out that this has something to do with four dead girls. I let him have the paper while the TV screen flashes images of gladiators. The boys are into it; the girls are texting. I'm staring at Irving.

At one point, he catches me, so I immediately shift my gaze to see a computer-simulated gladiator driving a four-pronged instrument of torture under the knee of an opponent.

"Ooh, sick!" one of the boys calls out.

"The only evidence of the quadrant's use is based on bones found by archeologists. . . ." The voice drones on as the weapon is enlarged with the word *quadrant* on the screen and suddenly, I'm riveted. I've seen that weapon. I've seen it . . . in the museum cave that Levi and I discovered.

But the narrator is saying that none have ever been found intact.

Is that cave some kind of archeological storage room? The video moves on to more gladiator brutality, but my mind is wandering. At the end of class, Mr. Irving waves me up to his desk, his expression a little dark and questioning.

"Are you doing this because of your brother?"

The question throws me so much I actually grip the desk to keep from swaying. "What?"

He waves the paper. "The scholarship? I remember he applied not long before . . ." His voice trails off in a fade I always

274

recognize. People don't like to mention Conner's death, especially teachers who knew him and loved him.

"What exactly are you talking about?" I ask.

"The Jarvis Aurelius Memorial Scholarship."

I just stare at him. "Jarvis . . ."

"I know he left big shoes to fill and that you want to be just like your brother, but that test didn't go well at all for Conner."

I still can't quite process what he's saying. "I don't want to be just like him," I manage to say. "But what test are you talking about?"

"The one you take following these instructions." He slides the paper I'd given him across the desk. "He talked to me the next day and he was upset. I never got the details because that was the day . . ."

The day he died. Which was two years ago today. "What did he tell you about the test?" I ask. "He didn't pass?"

He shakes his head. "Shocking, I know." Because Conner was better at Latin than I am. "But he did finish." He opens his desk drawer. "Not in enough time, but they gave him this consolation prize."

I feel myself stepping back, certain of what he's going to show me. Certain and terrified. Sure enough, it's a gold coin with the words *Nihil Relinquere et Nihil Vestigi* engraved on it.

Mr. Irving looks at it for a long time, turning it in his palm before holding it out to me. "Would you like it, Kenzie?"

"No, you keep it," I say. "He must have had a reason for giving it to you." Like he knew it had a tracking device in it.

"Oh, he had a reason." Mr. Irving gives me a slow, sad smile as he holds up the coin. "To warn other kids about the test."

My eyes pop open. "To warn them . . . How?"

"Do you know what these words mean, Kenzie?"

275

I nod without reading it. "'To leave nothing behind and no trace.'"

"No, no, on this side. Look."

I lean closer and squint at the words, certain there was nothing on the back of the coin that Josh left at the convenience store. So maybe this one is different.

"You can read that, Kenzie."

Secreta sodalitas sicariorum. My brain starts to translate . . . and a fine chill crawls up my spine and settles at the base of my neck, weighing me down.

A secret society of assassins.

"Assassins?" I can barely get the word out.

"In other words, the test is a killer even if you just take it online, and I wouldn't put myself through it if the only thing you're trying to prove is that you can walk in the shoes of your brother."

Assassins?

I take a step backward, my head spinning and light. "Then I probably won't take it," I say. And it's not online, but that seems to be what Mr. Irving thinks.

He gives me a smile and returns the coin to his desk. "Thank you for letting me keep it. Conner was one of my favorite students."

"He was everyone's favorite," I say, more out of rote than emotion.

"But you're actually a better student," he adds quickly. "You go deeper into the language and the culture. He just wanted to get his A and move on. This test really shook him up."

"How, exactly?" I ask.

"He didn't give me a lot of detail, but he did say not to let

276

any of my students go for it. He said it damn near killed him."
He cringes instantly. "God, that was . . . I'm sorry."

I shake my head and gesture for him not to worry about it.
But something did kill Conner . . . and maybe I had nothing
to do with that death.

I just had to stay alive long enough to prove that to myself.

CHAPTER XXVIII

By evening, I'm freaked that I haven't heard a word from Levi in hours. He texted in the middle of the day just to see if I was okay but didn't reply to my urgent message that I had news.

Frustrated, I hole up in my room and consider my options. I don't want to be specific about what Irving told me in a text to Levi, and I'm actually scared to Google anything. Maybe someone has my Internet access tracked, too.

I get a few texts from Dena reminding me that there's a meeting tonight, but I'm not sure if I should go. I could put an end to that curse business with my assassins news . . . except I don't know enough to do anything but get them all worked up.

To pass the time, I've completely translated the Latin paper, but the translations mean virtually nothing. They're just a set of unrelated statements that are like puzzle pieces with no picture to follow. I don't know where to begin with sentences like *A strong shield is the safety of leaders* and *There remains a shadow of a great name.*

I hear a car in the driveway and sit up, willing it to be Levi, even though I know he'd be on a motorcycle. But when I hear Molly's voice after Mom opens the door, a different kind of happiness rolls through me. I need her almost as much as I need Levi.

We meet halfway on the stairs and hug again.

"C'mon, let's go," she whispers.

"Where?"

"To the meeting."

I inch back and shake my head, immediately taking her up to my room so my mom doesn't hear us.

"I'm not going there with you," I say, pulling her in and closing the door. "And not because you don't belong there."

"I don't," she says quickly, with no bitterness in her voice. "But I belong with you. Come on, Kenzie, you know something bad could happen to you. You know you're next on that list. What if they're right? What if there is a curse? I'll go with you and be your bodyguard."

A surge of affection swells but I refuse the offer. "There is no curse, Molly. But . . ." I glance at my bed, where I've left the translations and all my questions. I have to share with someone. "But there might be . . ." *An assassin.* "A killer."

"What?"

"Shhh." I pull her closer, barely fighting the need to pour all this out on her. But is that fair? Is that safe? "There's stuff . . . going on."

She glares at me. "No shit."

"It might involve . . ." I close my eyes and say it. "Conner's death."

Sucking in her breath, she grabs me. "If you don't tell me everything, and I mean everything, right now, I will kill you myself."

I lose the battle and pull her to the bed, the whole story spilling out in nearly incoherent sentences, but she's smart and seems to follow it all well enough, knowing better than to interrupt me with a million questions.

When I finally finish, she grabs the paper and folds it up, stuffing it into my hand. "You are going to tell the girls everything and then, with me, we are all going to the police."

I stare at her. "You think we should? What if they get to me first?"

"They have to get through me, and I'm not on any stinkin' Hottie List, thank God." She pulls me off the bed. "I can find that trailer again. Come on."

God, I love her. "Okay, let's go."

She peppers me with questions during the drive out to the country, but I can't answer many of them. Including why I haven't heard from Levi in hours.

"Maybe that's how he wants it," she suggests.

"What do you mean?"

For the first time, she doesn't answer right away, pretending to be focused on the dark road and the beams of her VW headlights.

"Come on, Molly, you can't drop a bomb like that and not tell me what you mean."

"I mean . . ." She shifts in her seat. "I don't think he's good enough for you, Kenzie."

I grunt. "You don't know him."

"I don't have to know him. He's got a reputation."

"Like I said, you don't know him. You know his reputation, which is based on hearsay and rumors and, okay, maybe he had some issues back at his old school, but he's really trying to turn his life around."

"Are you going to just ignore the elephant in this car?" she asks.

"The elephant in the car?" I try for humor. "Who says that?"

She doesn't laugh. "He almost killed a girl in a stolen car. And that's not just a bad reputation, Kenzie. That's on the Internet."

I inhale slowly, a little sick that she cyberstalked him.

"Don't be mad," she says. "I'm your bodyguard, remember?"

"It was . . ." *An accident.* But I can't even say the words.

"And he admitted he was at the quarry. And he left Starbucks right before Chloe died."

"He was with me when Amanda and Kylie went off that bridge," I insist.

"A perfect alibi. What if something was done to their brakes?"

I hate where she's going with this. Hate it. He *has* been in the wrong place at the wrong time more than once.

She doesn't reply, but turns onto the dirt path and we drive in silence, the little Bug jostling us over the ruts, each one making my heart ache. Not Levi. Not Levi.

And then her headlights shine right onto his Kawasaki, parked directly in front of the trailer. *Oh, Levi.* I can't even breathe.

"What's he doing here?" Molly asks.

There are three other cars parked on the grass, and I immediately recognize them as belonging to Dena, Shannon, and Bree, who probably brought Candace and Ashleigh. They're all here . . . with Levi?

"What *is* he doing here?" I repeat Molly's question because nothing makes any sense right now.

"Guess we better find out."

As she stops the car, I put a hand on her arm. "Would you consider staying here until I find out what's going on?"

She smirks. "No."

I'm not going to fight her, so we get out and walk toward the trailer, the only sound some crickets and a soft night breeze, the only light a dim bulb in the living room.

"It's quiet," Molly whispers.

It sure is. What's going on in there? My heart is crawling up to my throat, the pulse so hard and steady it's vibrating my whole body. I walk up one step to the front door and raise my hand to knock.

"What's that smell?" Molly asks.

I sniff, getting a whiff of something putrid.

"Whoa, that stinks." She covers her mouth. "Like rotten eggs."

Everything inside me turns ice cold. "Oh my God." I slam my hand on the doorknob, not even thinking, not even caring what's on the other side. I recognize that smell. "It's gas!"

The door flies open with almost no pressure and I practically fall into the tiny living area, the smell so strong I nearly gag.

"Kenzie, look!" Molly points to the sofa, where Dena and Candace lie perfectly still, eyes closed. On the floor are Bree, Shannon, and Ashleigh.

I lunge toward them, thoughts of Levi gone as I pray they're still alive. Molly's already leaning over Shannon's body, lifting her wrist. I put my hand over Dena's mouth and feel the faintest of breaths.

Almost immediately I have a headache, the smell of gas is so strong.

"We have to get them out of here," I say, already pulling Dena.

"I'll call nine-one-one."

"There's no time!" I'm dragging Dena to the door. "They'll die. Let's get them out and then call."

"What about—"

"Molly!"

She shuts up and grabs Shannon, helping me drag two bodies out onto the grass. We leave them there. Sucking in clean air, we both tear back in for two more, finding superhuman strength as I pull Candace and Molly takes Ashleigh, who moans but doesn't wake up.

My arms are on fire as I clunk Candace down the single step and practically thrust her to the grass. She doesn't even flinch.

Oh, God, don't let her die. Don't let her die.

"Let's get Bree!" Molly says, and I start to run with her, then catch a glimpse of the motorcycle that shouldn't be here.

"You get her," I say, hauling past Molly to the back of the trailer. "He might be back there."

I don't know why or how, but I have to look.

Molly grabs my arm. "Don't, Kenzie!" She yells through the hand she has covering her mouth and nose. "We have to get out of here. This thing could explode any second!"

Horror rocks me. She's right, but . . . "Just let me look,

Molly. I can't let him die. Get her." I give her a shove toward Bree and bolt down a little hallway to a darkened bedroom.

"Levi!" I call, but there's only silence. I hear Molly grunt as she works to get Bree, and I peer into the bedroom, seeing no one. A wave of nausea grips me as the gas invades my body, making me gag, but I force myself to go over to the closet and throw the door open. I can't let him die.

But there's no sign of Levi. I stick my head in the dingy bathroom in the hall, also empty.

"Kenzie!" Molly screams at me from outside, a note of sheer panic and terror in her voice. "Kenzie!"

"Coming," I call, running back to the living room, the effort taking everything from me as weakness presses on my body. I take one second to look in the kitchen, fully expecting the gas burners to be on.

But the stove is electric and it's off.

So where is the leak?

I hear a clicking sound, a steady, insistent *tap-tap-tap* coming from somewhere. The walls? The floor?

There's a low rumble, like a volcano about to—holy crap, I have to go. Forcing myself to run, I throw my whole body outside, rolling on the grass right into Candace's body just as everything explodes, a mushroom of fire and heat like I've opened a furnace and stuck my face in.

Instinctively I throw myself backward, the noise of the explosion echoing over the forested countryside, a sickening, deadly sound I know I'll never forget.

I roll away from the heat, squinting into the reflected orange tinge of the lawn for Molly, scanning in panic when I don't see her.

"Molly?" I scramble to my feet, spitting dirt and ash from my mouth. "Molly?"

Is she at her car? Calling for help? Had she left her phone in the car? I cling to that hope, pivoting to check on the girls and nearly buckling in relief when I see Candace, Dena, and Shannon waking up. Ashleigh turns over and Bree starts to cough.

They're alive!

Still moving on autopilot, I know I have to find Molly. I run to the car, stumbling and coughing, certain I see her inside. I grab the driver's door because it's closest and yank it open, another wave of raw relief when I see her leaning against the window, eyes closed.

"Molly?" I slide in, reaching for her. Was she overcome by the gas? Did she faint from shock? What the heck? "Molly!"

Another smell sucker-punches me, this one pungent and sharp, like vinegar. What is that—

With a gasp, I whip around to the backseat, meeting the dark, threatening, murderous eyes of Jarvis Collier and the glint of a blade he slides right under Molly's jaw. In his other hand, he has a rag drenched in something that must have put her into a sound sleep.

"Obviously, it was a mistake to put you on that list." He gestures the rag toward the steering wheel and flashes the knife at Molly's neck. *"Age, Quinte."*

ge, age. Age . . . drive, imperative mood. *Quinte . . . Fifth.*

"Don't hurt her," I whisper, grateful I can make any sound at all as I turn to face the front and follow his command, stealing a glance at the burning trailer. I see the girls moving around, but I don't think they've even realized what happened or know we're in this car. I can't think beyond my best friend, inches from a killer's knife.

When he doesn't answer, I look in the rearview to see him. "Please, please don't hurt her."

He lifts a brow, the hollows of his angular face making him look even more menacing. "One more moment of hesitation and she's dead."

"Where?" I croak, stalling for more time. My fingers tremble as I turn the key, which was in the ignition, and the lights come on. Should I flash the brights? Honk? Signal for help?

"Don't even think about it," he says, leaning forward to

get his whole arm around Molly's neck. "Just go. I'll tell you where."

I take one more look at Molly, who hasn't stirred. "Don't hurt her. Hurt me. Kill me, I don't care, but don't hurt Molly."

"You should know me better than that by now," he says. "My work is so much cleaner. But if you don't drive this car, I will make an exception. They won't find her body for so long it won't matter how I kill her." He nods toward the steering wheel. "You have exactly five seconds to move."

I turn, my arm instinctively reaching for the seat belt, but I realize just how stupid that is. Anyway, I might have to leap out of a moving car.

No, not without Molly. I won't let him hurt Molly, no matter what he does to me.

Very slowly, I start to pull out of the rutted driveway.

"Move it!"

The order bounces off the metal and glass of the car, loud enough to make Molly stir and whimper. *Come on, Molls, wake up. Two of us are better than one against this maniac.*

I hit the gas, increasing the speed a little, working with everything I have to stop the trembling fear that shudders through me. As long as I'm alive, I have a chance. And so does Molly.

I struggle to find the high beams because I've driven this car only a few times. I turn onto the deserted road, willing a car to drive by. What will the police think when they investigate this explosion? When they see Levi's motorcycle?

I know he's innocent . . . so where is he?

I steal another quick look in the rearview mirror, but Jarvis is purposely sitting at an angle where I can't see him. He's still leaning forward and I know that knife is inches from ending my best friend's life.

Heavy silence thickens in the tiny space, the only sound my strained breaths. I blink when tears blur my vision, refusing to let him see how scared I am. He clears his throat and I brace for whatever order he's going to give now.

"*Lacrimis oculos suffusa nitentis.*"

Oh, for crying out loud. My head isn't clear enough for Latin.

"Beautiful words, don't you think, *Quinte*?"

I manage a nod, grateful to think in my native tongue.

"Translate," he orders.

Shit. "Can you, um, repeat the phrase?"

He chuckles. "Ah, memories of competitions. How I loved them."

Okay, maybe he'll talk. In Latin, about Latin, whatever. Maybe that will relax him and get me some answers and information . . . if I don't die tonight. Which seems pretty damn likely.

"Take the highway. West."

The highway is good—more cars. More chance of someone coming to our rescue.

"*Lacrimis oculos suffusa nitentis,*" he repeats after a few minutes.

I'm not listening, studying the other cars. Could I signal to one? Could I put an emergency call out somehow? What if I did something totally illegal and got pulled over? That would be brill—

"Translate!" he barks, and Molly turns and sighs.

"Okay, okay." I picture each word. "Eyes with tears?" He

doesn't answer. "Eyes that are . . . *'suffusa'*? Is that *suffused*? *'Nitentis'*?" I shake my head. "I don't know those words."

He snorts. "And you think you could win a competition? 'Her sparkling eyes bedewed with tears.' Book One of Virgil's *Aeneid*, line 228." After a pause, he leans closer to me. "Stop crying, *Quinte*. One of the reasons I chose you is that you aren't a baby."

"You *chose* me?"

"I choose them all, every year. But, it's over, sadly. This will be the last year of the list."

Despite the heat of the enclosed car, I feel goose bumps spread across my body. His arm is still over the seat, the knife millimeters from Molly's throat. "You mean . . . the Hottie List?"

"Ah, yes," he replies. "Who knew I'd still be using that expression long after it lost its luster? That's the thing about English. It changes too much. Not like Latin, right, my friend?"

I recoil at being his friend and force myself to be more aware of traffic. At fifty miles an hour, I can't risk hitting another car, but could I swerve like a drunk and get another driver to call 911? It's an idea.

"My invention," he says, pulling me back to the conversation.

"The list was?" Maybe talking and questions are the way to go. "Why'd you invent the list?"

He doesn't answer and I risk another glance over my shoulder. His eyes are narrowed, looking out the passenger side. "I invented the list because I needed a finite set of individuals who are easily controlled and can be victims of occasional accidents."

I feel my jaw slacken and my stomach turn as all thoughts of outsmarting him through conversation dissolve. "Oh."

He's a Virgil-quoting serial-killing lunatic who the whole world thinks is *dead*. Kind of an airtight alibi for a murderer—especially one who orchestrates *accidents*.

"You've really thrown me off my game tonight, *Quinte*," he says calmly, as if we're just cruising along for fun. "You should have come to the meeting on time like your boyfriend did."

"Levi? Where is he?" *Please, God, don't let him have been trapped in that trailer and I somehow missed him.*

"He goes where he's told. Well, he does when he thinks the text is from you."

So that's why Levi's bike was there. He thought I'd texted him.

"Where is he?" I ask again, my voice rising.

He ignores me. "Now I'm going to have to repeat the drive off the bridge, and that doesn't look good at all."

Look good to who? I shoot him a questioning glance in the mirror but he's not looking at me; he's thinking. Is this my chance to do something?

But then he glares at me. "Not that it's a competition," he adds, as if I have any idea what he's talking about.

"Then what is it?" I ask quietly.

His eyes narrow at me in the rearview mirror. "Take the next exit."

Molly shifts around again, whimpering a little and giving me hope that she's going to wake up. But what if she does? Will he kill her immediately? Give her more chloroform or whatever he smothered her with?

Jarvis has to lean even farther forward to keep the knife close to her, enough that I can slide my eyes over and see his face. It's set in a hard expression as his gaze darts around the highway, his tension palpable.

"We're almost at Birch Run." He sighs, sounding disgusted. "Not one of my favorites, but I'm a professional."

A professional *assassin*.

He's looking the other way, and the exit is coming fast. I keep my foot on the gas and hope he'll be distracted by his thoughts for the ten seconds it'll take to pass the Birch Run exit. I know that section of river, and I know that bridge. It's—

"Hey!" The knife comes at me this time, flashing in my peripheral vision. "This exit!"

I jerk the wheel to the right at the very last second, wishing I'd hit the guardrail, but I don't. I roll down the exit road and wait for him to tell me where to turn, even though I know exactly where we're going. An old bridge with rickety sides.

My mother won't even let me drive over the Birch Run bridge. And now I'm going to drive *off* it. At least, I think that's what the "professional" has in mind.

I can't let that happen to Molly. I *can't*.

Why is he doing this? "It doesn't make sense," I mutter, my brain short-circuited enough that I talk out loud.

"It makes sense to me," he says.

How reassuring.

"Juvenal said it best when he observed the dark side of human nature," he says. *"Et qui nolunt occidere quemquam posse volunt.* Don't you agree, *Quinte*?"

I don't have a clue what he said beyond *who does not want to* . . . something.

"I don't know," I admit.

"'Those who do not wish to kill anyone wish they were able,'" he says, followed by a slow, deep breath into his nostrils.

"And that's why no one else can do this and I have to prove that to them."

"To who?"

He doesn't answer and I decide to push it. "Your secret society?" I go a little further. *"Nihil Relinquere?"*

He turns sharply to me. "Of course I'll leave nothing behind. That's the whole idea, *Quinte*. No proof, no evidence, no clues, no suggestion of foul play."

"Then why do you leave those coins?"

"Proof that it wasn't an accident," he says. "Proof that only certain people in my society would understand and believe."

"I thought they tracked people. I thought that's why Josh left one at the convenience store."

"A rookie error, I assure you."

In my peripheral vision, I see a flash of black and white under a billboard. Hope surges through me as I realize it's a police cruiser waiting for a speeder. What do I do? Flash the brights? Hit the brakes? Speed like hell?

I go with plan C and smash my foot on the accelerator, the engine screaming.

"What are you—" He sees the cop and instantly leans forward. "Don't even think about it."

The cop pulls out but doesn't put on his lights. Next to me, Jarvis pulls Molly's sleeping body a little higher.

"You go one mile an hour over or under the speed limit, blink your lights, touch your brakes, or so much as think about signaling that cop and I will put this blade five inches into this girl."

I say nothing.

"Isn't one death on your conscience enough, *Quinte*?"

Does he mean the other girls, or Conner? How would he know I feel guilty about my brother's death? Nausea threatens to rise and I fight the feeling.

"You really didn't think you were on the list because of your looks, did you?" he adds.

I can barely breathe as we approach the bridge. The cop is letting us get ahead, and he still hasn't turned on a siren or flashed his lights. If he does, surely this madman wouldn't risk being pulled over and having a cop find a dead body? Should I—

"Did you, *Quinte*?" he demands. "Did you think you earned a spot thanks to your great beauty?"

Oh, God. This has to do with Conner. I'm on the list because of Conner. My whole body shudders like I've just dropped off a ten-story building. I sneak a look in the rearview mirror; the cop is still back there. Way back there.

"If you'd done your research, you would have seen that many of the girls on the list fall into the category of not so hot, but so very . . . vulnerable. Like you, they also have weaknesses and tendencies and allergies and histories. I'm very careful who I pick. Turn here. Right here. And use your signal. I see the damn cop."

I follow the orders and we head back up a hill, away from the bridge. That's good news. The bad news: the cop doesn't follow.

"Stay on this road. I have another plan."

Of course he does. "Where are we going?"

"No more questions. You can't keep doing this to me."

"Doing what?"

"You escaped the cut brakes, you found the gas leak, and I

couldn't flatten you on your bike. But your luck has run out. *Memento mori, Quinte. Memento mori.*"

I don't have to dig too deep into my translation well for that one. *Remember to die . . .* or, figuratively, *remember you're going to die.* Yeah, how could I forget?

CHAPTER XXX

I'm not completely surprised when Jarvis directs me to Nacht Woods, although we're far from the Collier property. This section of the woods is at least a mile from any homes, a desolate and dense forest that only the most seasoned hiker would attempt to enter. I don't know what to expect, except that it can't be good.

Next to me, Molly grunts softly, surely coming out of her sleep. Two of us can take him down. Molly and I can silently communicate and beat this nutcase at his game . . . unless he kills her first.

No matter what, I have to protect Molly. I have to outsmart him because he might be crazy, but he's smart. That's what I have to be, too.

"Up that hill," he orders. "Cut through those trees and find the path."

My lights slice through the densest section of evergreens. "Through them?"

"You'll make it. Might scratch your pal's nice ride, but she and her car are about to go through worse."

Not if I can stop you.

But how? I have to gun it to get up a steep embankment, the path carpeted with slick leaves that make the tires skid. I manage the climb and cringe when the needles scrape over the car like nails on a chalkboard.

Then I realize we're driving up to Stony Creek Cliff, the very place a hiker was . . .

"Stephanie Kurtz." The woman's name pops into my head and out of my mouth. She wasn't a teenager, but a young mother who graduated from Vienna High and had probably been on the list.

"Mmm. That was a good one. A flawless accident, orchestrated with perfection."

To fall off the cliff onto the rocks of the creek below?

"I called her *Septime*."

I don't get it. "You mean you killed seven that year?" I can hear the breathlessness in my voice. "Women who were once on the list?"

"I didn't kill her," he says. "I merely choreographed that one and let one of the trainees take the credit. This year's different."

"How? Because everyone dies? In order?"

"Getting the order right is just, shall we say, a flourish on my signature. Not as necessary as getting all ten taken care of."

"Why?" I choke out the question.

"Let's just say the stakes in my business got higher, and I have something to prove to get a promotion."

"You kill people to get a promotion?"

That makes him laugh. "I kill people for a living, Quinte. I do it better, cleaner, and faster than anyone else and I get the promotion. It's really like any other job."

It's his job. Sick to my stomach, I force myself to focus on all that matters right now: staying alive and saving Molly. And then . . . Levi. I have to find him, too.

I cling to those goals and inch the car up the glasslike surface of stone and rock, heading toward the embankment about fifteen feet over Stony Creek.

In my pocket, my cell phone vibrates.

"Give it to me," he says.

Can I swerve the car when I reach into my pocket? Is this my chance? When he reads the phone? Or should I press the call button when I hand it to him and have whoever is calling hear what's happening so at least someone will know the truth?

"Why are you doing this? Aren't you supposed to be dead?" I practically scream the questions that won't stop.

"Death is an illusion, *Quinte*. At least, mine was, allowing me total freedom. Give me your damn phone. Now!"

I reach for the phone and swerve to the left. In an instant, Jarvis pulls up Molly's limp body with one hand, the knife poised at her throat with the other.

"Don't make me ruin a perfect record, *Quinte*! I will do what I have to do."

Shaking, I manage to dig the phone from my pocket and hold it up. He drops Molly and grabs the phone before I have any chance of hitting the screen.

Wordlessly, he uses his free hand to open the window, and my phone goes sailing out.

We're nearing the top of the cliff and the road roughens and flattens. Ahead of us is . . . nothing. A long drop straight down that we'll never survive.

"Put the car in neutral," he demands.

I do, my mind whirring with possibilities of how to escape this, coming up with none. He has to get out of the car at some point if I'm going to drive it over the cliff, right? That's why he wants the car in neutral—so I can't back up and drive down the hill in reverse.

But I can try.

"Get in the backseat," he orders.

I don't move, thinking too hard about my options.

"Move it!"

His command is loud enough to make Molly stir and shift in her seat. Oh my God, these might be her last moments alive. All because of me.

I open the car door and he does the same. Okay, now Molly's not in danger. Well, not from a knife, anyway.

Jarvis is over six feet tall, and strong. I don't stand a chance against him and his knife. I have to look up at him, way up, and when I do, I meet the ice-blue eyes of a killer.

"Okay," he says. "This can work but we have to think about how the evidence looks when they investigate." He's nodding, calmly thinking things through. Why can't I be that calm? Instead, my whole body is quivering and my brain is flatlining.

"Sure, there will be evidence of a murder," he continues. "The one *you* committed. And then you'll jump off the cliff in remorse." He tapers his eyes to angry slits. "I'll still prove my point to them."

To who?

"*Nihil relinquere et nihil vestigi.* That's how we work."

"Who is that?"

His smile is slow. "*Sicarii.*"

Assassins.

Before my next breath, he grabs my arm and whips me away. I go sliding on the slick surface, tumbling face-first, my hands slapping hard right before the rest of me does. I lift my head just as he's pushing the car, standing behind it and giving it a solid shove to send Molly to her death.

I swallow my scream, instinctively knowing that will only make him more determined, and vault to my feet just as the car starts to move and the two front tires pop over the edge of the cliff.

He sees me, but if he stabs me to death, then his setup of a murder-suicide won't work. So I run full force toward him. He turns, straightening the blade and aiming it right at my stomach. His face is contorted in frustration and fury at how I'm testing him and messing with his plans.

I keep plowing forward, straight at that blade, imagining how it's going to feel, cold and sharp.

The world's in slow motion—my feet stomping over the leaves and stone, the cold air whooshing over my face, the deadly expression in his eyes as I reach him. In the distance, muffled, a girl screams. Molly!

"Damn you!" He flips the knife away and I pounce, surprising him and getting help from the slippery leaves. Off balance, he slides down, his full weight on top of me.

I hear something hit the ground and know it's the knife. At least he can't stab me, I think, as his knee slams into my gut. I let out a grunt of pain, then reach up to grab his hair and pull like hell.

He's swearing as his fist slams into my face, and I can hear my jaw crack. I don't care. Break my face. Break my body. I just have to fight him long enough for Molly to get out.

Is she awake? Coherent? *Come on, Molls!*

He gets his hands on my throat and I feel him squeeze, then relax, anger flashing in his eyes, and I know why. He can't kill me like this. It will ruin his plan.

I manage to grab his shoulders and push him off, then try to scramble away. I don't get far. He lifts both legs and aims right at the VW's bumper. With another solid shove, I hear the undercarriage scrape against the side of the cliff.

I flail sideways to get away, but he snags my arm and drags me closer, something jabbing hard into my hip on the way. Not something, the knife. The knife is under me.

Once more, he slams me onto my back, my head whacking against the stone. I see stars for a second, but manage to get the fingers of my right hand around the knife handle.

"I don't care." He grinds out the words as his hands close on my throat. "I don't care if it costs me everything."

He squeezes my neck, instantly cutting off my air. I have seconds, if that. There's no pain, just relentless, blinding pressure.

"You will *not* ruin this for me! I've worked too hard, too long, given up too much. *Morere, Quinte! Morere!*"

"No!" I rasp and choke as I lift the knife, twisting my wrist. "I will not die!" I thrust the knife with all my strength, aiming for his neck and nailing it, blood splattering all over me as the blade slides into his flesh.

He shoves my hand away and kicks backward, the screech of the car sliding farther over the cliff almost drowning out his gurgled cry of disbelief. I push him off and this time it's easier, my effort rewarded by him rolling away.

I slam my hands on the ground and push myself up, just in time to see the car teetering at the edge.

"Molly!"

The car is tipping forward, sliding and dragging to the edge just as I see the passenger door fly open. I scramble forward as the car teeters and Molly rolls out of the side onto the ground. I manage to reach out and snag her hand, pulling her away just as the VW loses the fight with gravity and goes headlong down to the boulders of the creek below.

Tears are streaming down her face, her eyes vacant and shocked as she suddenly leans over and retches.

I whip around frantically, certain Jarvis will be coming after both of us now, and freeze. Nothing.

He's gone. Absolutely . . . disappeared, like a ghost. Who took his knife with him. Of course he did—he's an assassin.

And he's not the only one. *Sicarii* is plural.

"I'm dying!" Molly rolls into a ball but I immediately grab her arm.

"Not on my watch." I pull her up, not caring that she's stumbling. "Run!"

"I need to barf!" She clutches her stomach and gags again but I refuse to wait.

"Barf and run," I tell her, wrenching her arm and practically dragging her to the bottom of the hill.

"Kenzie . . ." She moans but staggers along as I squint into the darkness. I can't see two feet in front of me and Molly can barely walk, let alone run.

"Just be quiet, Molly," I tell her. "Don't make noise if you can help it, and force yourself to run."

She folds over again, her knees buckling. "Can't. Sick." She pukes again and my heart rips in half, but I don't give in to the urge to comfort her.

"Come on, Molly."

She's starting to collapse, so I scoop her up by the armpits, making her groan and give me an ineffective swat. "I swear you'll thank me if we live through this."

I wrap an arm around her and drag-walk her about twenty or thirty feet, my shoulders already aching from the effort. As we near the middle of the incline, I remember my phone and steal a glance in the general direction of where Jarvis threw it, praying for a miracle.

Like, that it would ring at that moment and I'd see it light up.

"Molly, do you have your phone?"

She shakes her head and moans. "He took it."

I can't afford to stop and look for mine, so I stumble us both farther down the hill, hauling Molly, who somehow manages to get one foot in front of the other.

I follow the path as best I can, finally on soft pine needles and not sliding on leaves over stone. After what seems like an eternity but is probably only thirty seconds, I risk stopping, giving Molly a chance to bend over and throw up again. After a second, she moans, wiping her mouth.

"Where are we?" she asks.

"Nacht Woods. It's Jarvis, Molly. He's not dead. He's crazy.

He's some kind of assassin. I stabbed him but he's not dead." I seize her arms and squeeze.

"I'm so sick. I'm so . . ." She closes her eyes as a wave of nausea passes through her. "I can't."

"You have to." I pull her along. "We have to get out of here before he kills us both."

Her eyes focus enough for me to know I got through to her. "'Kay."

"You can do this," I tell her. "One foot in front of the other and stay standing."

She gives me a limp, pathetic nod and I swell with sympathy and regret. I shouldn't have involved her. She almost died . . . because of me.

"Come on," I say again, urging her forward.

She allows me to help her, her arm over my shoulders pressing on my sore neck, still bruised from being strangled.

She's whimpering in my ear as we head down a path I'm relatively certain will get us back to the road.

I can't believe I didn't kill that son of a bitch. How did he get away from me?

The path narrows and there's another split-off that I don't remember because I was so distracted when Jarvis made me drive here. Which way do I go? I hesitate just one second and think I hear—no, I *do* hear footsteps. Fast and furious and getting louder.

"Molly," I whisper frantically. "We have to move."

She looks at me, silenced for a moment; then her eyes widen as she hears the footsteps, too. We both run a little but the path is narrowing quickly, the trees coming together like a wall of evergreens.

How will we get through that? I look around, my eyes

slightly adjusted, my ears completely in tune with the footsteps that could be fifty feet behind me . . . or five.

And then I see the tree—a tree that's not a tree. It's a telephone pole, and it has the two-by-four steps leading up. I stop and lean back to see how far up it is—oh, Lord, *far*—and squint into the starlight to catch a glimpse of a zip line.

A zip line that would take me over the trees and far away fast. Surely a man bleeding from a knife wound wouldn't have the strength to follow us up there and get on that line.

"We're climbing," I say to Molly.

"What?"

I don't explain but drag her to the pole and place her hands on the closest piece of wood. "Up!" I order. I have to go behind her so I can push.

She looks at me like I've lost my mind but I just shove her up the first step. "Go or die!"

That works. She starts to climb, slowly, but then I get on the ladder rung under her and shove her butt up each rail, refusing to let her slow down.

She pauses just long enough to turn her head and look down at me; then she sways and slips.

"Don't look down, Molly," I order. "Just look straight ahead. Go."

She follows the instructions and climbs, reaching a narrow hole cut into the platform. It's only big enough for one of us to squeeze through at a time, which she does without even consulting me.

As soon as she disappears through the hole, I follow, hoisting myself up to find her in a fetal position on the platform, covering her mouth either to stay quiet or keep from throwing up.

"Oh, God, how long do we have to stay up here?"

Right then, I realize there isn't one zip line; there are three. Levi's words come back to me. *When you get up there, you don't know which line to take, since there are two or three or even more. One takes you farther into the course, the other two dead-end on the ground and you have to start over.*

Damn. I peer at the three lines, each going in a different direction. I'm so turned around I have no idea which would take me where.

But didn't Levi say there were instructions? Weren't they burned into the wood? I look around, squinting in the darkness, the thick cloud cover making it almost impossible to see three straight lines scratched into the wooden platform. I look harder at the marking, noticing there are two more running perpendicular to those three on the top and—

"Oh, jeez," I say, not even able to believe I didn't see that Roman numeral. "That's a three." So now what? How do I find the . . .

Instructions!

I stuff my hand into my back pocket and exhale with relief that the sheet of paper Molly made me bring is still there. Could these phrases help me navigate the course?

I open the paper and try to angle it to catch any light available and read the list in Latin, my gaze going right to number three.

MEDIUM TENUERE BEATI

That means . . . *middle* . . . *kept* . . . *happy*. I know this one. I can hear Mr. Irving's voice: *Blessed are those who have kept the middle course.* Bingo.

305

I choose the line in between the others and reach for a small silver clip, knotting the rope that hangs from it.

"You're kidding, right?" Molly whispers from the platform, slowly getting up to her knees as she realizes what I'm doing.

"Actually, no."

"Kenzie, I can't."

"I'll hold you."

"I *can't.*"

We both hear the first footfall on the bottom rung. I peer down the hole and see the shadow of a man starting his climb. "We have to," I whisper, reaching for her.

She hesitates only long enough to hear another footfall, then her hand closes over my wrist and she lets me pull her up.

"Hold on," I say, opening my arms so she can wrap herself around me.

For one quick second, we are face to face and eye to eye, best friends who need each other more than any two friends ever had. "I won't let you fall," I promise.

"I just hope it holds us both."

The whole platform shakes with the weight of a man climbing closer. "I do, too." I dry my hands on my jeans, letting go of Molly completely as I reach up and close my hands over the rough rope, anchoring my wrists against the knot. I have no idea how far this line goes or if it will break or whether we'll live or die.

"Lift your feet, Molly."

She does and I do the same, closing my eyes as a fat drop of rain hits my face and we fly.

CHAPTER XXXI

Wind whistles over us. Raindrops pelt our faces as we sail above the treetops, some so close they brush the bottoms of my sneakers. My hands already ache and my whole upper body is throbbing with Molly's additional weight.

Every second feels like an hour, every foot a mile, regardless of the fact that we're going fast. The ride starts to slow and drop, not to the ground but to another platform. We almost crash into it, but I steady us and we tumble across the wood, Molly grunting and crying out in pain.

"Are you okay?"

"Yeah, yeah. That actually cleared my head." She manages to get up and we both look around to get our bearings. "Now what?"

We're definitely lower, but not, I realize, low enough to jump off the platform. As I sit up, I look around and see no lines and, of course, no railing—just rain.

There's no way down . . . only up. Way up. There's a platform about twenty-five feet overhead, then another built off
that one that is higher and farther out, then a third, even
higher, in the opposite direction. It's like a giant spiral stair-
case that leads at least fifty or sixty feet in the air.

They all have multiple zip lines, and each one looks more
impossible than the last. *Please, God, don't make me climb to the
top.*

I peek over the edge of our platform. "What do you think
of jumping?"

She leans and looks down. "Not a chance one of us wouldn't
break something. Probably both of us, and it could be our legs."

She's right. "Anyway, we're so deep into the woods I wouldn't
have a clue how to get out without getting completely lost."

"Could we just wait here until morning?"

I consider that but shake my head. "This guy's a killer and
he built this course. He's going to know how to find us." I look
up again. "But if we go higher, we might see a road and get a
sense of which direction to go."

"And then we ride again."

I dig up a smile and nod. "Let me consult my instructions."

As I read, Molly pushes up to stand, swaying a little but
holding on to the post attached to the platform. She leans
closer to read over my shoulder.

I point to the bottom of the page, at number nine. "I think
that's where we are. See how there are three lines of text? Wild
guess, but maybe one for every platform."

"Maybe. What do they say?"

The first clue is *haud passibus aequis.* "'Not with equal
steps.'" I frown. "What the heck does that mean?"

She looks at the wooden rails that lead upward. "They're perfectly equal in size and distance."

"Maybe it means not to take the zip line from the platform that has equal steps?" I suggest.

"I guess we have to get up there to find out. What's the next line say?"

Sweat beading on my neck despite the cold, I study the words: *alia tendanda via est*. "'Another way must be tried.'"

"Great, Yoda wrote the directions."

I almost smile, more encouraged that Molly is back than by any humor in the situation. "It's Latin," I say. "But maybe it refers to the second platform? Let's climb and see what we find."

Molly turns and immediately puts her hands on the third rung. "I'll go first."

As I fold the instructions to keep them dry, she starts to climb, but suddenly I hear a loud crack and her gasp as she falls backward.

"Molly!" I leap to her but the platform board under her gives way and she tumbles into space. I dive after her, our hands flailing to find a grip on each other before she falls all the way to the ground.

I just manage to snag the sleeve of her hoodie and stop the fall. "Don't move, Molly," I tell her. If she squirms, the jacket could come right off.

She looks up at me, dangling in open space, horror in her eyes. "What do I do?" she whispers, as though even talking could end in a fall.

"Hold on." With strength I don't even know I have, straining every muscle to its snapping point, I fight to hoist her back up. Her wet hand nearly slips through mine, but I grip so hard I could break her wrist.

I will not drop Molly. I will *not* let her die. I don't waste energy talking but pull with everything I have, one agonizing inch at a time, until she can finally grab the wood and climb back onto the platform.

We both collapse and let out a breath I think we started holding when the step fell.

"Well, now we know," she pants.

"Know what?"

She lifts a shaky arm and points to the ladder. "Why we have to take unequal steps."

Scrambling to my knees, I nod. "Skip every other step."

"And pray."

We do both and get to level two without a mishap, but there's no clip on the zip line. "So this is the part where we 'try another way.'"

"The way up." Molly points.

In silence, we climb to the next platform, the wind strong enough up here for the rain, now a light shower, to sting our faces. As I poke my head through the opening to the next level, I get the best view of the woods I've had yet. Molly's already kneeling on that platform looking around.

"Look, Kenz." She points to a golden glow on the horizon.

"That's probably the lights of Vienna. Good, that tells us where we are." I turn and peer to the north.

"That's the direction where the cave and that room was," I tell her. "Where all that art is hidden."

"I was thinking about that," she says. "Maybe that's why he faked his own death, because he's some kind of international art thief."

"And a serial killer? That's pretty bizarre."

"Yeah, 'cause the rest of this is so normal."

Staring in the direction of town, I swear I see a light moving. It flashes, disappears, then flashes again. Is that Jarvis on the hunt? "Whatever he is," I say, "he's out there and he's looking for us."

I scan our platform and plan our next move. There's one line connected to the next level, but as we examine it, we both see what we have to do to get to it—balance on a series of six logs suspended from ropes that lead to the start of the zip line.

"Holy crap," Molly mumbles.

"Yeah," I agree.

But we manage our way across the logs to the zip line. This time we move like a team, Molly wrapped around me, the zip-line rope firmly in my hands. When I let go, the ride seems smoother and faster, ending not on another platform but a soft mound of pine needles. We fall, safe and alive.

"I know where we are," I say as we brush off and look around. "Levi and I were here the other day. We just have to jump that overhang where the cave is, run to the right, then the left, and straight to a road."

"Thank God." We bolt together to the cliff, stopping when we reach it to look over the embankment.

"Levi helped me do this," I say. "Hold on to me and I'll dangle you, then it's not so far to fall."

"'Kay." She scoots down to the ground and we clamp our hands around each other's wrists. As she gets into position, she looks at me and smiles. "Thanks for saving my life, Kenzie."

I just nod. "We're not out of the woods yet."

She manages to laugh at my pun. "Seriously. You're the best."

I give her wrists a squeeze. "Remember that the next time you want to be popular and cool," I joke as I let her down.

"So overrated."

She's swaying in the air, her sneakers about five feet from the ground. "Ready?" I ask.

"Let go."

She falls with a soft thud, rolling under the overhang so I can't see her. "Here I come," I say, turning and hoping I can do this without help, like Levi did.

I get a grip on some rocks sticking out of the ground and slowly lower my body until I'm hanging. "Watch out so I don't land on you," I call to Molly.

Three, two, one, and I let go, hitting the ground with a jolt.

"There, now we . . ."

When I get up, I scan the area. "Molly?" I turn again, peering into the bushes that cover the cave. Did she go in there? "Molly?"

I push back the foliage to peer into the darkness, and hear the distant, muffled sound of running footsteps from deep inside the cave. And then, silence.

CHAPTER XXXII

It takes me no more than five seconds to decide what to do. I can't leave. By the time I find my way out of the woods and get help, Molly could be dead.

Shoving the branches and leaves away, I'm swallowed into the blackness of the cave, longing for Levi and the light we had last time we were in here. I stick my hand straight out and shudder at the sudden cold.

I stay still, listening for any hint, any sound other than the relentless hammering of my heart, clobbering against my chest. How could he—or someone—have gotten Molly so fast?

I have one advantage: I've been here before. I shoot one hand out and use the other to hold on to the cold stone wall to walk through the darkness, utterly alone and wretchedly scared.

As I concentrate on each step, I follow the corridor to a lower level on the stone path, trying to imagine the footpath

I'm on. I pause, my hand still on the wall, remembering the engraving.

Many are called, few are chosen.

Yes, Levi was right that it's a Bible quote, but the phrase was also used by Romans to mean that only the elite could do something.

I let one of the trainees take the credit.

Training for what? Professional killers?

I reach the dead end, my heart sinking because there's no sign or sound of Molly. Is she in that room? Is she still alive?

I don't really think about whether or not to go in—it's more about how. Remembering the force it took Levi, I place my body against the stone wall and push as hard as I can and—

It slides right open and I'm back in the museum meeting room. I think. It's dark now, pitch black and airless. I stay perfectly still and listen for any sounds. Even . . . breathing.

It's as quiet as a tomb.

I work my way along the side of the room, my arm brushing a tapestry as I move very, very slowly to not give myself away. My sneakers are silent, and I'm barely breathing, bracing for an attack at any moment.

Is there another way out of this room? Another secret door?

Gingerly, I reach over to the wall and touch a glass box, then the stone wall again. I move ahead another few feet and touch something cold and sharp. A sword. For a moment, my fingers linger on the weapon.

I close my hand over the hilt and try to lift, but it barely moves. I'm no gladiator. I can't lift—

Gladiator! This is where that four-pronged knee-buckling

thing was. The quadrant, right on this wall. I flatten my hand and inch to the right, remembering exactly where I saw the ancient weapon, my fingers touching the rough-hewn metal almost immediately.

It lifts off the hook, no more than a few pounds, and it fits fairly neatly in my hand. It's warm and . . . deadly. Actually, it doesn't necessarily kill, if I recall what I saw in the video in my Latin class. But the quadrant can bring a man to his knees, and since it's the only weapon on this wall I can handle, that'll have to be enough.

Tucking the quadrant into my jacket pocket, I take a few more steps, carefully navigating around a large clay vase, then—

"Hello, Mackenzie."

The room is suddenly bathed in light and I whip around with a gasp to meet the steel-blue gaze of Rex Collier.

"We've never had a woman in here, let alone an expert in the classics. What do you think?"

I can barely blink or breathe, let alone think. He looms over me, taller than I remember, more regal, far more threatening.

"Jarvis said you'd be a handful when we put your name on the list." He barely smiles. "He was right."

My head is humming, questions buzzing and colliding with exclamations of fury and the need to hurt him and get out of here. But I don't move. Does he know where Molly is? Did he take her?

"What do you think?" He gestures toward the tapestries. "They're all real," he says. "All in my family for centuries. Payment for the job."

"The job?" I practically spit the words, angry at myself for even asking questions when all that matters is getting out of here alive with Molly.

"It's dirty work, but someone—someone quite talented—can do it. This way, Kenzie." He indicates a space in the wall between a carved bust and a glass box with a leather-bound book inside. Pausing, he points to the box, but my mind is whirring. I have to get out of here. I have to do something drastic.

"That's the Persius Cipher."

Can I lift a chair and hit him over the head? Hoist one of those clay vases and knock him out? I have to think, buy time, and be clever.

"The Persius Cipher?" I ask.

He gives me a smile. "You've heard of it, of course."

Never in my life. "Of course. Can I see it?" Maybe if he opens the glass, I can break it and slice him.

He gives me a wary look, as if he can read my mind.

"I've never touched a manuscript like that before." I try to sound convincing. Will it work on him? "Could you take it out of that box and let me examine it?"

He steps aside and opens his hands, giving me permission to go to the manuscript. I put my hands on the clear glass, saying a silent prayer of gratitude that it really is glass, not plastic. I squeeze, lift, and in one lightning-fast move, crash it against the pedestal, holding on to one long shard as I pivot, ready to dive at him.

And I come face to face with the barrel of a pistol.

Rex Collier just smiles. "Nice try, but you really need to work on your timing." With his free hand, he touches the wall and it slides open, revealing another corridor.

So much for thinking on my feet.

He takes the shard of glass and gets next to me, the gun in my back. "Still, you get points for creativity, which we value above all else."

I close my eyes, biting back a retort that could get me shot. Except his words are settling into my brain. "They" value creativity; "their" killings are clean. So, maybe he won't shoot me.

"Where are we going?" I ask.

"Toward the house, but you can't go to the party tonight, I'm afraid. Even though your friends are there."

I stop short. "Molly?"

"And your boyfriend." He sighs heavily. "I hate when we find one with such potential who can't pass the simplest, earliest tests." He takes a few more steps. "Then there are those who can pass every test but just can't be lured with the astronomical amounts of money we make." He gives me a look rich with meaning, but I'm not able to decipher what that meaning is.

Except, deep in my heart, I know. *Conner.*

"They'll be gone soon," he says, pulling me back to the moment. "Levi went back to the house with Josh, thinking that's where you are. When he finds a drunken Molly, he'll be taking her home in a car that is rigged to have an unexpected fire and explosion just ten minutes after he turns on the engine." He pauses dramatically. "That leaves us with only you to deal with. One more *accident.*"

He pushes me toward an unexpected turn, a dark corner off the corridor.

"You'll never get away with this. Eventually, you'll be caught." My voice is thick, trapped in my throat.

"We've gotten away with it for two thousand years. *Nihil* was formed in Rome, started by slaves who took money for killing noblemen as a favor to other noblemen. Nothing's changed now. Only instead of a patrician who falls into a well, it might be a CEO in a freak biking accident, a hedge-fund trader whose private jet goes down. Assassinations are nothing new. Neither are assassins. We're all over the world, working quietly, killing neatly, amassing fortunes for our work."

I stare at him. "But why would you kill innocent girls?"

"Our members have to train on someone, Kenzie. That's why we make a list of easily manipulated girls. And, of course, boys who help us manipulate them. Not all those boys know why, just that they're getting much-needed cash. But the organization is undergoing some drastic changes and, well, Jarvis wanted to make a point. He's my son and I brought him into the business. I have to support him."

"Is Josh in on this?" A wave of disgust rolls over me. Did I kiss a killer? An accomplice? An assassin?

"Not fully, but *Nihil* is in his blood. Of course, he thinks he's being groomed and tested for something a little less . . . deadly. Tonight's one of his exams. He has to make Levi think he's being a hero, stealing a car to drive a drunk girl home."

Levi wouldn't steal a car to drive a girl anywhere. Unless he thought he was saving her.

"Once that's done, it will be time to tell Josh exactly who he is and what family he is part of. I have great hopes he'll be overjoyed to learn his father is alive."

Only his father. "But his mother was one of your victims, wasn't she?"

"One of Jarvis's victims," Rex corrects. "In fact, getting rid

318

of his wife was his first official training assignment with *Nihil Relinquere et Nihil Vestigi*. They're all much easier after you prove yourself. We ask all trainees to assassinate someone they care about. A sort of hazing, if you will, with the same benefits. It would have been interesting to see how Josh did with you. He *does* care about you, you know."

I'm sick as I process this secret society of assassins, training on innocent people. "Is it only Josh?"

"This year, yes. We haven't had a good recruit in years." He makes a low grunt in his chest. "Came so close two years ago. So close."

I know exactly who he means.

He inhales slowly, as if savoring the moment. "An extraordinary young man, Conner."

Yes, he was. I fight the urge to lunge, but only because of the gun pointed at me.

"Training is important, of course, and all the assassins of *Nihil Relinquere* undergo rigorous training all over the world. But recruitment is so important, and it's my forte. That's why we run the scholarship program, which is really a way for me to spot talent. Of course, it is a legitimate scholarship. But sometimes . . . I recruit."

"And Conner?"

"Such potential," he says again, slowing his step to look at me. "But sadly, he had morals. That will never do in this job. So he had to die."

I ball my fists and grit my teeth. "You killed him."

Very slowly, he reaches into his pocket and pulls something out, lifting it close to my face so I can see what he's holding.

319

"No, Mackenzie. You did. Remember?" The necklace dangles from his fingertips, and my eyes immediately find the gold M with fourteen diamond chips.

I can't breathe. I can't move. "How did you—"

"Oh, child, that was an easy accident to arrange. You merely helped us by setting up the situation. Jarvis would have gotten your brother in the basement of that pharmacy. He was right there the whole time, shopping and watching you."

Hate and resentment and the unyielding need to destroy him bubble up in me and make me quiver. He laughs.

"Here, take it. You can wear it when you die." He shakes the necklace and I reach for it, closing my fingers over what has been the symbol of my brother's death for two years.

He steps back as a noise on the floor pulls my attention. Very slowly, the stone beneath us begins to disappear, rolling away like some kind of conveyor belt, leaving a huge, gaping hole.

Deftly, Rex presses against the wall and I do the same next to him, gagging as a disgusting smell rises up.

"*Odor mortis,* as you linguists would say."

The smell of death.

He waves the gun toward the hole. "As I mentioned, sometimes we have to do things the old-fashioned way. So, down you'll go, where some others have gone before you. I'd love to have you be Josh's first true test, but we simply don't have the time to arrange that. So . . . go."

There's nothing down there but blackness. Endless blackness.

"It's a long drop with a lot of jutting stones," he says as calmly as if he's describing a walk on the beach. "Your bones

320

will be broken by the time you hit bottom. You'll be dead before long, I assure you."

All the air is whooshing from my lungs and my whole body starts to shake. I don't want to die this way. I don't want to die any way, but definitely not this horrible, horrible way.

"We got this from the ancient Romans, too. No one knew about this form of killing until archeologists found the broken bones and, trust me, no one will know about this under my house for two thousand years, either. Now it's your turn, Kenzie."

The ancient Romans. For the first time, I remember the quadrant. I slip the necklace into my pocket and my knuckles brush the weapon.

"No!" I flatten against the wall. "I won't."

He lifts the gun. "You prefer to die first? I suppose I could grant you that, though I pride myself on never having to use a gun."

My fingers squeeze the quadrant, meant to make a man's knees buckle. If his knees buckled . . .

How can I do it? I have to get down, low enough to get to his knees . . . almost *in* that hole. I close my eyes, visualizing the video clip I'd seen of the gladiator using the quadrant and how it had to fit just under a victim's knee.

"Don't shoot me," I say quietly. "I'll just . . . go."

He lifts a brow. "Think you can outsmart the system, Mackenzie? Drop down slowly, maybe not break a bone, escape somehow?"

The foul smell roils my stomach. "Yes," I say.

"Fine." He waves the gun. "Go."

I consider jumping him, going for the gun, trying to push

him in, but he's a trained assassin. I'm a sixteen-year-old Latin nerd. And only a Latin nerd would know how to use this quadrant.

Very slowly, I crouch down. There's not quite a foot of space around the hole, and the smell makes me dizzy. He doesn't seem to mind. Of course not: this killer loves *odor mortis*.

I get on my haunches.

"Down, Mackenzie."

I bend over like I'm going to jump, inching a little closer to his legs. Then I turn so he can't see my hand, very slowly inching out the metal quadrant.

"Jump!"

"I will." My hands are shaking, the palms wet with sweat. I have to do this. I have to hit him directly below the kneecap, in the soft tissue. The right spot, and he collapses. The wrong spot, and I'm dead. After I lie with broken bones in an underground graveyard.

"Now."

"Right . . ." I inch my hand back. "After . . ." I suck in a breath. "You!" I thrust the tool right at his knee, and the simultaneous sounds of his cry and the crack of his knee echo around me.

Directly in front of me, he buckles, losing his balance and tumbling toward the hole. Screaming an obscenity, he grabs for me, but I slip out of his grasp, using the quadrant to poke at his hands furiously, crunching his bones with each stab.

"Goddamn you, Goddamn—" And he disappears, a thudding sound like a person falling down steps, his voice nothing but a moan of agony and despair as he goes farther and farther into the pit.

"No, Rex. God damned you when you killed my brother."
Slowly, I stand up, worried that my shaking legs will betray me
and I'll be following him, but I manage to step away to solid
ground.

I think about throwing the quadrant in after him, but then
I realize I'm not done being a gladiator yet. I still have to find
Molly and Levi, and if I have to kill to save them . . . Well, I
guess I've proven I'm capable of that.

CHAPTER XXXIII

I worm my way through more corridors, frantically slamming on the walls as I search for openings. I finally find a stairway that leads up, taking me into a cave, and when I get out, I step into a heavy rainfall.

Still, I'm able to see the lights of the Colliers' house from where I'm standing.

As I run toward the house, I blink into the raindrops to see a car careening down the driveway.

Levi! In the car that's going to explode? Is he driving Molly away? I run at full speed, waving wildly as I reach the driveway, but the car's headed onto the road, the engine and rain both too loud for him to hear me screaming at the top of my lungs.

"Noo—"

A hand snakes around my waist and clamps hard, yanking me into a solid body. "What the hell are you doing, Fifth?"

"Josh." I barely breathe his name, trying to wrench away, but he holds me tightly. "Who was in that car?"

He shrugs. "Some kids. What're you doing out here, Fifth?"

I try to step away but he won't let me go. I can barely look at him, considering I just killed his grandfather and tried to kill his father and I might want to kill him, too.

"What kids?" I ask. "Who was in the car, Josh?"

"Don't worry. My grandfather already called the cops. They'll be pulled over before they get far. Sorry, but that prick's going back to juvie, where he belongs."

"No," I say, shaking my head, fury and fear rocking me as the rain intensifies, soaking me completely.

"Molly showed up wasted, so he poured her into my grandfather's Beamer and took off like a bat outta hell." He starts pulling me toward the house. "Let's get dry."

"They're going to die," I sputter, praying this is a surprise for him. *Please don't be part of this, Josh.*

His reply is drowned out by the sound of a motor, growing louder, and bright lights bearing down on us. We both start to run, but the black pickup screeches to a halt on the grass. The driver's door pops open and Jarvis emerges.

I recognize the hood over his head, the shape of him. His voice is thick, like he's drunk, and he holds his hand over a dark bandana wrapped around his neck.

"Who the hell are you?" Josh asks. As I back away in horror, Josh reaches for me. "Do you know him, Kenzie?"

"He's—"

"Take her inside, Joshua."

Josh bristles at the order. "What? Who *are* you?"

As much as I'd love to stay for the Darth Vader moment, I have to get Levi. "Let me go, Josh!"

"Don't let her go, Joshua. Inside, now. I'm bleeding."

"Not enough," I say, frantically trying to loosen Josh's grip on my arm and get away.

"No, maybe we should listen to this guy," Josh says, eyeing Jarvis. "He might, uh, work for my grandfather."

I've got one card left, and I have to use it. "You think he's going to help you?" I demand. "You think this guy is going to make your life better, Josh? Make you do things that your grandfather says will give you power and money and control?"

He staggers back at my words.

"Inside!" Jarvis growls.

I manage to twist around, slipping in the wet grass. "Look at him, Josh! Don't you see the resemblance? Don't you see? This man, this murderer, this *assassin*. He's your father."

Josh's hand loosens but not enough for me to get away. Jarvis is silent. Josh pales visibly. And all I can think is that Levi and Molly have about eight minutes left to live.

"What?" Josh says, narrowing his eyes at the other man. "My father is dead."

"We need to eliminate her," Jarvis finally says, taking a few steps closer to me.

But Josh moves to block him. "My father is dead," he says again, grinding out the words.

For a long moment, they stare at each other, two sets of steel-blue eyes locked like swords.

"Not exactly *dead*," Jarvis says calmly, a scary smile on his face. "I'll explain, but first we have some business to take care

326

of." He lunges at me and grabs my other shoulder. "We have to kill her."

"Wh-what?" Josh stammers.

"More specifically, you do." With his free hand, Jarvis reaches into his pocket. "This pill will replicate the symptoms of alcohol poisoning. A bit of a cheat, I agree, but you put it down her throat and I'll count it as a pass."

I stare at Jarvis's hand. I will not take that pill. I'll rip his flesh with my teeth if I have to.

Josh is staring, too, in speechless shock, pain etched on every feature. "My . . . mother?"

"She *did* die in the boating incident." Jarvis steps forward, letting go of his bloody bandana to reach into his pocket. Out comes the knife again.

"What are you talking about?" Josh's voice is barely a whisper.

"Later." Jarvis positions the knife under my neck, the blade pricking my skin, and extends his other hand to Josh. "Put the pill in her mouth, son."

He doesn't move. "I'm not your son."

"We'll see about that." Jarvis holds his hand steady in a fist. "Take this pill and put it in her mouth."

I fight the urge to lunge away, but my pulse is pounding right into the blade. One move and I'm dead. So I just shift my gaze to look at Josh. Tears have mixed with the rain now.

"Do it!" Jarvis practically spits the order. "It's your legacy. It's in your blood. It's your destiny."

Josh's eyes widen. "You killed my mother."

"Sometimes there is collateral damage." He shakes the knife slightly. "Even girls we're a little fond of."

"My *mother*?" Josh's voice rises to a bellow now.

"Calm down, son."

"You bastard!" Josh leaps forward, pushing Jarvis away from me as they both roll to the ground.

I'm free, but I freeze for a second, torn between helping him and going after Levi. I see the knife slice through the air, and I know someone is going to die.

They wrestle on the grass, grunting, until Josh flips Jarvis and slams his head to the ground, pinning his arms.

"You killed my mother!"

Jarvis just fights for breath, staring up at Josh. "You'll get over it."

"What?" He lifts him and smacks him down again.

"You'll get over it," Jarvis says. "The rewards are too great. And if you don't accept that, you're next to have an accident."

"Kenzie!" Josh doesn't take his eyes off the man on the ground. "Get the pill from him." When I don't move, he screams, "Get the pill from his hand!"

I know what he wants, or at least I think I do. Without debating, I fall to my knees and grab Jarvis's fist. Josh twists his hand like he's going to break the bone, and Jarvis's fingers unhinge so I can get the pill.

"Put it in his mouth, Kenzie."

"How?" I ask, seeing Jarvis clamp his lips together.

"Like this." Josh rises up and slams a knee right into Jarvis's solar plexus, and the older man throws back his head to howl.

I toss the pill down his throat without hesitation.

"Now, go, Kenzie. I'll take care of him."

I don't waste one second. I run straight to Jarvis's truck,

which is still running. Gripping the giant steering wheel like it's a bus, I peel out to the driveway, heading in the same direction Levi went, imagining the route he'd take. I slam on the accelerator and pray they've hit every light and that I can get them in less than . . . seven minutes.

That's all they have left.

I turn onto Route 1 and pass a 7-Eleven, considering all my options. I could go in, make a call, get the police—and that would take so long they'd be dead. I press the gas harder, fly past a much slower car, and power into the left lane spraying water, fussing with the windshield wipers to get them up to high speed.

The rain makes it that much harder to find the white BMW. I squeeze the steering wheel and let out a long, low howl of pain, my whole being electrified with the need to get Levi and Molly out of that car.

There's almost no traffic and I'm hitting sixty, but the big-ass truck doesn't hydroplane like my old Accord. Gauging where I am by the stores I recognize, I have a few more lights before the turnoff to Molly's house.

I run a yellow light, then another, then whip over to the right to take the next turn, weaving through some residential streets just as I see a white sedan cross in front of me, heading back to Route 1.

Is that him? I follow, just about to flash my brights frantically when I see him turn again. What the—

Oh, God. Of *course*. Levi thinks I'm Jarvis in the black pickup. He thinks I'm following him.

He'll never stop for me!

I whip to the left, taking a side street, praying he's headed back to Route 1. Each thump of the windshield wipers matches my heart, slamming against my ribs, ready to explode.

"Levi!" I scream into the night, my voice echoing in the truck.

I barrel onto Route 1, rolling down the right lane, squinting into the night, when I see him approaching the intersection. I have to beat him. I have to stop him.

I'm flooring it, sweating, grunting, bracing to beat him there, and I have him. I'm going to do it. I get to the middle of the intersection and slam on the brakes, somehow stopping the truck as the BMW keeps coming faster and faster.

He's going to hit me!

I push the window button and lower the passenger side down so he can see who is driving, screaming his name, willing him to stop. All I can see is the two white headlights bearing down on me, coming closer and closer. I squeeze my eyes shut and brace for impact, hearing the screech of brakes and horns and preparing for the jolt . . . that doesn't happen.

I open my eyes to see Levi stick his head out the driver's window, rain drenching him. "Kenzie! What the hell are you doing?"

"Get out!" I holler, throwing my door open. "Get out of the car! Both of you!"

He climbs out just as I reach him, spitting water out of my mouth. "Get Molly out, too! The car's going to explode!"

We both run to the passenger side, where Molly is passed out. I yank the door open and he scoops her up in his arms.

"Hurry!" I scream. "Get away from the car! Away!"

Together, we bolt across the street, Levi carrying Molly and jumping over a guardrail and rolling to the grass just as the night lights up and rocks with the power of a deafening explosion.

Levi is on top of us, his body pressing Molly's into mine as the sound and heat roll our way. I manage to open my eyes and peer through his elbow and over Molly's head, looking straight at a set of golden arches next to the road.

For a moment, I can't breathe or think or do anything except embrace the reality that I am alive.

And so are my two closest friends.

CHAPTER XXXIV

The graveyard where Conner is buried sits on the side of a hill overlooking the farmland of western Pennsylvania. The trees have shed almost all their leaves now, but a rare late-autumn sun warms my face as I climb out of my car and stand by the door.

"You want company?" Levi asks from the passenger seat.

I look at him, then glance at Molly in the back. "Do you guys mind giving me a few moments alone?"

"Not at all," she assures me. "We're here for moral support."

I give her a grateful smile and reach to give Levi's hand a squeeze. "I'll just be a minute."

But it takes longer than that to meander through the cemetery, pausing to glance at names and dates, fighting that sense of injustice because almost all of those birth-to-death dates span many, many years.

But not Conner's. He didn't even make two decades.

I reach his grave and know instantly that Mom and Dad have been here recently. Since we learned the truth about Conner's death, they've been up here a lot. *Together.*

I eye their work, noticing the plot is neat, the flowers fresh, and the last leaves from a nearby maple have all been raked away.

If headstones are supposed to represent a person's life and character, then we really missed the mark on this one. Unlike Conner, his grave is unassuming, with a tiny stone flat in the ground. It says his name, his dates of birth and death, and one simple word: *Unforgettable.*

I stare at the carved letters, then let my knees fold so I can sit on the grass next to him. I try to think of a joke or at least something witty, but my eyes are filling up, and heck, I'm not Conner. He always knew what to say.

"I miss you," I whisper, closing my eyes to see his face. His square jaw, his laughing eyes, those big white teeth always exposed in a smile.

I wait to hear his voice, but there's only a bird singing in the distance and a breeze in the bare trees. If only I could remember his voice.

"I want to give you something, Conner." I reach under my hair and slip my nail into the necklace clasp. "I guess it's more like I want to get rid of something."

I let the necklace fall onto the grass, then lean over and cup my hand to dig a small hole in the dirt by the stone. "Some things need to be buried," I say. "Regret, second guesses, doubts, and guilt. I want them buried forever so that I can stop thinking about me when I think about you."

The words make me smile. I never realized that was what

was bothering me the most. Memories of my brother were so clouded and crowded by self-hatred that I could never just enjoy the life he had.

"We got the bad guys, Conner," I add, leaning over his grave to run my fingers over the word *Unforgettable*.

But that's not what I came here to talk about. I'm here to let go of my guilt and start a new relationship with my brother. Instead of feeling only pain, I want to remember him as the amazing boy he was.

"You probably wouldn't like my boyfriend," I say to him. "Not until you get to know him." I blow out a breath and think of all the things I want to tell him, finally free to come here and not imagine him watching and blaming. "Oh, and guess what? Because all those FBI agents had to go through your room and all your stuff, Mom's decided to put the house on the market and she and Dad are going to get another one together. Isn't that—"

"Kenzie!"

I turn at the sound of Levi calling me, pushing myself up and brushing off dirt to see him and Molly standing by my car talking to two men. . . . No, that's not a man. That's Josh Collier, who I haven't seen since the night I left him on his lawn three weeks ago.

I put my hand on my chest, stunned by the sight of him. We'd been told he was in special custody and working with the FBI, but that's all I've heard. Of course, the vacuum of information surrounding the events has been suffocating. All those deaths and not one of them has been in the news as murder.

The FBI gagged us. No one knows the truth about all those

accidents except a few of us, and for some reason, that's how the authorities want it. I squint into the sunlight and look at the other man in dress clothes. Speaking of the FBI . . . I can now spot a fed from a mile away. Levi gestures for me to come down and I hold up my hand to let him know I will.

Turning back to Conner's grave, I sigh. "I need to go, big bro." I reach my hand out as if I can touch him, my heart aching for one last hug. "I'm happier now and I hope you are, too." I take a few steps away and turn back once more, still waiting for the sound of his voice in my head. His baritone. His laugh. His constant talking. After fourteen years of hearing Conner's voice, why can't I remember it?

But I can't hear anything. "I love you, Conner."

The only answer is the wind. I jog down to the car, unable to take my eyes off Josh. He looks bigger, stronger, bolder. His jaw is set and his eyes look angrier than I can ever remember. Well, except when he was beating the crap out of his father.

He doesn't nod or acknowledge me when I reach the car, but the older man holds out his hand. Light hair and gold-rimmed glasses give him a more intellectual look than the average FBI agent.

"*Salve,*" he says in greeting, pronouncing it correctly, with the *v* as a *w*.

I laugh softly. "A Latin-speaking FBI agent?"

"There are plenty of us in the bureau," he says. "I'm Special Agent Stewart with Art Crimes. I hope you don't mind the intrusion. Your parents told me I could find you here."

I cast a quick look over my shoulder to the graveyard. "I was just visiting my brother." Finally, I catch Josh's eye. "Hey."

He nods, silent.

Special Agent Stewart clears his throat. "I—*we*—wanted to talk to you privately. You have no idea how much you've helped us, Ms. Summerall."

"Kenzie," I correct. "It was a group effort." I nod to my friends and add a tip of my head to Josh. "Are we allowed to go public with this story now?"

"No," he says simply. "But I am here to tell you more. And ask you . . ." He shares a quick look with Josh, who nods as though he's giving permission.

"A few years ago," the agent says, "I was brought into an unusual case when the bureau found a treasure trove of artwork and antiquities very similar to those you discovered." He leans forward. "The artifacts were in a bunker-style basement outside of Los Angeles."

I feel myself tense. "Did Jarvis work out there, too?"

"Not as far as we can tell. But when I ran the artwork through the bureau's computer, I was contacted by a detective from Scotland Yard; they'd also found a basement full of ancient art. I went to see him and look at the works, and we found several of these."

He opens his hand to reveal a ring much like the one Jarvis wore. I hear Josh swallow hard as we all look at it.

"You're familiar with the words on the inside," Special Agent Stewart says to me, pointing to the tiny inscription. *Secreta sodalitas sicariorum.*

"That's a secret society of assassins," I say.

"Plural," Josh says, the first word he's uttered.

"Yes," I say, too curious to explain why. "That spelling does means more than one assassin."

"Many more." Stewart pockets the ring and stares hard at

336

me. "The bureau now believes *Nihil Relinquere* is a large secret society with members around the world, all working and training to kill people without leaving a trace of evidence that there's ever been a crime."

I can barely process that. "Why?"

"Assassination fees are high. And all the members as they move up the ranks of the organization are rewarded with rare and ancient artifacts, which is one of the things that connects them."

I can't breathe as I realize the implications. That means . . .

"Many assassins," I whisper. "Many trainees."

The agent nods. "And many 'accidents' that kill innocent people strictly so that assassins might perfect and train for the trade. The victims are most often innocent teenagers who are easily grouped and manipulated. Like the list of girls in your class or members of an extracurricular club, any group that can be created or convinced to be in a certain place at a certain time. The *Nihil* use advanced technology—like the ability to delete texts—as well as creative weapons and effective techniques."

I'm speechless, but Molly steps in closer. "So there are groups and clubs and lists of kids who are targets for assassin trainees . . . all over the world?" she asks.

Stewart nods. "Based on what Josh has been able to help us piece together, we think *Nihil* meets regularly, perhaps in a place like Collier's underground museum, and there's quite a friendly competition among them. For instance, the warning text you received after your accident, Kenzie? Possibly someone from another cell trying to sabotage Jarvis's efforts to kill all ten members of his list, which isn't how they work at all.

Usually there is no more than one every few years from these lists."

"But this year was different," Josh says. "Before my—before Jarvis died, he told me there was an internal competition for power and control that he was trying to win. Obviously, he's not the new boss of *Nihil Relinquere*. But someone is. And they're out there . . . killing." His voice is cold, his eyes dead. "Unless we stop them."

"We?" Molly, Levi, and I say the word in perfect unison.

Stewart puts his hand on Josh's shoulder. "This young man has an idea and I have to say, I like it. You have some extraordinary qualities, Kenzie. You know their language, and now you've been deeply exposed to the culture. And you—and I do mean all of you, because we'd need a team—can fit in if we wanted to infiltrate a cell and help us identify the assassin manipulating it."

"I'm going to do it," Josh says. "With or without you." He glances at each of us and for a long moment, he and Levi hold a gaze. "I think we could work really well together. All four of us."

Levi inches back, surprised, and Molly's jaw drops. But I know where I stand. "I'm pretty certain that's one parental consent form my mother would never sign."

"We've already approached her," Stewart says. "She and your father agreed to let us talk to you about it, so I believe they are supportive." His gaze shifts over my shoulder to the cemetery behind me, and really, he doesn't have to say anything else. I know why Mom will let me do this: so no other mother will have to lose a child like she did.

"What about school?" I ask.

"You'll continue your education right here at Vienna, but you may have to take a few extended trips. We can work out the details. You three—you *four*—have to decide if this is something you want to do."

"I already know what I'm doing," Josh says. "And it is *not* continuing the family business."

"Talk it over." The FBI agent puts his hand on my shoulder. "I'll be in touch." He nods goodbye to Josh and walks to a sedan parked across the street, leaving us in a minor state of shock.

"Holy heck," Molly says, sounding like she just let out a breath she'd been holding for a while. "Infiltrate these cells and figure out who's orchestrating accidents? Sounds . . . cool."

I give Levi a questioning look, which he returns with a smile. "Guess that would take me off probation permanently."

All three of them look at me expectantly. I blow out a breath and turn to the hill behind me, my gaze moving to Conner's barely marked grave.

Nobody says a word and yet . . . I can hear something. A familiar voice in my head that's been silent for two years.

Go get 'em, Mack.

Finally, I can hear Conner's voice again. And I know exactly what I'm going to do.

ACKNOWLEDGMENTS

My team makes this look so easy, but they must get some praise and love. . . .

Tremendous gratitude to the professionals at Delacorte Press, especially editor Krista Vitola, whose gentle touch and keen eye can be felt on every page. As always, huge appreciation to literary agent Robin Rue.

There's a lot of Latin in this book, all graciously reviewed by Adam Mize, master of Latin and teacher of greatness! Any mistakes are mine, not his. *Gratias,* Mr. Mize.

The professionals at TreeTop Trek assisted with information about zip lines and rope courses . . . all without managing to kill me. Former FBI agent James Vatter also deserves a nod for his help regarding federal investigations.

I'm surrounded by awesome friends and writers for every book I write, and this one was no different. My love goes to the team at Writers' Camp, who cheered me on and helped complicate the plot every chance they could.

I have the best family in the world. I love you guys.

And finally, *soli Deo gloria.* Always.

Stanley Studios

ROXANNE ST. CLAIRE is the *New York Times* and *USA Today* bestselling author of more than thirty novels of suspense and romance for adults and teens. She has lived in Pittsburgh, Los Angeles, Boston, and Miami, and currently lives on an island off the coast of Florida with her husband, their son and daughter, and their dogs. When she's not writing, she can be found at the beach or on the Internet.

Visit her online at roxannestclaire.com